SUN OF SILVER, MOON OF GOLD

Sw 3/10	KN 9/10	BE 04/13	
BI 3/12	MA 9/12.		

SUN OF SILVER, MOON OF GOLD

MAUREEN PETERS

THORNDIKE
CHIVERS

This Large Print edition is published by Thorndike Press, Waterville, Maine, USA, and by BBC Audiobooks Ltd, Bath, England.

Thorndike Press, a part of Gale, Cengage Learning.

Thorndike Press® Large Print Gentle Romance.

The text of this Large Print edition is unabridged.

Other aspects of the book may vary from the original edition.

Set in 16 pt. Plantin.

Printed on permanent paper.

LIBRARY OF CONGRESS CATALOGING-IN-PUBLICATION DATA

Peters, Maureen.
  Sun of silver, moon of gold / by Maureen Peters.
    p. cm. — (Thorndike Press large print gentle romance)
  ISBN-13: 978-1-4104-0982-9 (hardcover : alk. paper)
  ISBN-10: 1-4104-0982-1 (hardcover : alk. paper)
  1. English — United States — Fiction. 2. Indians of North America — Fiction. 3. United States — History — 1849–1877 — Fiction. 4. Large type books. I. Title.
  PR6052.L335S86 2008
  823'.914—dc22   2008020070

BRITISH LIBRARY CATALOGUING-IN-PUBLICATION DATA AVAILABLE

Published in 2008 in the U.S. by arrangement with Robert Hale Limited.
Published in 2009 in the U.K. by arrangement with Robert Hale Limited.

U.K. Hardcover: 978 1 408 41235 0 (Chivers Large Print)
U.K. Softcover: 978 1 408 41236 7 (Camden Large Print)

Printed in the United States of America
1 2 3 4 5 6 7 12 11 10 09 08

SUN OF SILVER, MOON OF GOLD

ONE

August, 1847

Much of this journal is taken up with mundane affairs, the price of maize, whether the mare is in foal, how many can comfortably be seated around outside the barn when the fireworks are let off when we have our Thanksgiving Day. But sometimes when the yellow tips of maize are silvered by the close creeping night and the branches of the trees make music across the river, I remember her. I remember how her blue eyes mirrored every changing mood and how, when she talked, her hands wove patterns in the air. And sometimes I lean against the picket fence and listen for the songs of the vanished children. Only the trees rubbing their branches together to make a sighing melody below the wind sing of what was and, by day, their voices are muted, drowned out by the rumble of cartwheels, the sloshing of water in the pails, the barking of the house dog to warn us that visitors are coming down the dusty track with news of the world beyond. But all the events that happened unroll behind my closed lids when I lie down at night when I seem to stand outside my own life and watch myself as if I am a stranger whose ways are foreign to me. So it is as an observer that I shall tell my story and in the telling perhaps many things will become clearer to me.

The Scott family sat in the study discussing Flora's future while the subject of their conversation sat upright in one of the high-backed leather chairs and fixed her gaze firmly on a solitary bird sipping from the birdbath in the garden outside. It was, she had discovered, much nicer to think of other matters while the family talked about their plans for her. So far in the many earnest discussions that had taken place nothing definite had ever been decided but the letter from Uncle Frank had changed all that.

'It's a wonderful opportunity,' Uncle Edward mused.

'Certainly Flora cannot hope for a better one.' Uncle Rupert nodded.

Of all the names to choose, she thought,

Flora had proved to be the most inappropri-
ate!

'More like a weed!' her brother, Samuel,
had teased.

As a child she'd slapped him for impertinence but as they grew up she had learned
to treat his remarks with lofty disdain. If
she was honest with herself she had to admit
that she'd never liked her younger brother
very much, and she'd liked him less when
he came swaggering home from college after
their father's death, greeting their mother
with an airy:

'Cheer up, Mater! We can't all last for
ever, you know!'

He'd been rather less cock-a-hoop when
the will was read, the late Mr Scott's share
in the family business having gone to him
as was only right and proper but with the
proviso that he could only draw on the
interest and Uncle Edward and Uncle
Rupert would administer the bulk of the inheritance until Samuel was thirty-five. Flora
was sure that, despite his fondness for his
son, her father had known only too well how
money slipped through Samuel's fingers.

The house had been willed to Mrs Scott
during her lifetime and after that it would
be Samuel's. Neither had Flora been forgotten. She had been left an income of £200 a

year and the right to live in the house until she married.

Mr Scott, so clever in many ways, had always believed firmly that his daughter would grow up to be a beauty and marry well.

'It's a plagued long way to go,' Samuel said now. 'Strikes me as a gross piece of impertinence to expect Flo to go traipsing off to the other side of the world because Uncle Frank is in need of a housekeeper.'

'A hostess,' Uncle Edward said quellingly. 'Frank never wed and now that he stands in such good odour in the town he needs to entertain more and enable his clients to meet in an atmosphere of civilized conviviality.'

'Did Frank really say all that?' Mrs Scott asked timidly from the layers of black crêpe in which she was shrouded.

'He implied it, my dear sister-in-law. He implied it,' Uncle Rupert said with a slight air of reproach. 'My own opinion is that Flora should take advantage of this invitation and go out to Chicago for a year or two. Frank's getting on in years and being still a bachelor has no children.'

Which meant, Flora thought, that Uncle Frank had nobody to leave his money to. He had sailed away to the New World when still a youth, determined not to be sucked into the family mercantile business. His brothers spoke of him as a colourful and daring creature who had made good without female influence.

'I'm sure it would be a great advantage for Flo,' Mrs Scott said.

'Depend upon it but it would be the making of her,' Uncle Edward agreed.

'Does my opinion count?' Flora enquired frostily. 'After all it's my future that we're discussing!'

'Take a turn in the garden with me, Flo.' Uncle Rupert rose, darting a warning glance at the others, and offered his arm to his niece.

The garden was a fair-sized plot of land, nodding with jonquils and daffodils. A bench was set beneath a chestnut tree and there was a rockery at the end of the garden. Beyond it, behind a low wall, the Thames flowed deep and strong.

Seating herself obediently Flora hid a wry smile as she recalled the romances she had borrowed from the circulating library. They always seemed to end with the handsome hero proposing to the charming heroine on a similar bench in some sylvan glade. That she herself had occasionally yearned to be one of the principal characters in such a

11

scene was a fact she chose to forget.

'Flo, may I speak to you frankly?' Uncle Rupert now asked.

'Of course, Uncle,' she said politely.

'Edward and I have always had your best interests at heart,' Uncle Rupert said in his slightly self-important manner. 'Since your father passed away we have kept a close eye on affairs, for I tell you honestly that Samuel is not cut out to be a man of business. Until he is of more mature age the capital is safe in our hands, but after that he has the management of it. Both Edward and I will ensure that your mother has a regular income as well as her home but you . . . We have families of our own, my dear Flo, and must provide for them.'

'Uncle, I have two hundred pounds a year of my own,' she reminded him.

'Which would keep you in modest comfort but I have a shrewd suspicion that your brother won't be too happy to have you live at his expense. He will also very likely wed and you are too proud to relish the notion of being the spinster sister-in-law, at everybody's beck and call.'

'And I'm hardly likely to marry,' Flora said.

'When a young woman reaches the age of twenty-seven without a single offer from any suitable gentleman it is perhaps time to look reality in the face,' he said.

Flora, who had been staring reality in the face since she had been old enough to see herself in a mirror, bit her lip. She knew by heart her broad forehead, her jutting nose — a Roman nose her father had called it — her slate-grey eyes above high cheekbones, her wide mouth and curly brown hair that refused to be soothed into the fashionable ringlets craved by every young lady. The fact that she possessed a good complexion, white teeth and well-shaped hands counted for very little. These admirable features were rather countered by the fact that she stood five feet eight inches in her stockinged feet and was long-legged and slender with none of the rounded curves so admired by gentlemen.

'You would like to be married surely?' Uncle Rupert probed.

To lie in strong arms at night and feel male hands caressing one! On the rare occasions when she allowed herself to indulge in such thinking her cheeks grew hot and forbidden desires surged into her imagination.

She said defensively, 'Only if I met the right person, yes, I suppose so.'

'In America men outnumber the women by fifty to one.' Uncle Rupert apparently addressed his remark to the chestnut tree since he had leaned forward and was studying its branches intently.

'I refuse to allow myself to be packed off to America to go husband-hunting,' she said crossly.

'American gentlemen are said to be taller than we are in the main,' Uncle Rupert said, still apparently talking to the waving branches of the tree. 'Not that that signifies! Nobody is forcing you to take a husband, my dear niece. But consider the alternatives! You can stay here with the probable consequences I've outlined to you or you can travel out to Chicago and keep house for your Uncle Frank. You'll scarcely remember him but he was always an amiable fellow. Even if you choose never to marry you can be assured of a most comfortable home with him, you know. He was, after all, your godfather.'

'What of Mama?' Flora countered. 'She will miss me.'

'Of course she will! We shall all miss you,' he said briskly. 'But we all live near enough to ensure she is never lonely. Your cousins are most attached to her.'

Her female cousins were small and neat

with shining ringlets and small mouths and brothers who went dutifully to work everyday and treated them with amused respect. Though her mother was too kind to say so openly, Flora knew that she compared her unfavourably with them.

'For a year or two?' Flora said, reluctantly considering.

'For as long as you wish.' Scenting victory Uncle Rupert patted her shoulder. 'Your allowance can be paid into a Chicago bank or you may take two years' allowance in notes of hand as well as silver. It will be an adventure for you.'

An adventure! The word stood out on the surface of her mind as if it had been there all along and she had only just noticed it.

She'd read of adventures in books, had listened to her uncles talking of the many countries where their cloth and lace and silk were sold. And deep inside she had craved an adventure for herself.

'Very well,' she said at last. 'I will go out to stay with Uncle Frank for a year or so.'

After that there were endless preparations to be made, a ticket to be bought that would land her in New York, after which she would travel overland by stage to Chicago. Letters must be written to Uncle Frank, farewells made to the neighbours who, in the main,

15

failed to conceal their belief that she was going out to catch a husband. There was teasing from her female cousins, who shook their curls and twittered that she was terribly brave and they simply would not dare venture, but it was obvious that they too knew very well that she was being packed off to spare the continuing embarrassment of her mother at having a plain, unmarriageable daughter.

There were also garments to be made! The uncles obviously had dreams of extending the family business and regarded their niece as a walking advertisement for the fine quality of their materials and the stylish cut of the garments. So there were winter dresses in fine checked wool, sprigged muslins for the summer, basque jackets edged with ricrac braid, a travelling cloak of dark velvet edged with fur, ball-gowns with wide spreading skirts looped up with flowers and bows, and half a dozen bonnets, two of them shaped like oriental turbans with swathes of striped silk.

'Your uncle probably entertains a lot and you ought to be suitably clad,' Mrs Scott said.

Mourning for her father was evidently to be abandoned in favour of attracting a suitor, Flora thought cynically. It also struck

her that Uncle Frank would have to entertain all day long if she was to get sufficient
wear out of all the finery. On the other hand
she liked beautiful clothes as much as the
next woman.

'Were it anyone else I would insist on a
chaperon for her,' Uncle Edward said tact-
lessly, 'but Flora is a sensible girl and it's
not as if —'

'As if men were standing in line hoping to
marry me,' Flora finished for him as he
hesitated slightly. 'It's perfectly all right,
uncle. I know my limitations very well and,
to be honest, I would hate having to travel
with a chaperon like a silly schoolgirl. I shall
manage perfectly competently, I assure you!'

'Of course you will, my dear!' He beamed
at her. 'And you need have no concern for
your mama since both Rupert and I will
keep a close eye on her.'

She thanked him, knowing that he would
keep his word. The family had always been
fond of the delicate, pretty Mrs Scott who
conformed so neatly to their notions of what
a female should be like.

It was coming towards the end of June
when she sailed. Her Uncle Rupert escorted
her to the ship after a long journey by post
chaise to Devon.

'The voyage should take no more than six

to eight weeks, depending on the weather,' Uncle Rupert assured her. 'Once I have seen you safely aboard I have business to attend in the town so I am in a way killing two birds with one stone if you will forgive the rather vulgar expression.'

Meaning, she thought, that her departure would free him to increase the Scott profits. There was no point in feeling any twinge of resentment however. Her four trunks had been sent ahead on to the ship; money was sewn into her corsets and arrangements made to enable her to draw on further funds in a Chicago bank.

'Your uncle has made it plain in his letters that he expects you to live at his expense,' Uncle Edward had informed her, 'but it is pleasant for a young woman to have funds of her own to draw on for gewgaws.'

She had seen Uncle Frank's letters, written in a slanting copperplate hand and affectionate in tone, but they told her little of the man himself. He had, she knew, had the courage to emigrate and make a success of himself in a strange land but the polished phrases of his letters revealed little of his feelings or intentions.

'It's more than twenty years since he left,' Uncle Rupert said as he escorted her to the quayside. 'No doubt he will have acquired an American accent by now.'

Flora had studied the address at the top of his letters.

'Pine Creek Ridge, Chicago, Illinois,' she said now thoughtfully. 'It doesn't sound much like a town, does it?'

'I imagine the well-to-do have moved out to the nearby rural areas,' her uncle said, eyeing the bulk of the sailing ship anchored off the wharf. Passengers were already streaming up the gangplank and on the quayside groups of people were waving to relatives already on deck.

'I hope you will settle happily,' Uncle Rupert said, having armed his tall niece on to the vessel and ensured that her luggage had been safely stowed and that her cabin was comfortable.

He meant to be kind, she knew, but the very word 'settle' implied that in the opinion of the family sufficient had been attempted to launch her in the marriage market and she would be expected to remain a long time at the other side of the Atlantic.

Accordingly, having kissed her cheek and warned her not to neglect summoning the ship's doctor should she feel the least twinge of sickness, he took his leave, pausing on the quay to wave his hat briskly in her direction before he disappeared into the crowd.

Flora had tried not to anticipate what a long sea voyage would be like but inside her, where her locked feelings slumbered, she couldn't help hoping for some adventure, no matter how mild, to befall her. Had Uncle Rupert personally ordered it the weeks of the voyage could not have passed more serenely. Within twenty-four hours she had discovered that she was an excellent sailor with no tendency to sickness, that her cabin, though well-appointed, was somewhat cramped, and that her fellow passengers were mainly composed of small family groups, women and children going out to join husbands and fathers, and a couple of teachers going out to posts in New York.

The weeks passed pleasantly enough. Flora put on a cloak and sensible shoes and tramped round the upper deck for exercise every morning. She read the books in the ship's library observing with some amusement that stories of seafaring disasters were notable by their absence, exchanged the customary greetings with her fellow passengers when she saw them at table or on the deck and was obliged to accept the fact that though everybody was courteous not a single gentleman fell in love with her. When the ship docked in New York harbour she shook hands with a few of the passengers with whom she had exchanged the odd snatch of conversation, slipped some coins into the steward's hand and, with a porter shouldering her luggage, disembarked leaving not one broken heart behind.

She had half-expected that Uncle Frank might have come to meet her, but on the quay she was approached by a thin little man whose appearance gave the lie to her uncle's belief that all Americans were tall.

'Miss Flora Scott? I see the labels on your bags,' he said. 'I shall take you to your hotel and return tomorrow morning to see you safely aboard the stage for Chicago.'

He had a rasping, nasal voice. He informed her when they reached a brownstone hotel near the harbour that he was called Wallace Brown, was a New Yorker born and raised, and carried out small commissions for her uncle from time to time. He then shook her hand and was gone as if life was hurrying at his heels.

Though the hotel was obviously respectable and catered for travellers on their way to other places, Flora felt a little spark of excitement reignite inside herself when she opened the window in her chamber and heard the varied sounds of the city float to her from the streets below. She would have liked to explore a little but prudence kept her within doors, where she ate an excellent meal, took the first decent bath she had enjoyed since setting out on the journey, and climbed gratefully into a high and somewhat hard bed.

She had hoped to sleep soundly but the contrast between the rolling motion of the ship and the calm vastness of the surrounding sea seemed to have got into her bones, as each time she settled into a doze the rolling motion seemed to return until dizzily she rose, put on a dressing-gown and sat by the window for a while, listening to the voices, the clattering of wheels and neighing of horses from below. New York, it appeared, never slept. It was, from the very little she had seen, a thrusting, cut-throat place packed with people intent only on getting on in the world, a place where the weak might easily go to the wall.

She was trying to imagine whether the same atmosphere would prevail in Chicago when she found herself nodding off to sleep and thankfully climbed back into bed.

'I reckon you were getting back your land-legs, Miss Scott,' Wallace Brown said when, after she had done her best with a breakfast far too lavish for her to finish, he arrived with a porter in tow to take her to the stage. 'They say sailors walk with a rolling gait because the land just won't stay steady under their feet! Now the journey'll take from three to three and a half weeks, depending.'

'On what?' Flora enquired with interest.

'This and that,' he answered vaguely. 'Meals and stop-over beds are provided of course, though I don't vouch for the quality of 'em. You needn't fear attack. The roads are good and the drivers well armed. Have a good journey, ma'am, and give my regards to Mr Scott.'

Flora promised to do so and settled herself into a corner seat, having sensibly decided not even to consider the possibility of attack. The few local Indians who remained in the area were too busy wheeling and dealing to bother attacking anybody, so she gathered from the scraps of conversations she heard in the dining room.

Expect nothing and you'll get a pleasant surprise if anything interesting happens, she told herself firmly, making herself as comfortable as possible as the stage lurched forward, its driver blowing a horn loudly.

This, then, was it. She was on her way,

the slight rolling of a vessel replaced by the jolting of the coach as it left the city behind and gained more open country.

Wallace Brown had spoken truly when he had assured her of a trouble-free journey. In the days that followed Flora found herself wishing that something out of the common run might happen to stir her fellow passengers out of their torpor and make her feel for the first time in her life that something unexpected might alter its course.

Apart from a wheel that wobbled loose and had to be fixed and a slight delay when one of the male passengers lost heavily at cards during a night spent at a hostelry and drowned his ill-humour in a bottle of rum, the fumes of which he generously breathed out over everybody, the stage made its uninterrupted way, the journey varied only by the little townships through which they drove, and the glimpses of thick forest and tall wheat reaching to the horizon which she could see through the windows.

Passengers were regularly disgorged and others taken on. Elderly women eyed Flora with complete indifference and were greeted by sons or husbands when they reached their destinations: serious-faced men either folded their arms and went to sleep, snoring a little, or filled the carriage with cigar

24

smoke with scant regard for anybody else; and a couple of lanky men with pistols strapped to their legs produced an ancient pack of cards with which they proceeded to play some complicated game that Flora couldn't believe was serious, especially when one man ended up owing the other a million dollars.

The weather was warm, too warm for the thick cloak she was wearing, and she was only too aware of the drops of warm sweat trickling down her neck and forehead and making her nose shiny.

Had she been the prize in a card game, she reflected, nobody would have bothered to play. That reflection amused her despite herself and she bent her head, choking back laughter.

On the twelfth day, after a night spent in a staging post opposite a tavern through whose swinging doors customers were regularly ejected, she boarded the stage for the last part of the journey and found her interest reawakening as she gazed through the window at the dusty road with its borders of grain which looked parched through the dust clouds thrown up by hoofs and wheels. The windows had been closed, yet a sickly-sweet smell pervaded the carriage.

'Rotting vegetation, ma'am,' said a man seated in the opposite corner and speaking to her for the first time. 'Chicago is built on a swamp, d'ye see, and it sure does smell mighty loud.'

'And 'cause of that the sewers ain't none too sweet neither,' another passenger offered as his contribution.

Flora smiled faintly, resisting the urge to retch. Through the dirt encrusted glass she could see more traffic on the road, farm wagons with bonneted women holding the reins, solitary riders with holsters at their hips, an occasional pony cart.

They bowled at last into a yard with other vehicles drawn up in it and a line of horses with elaborately decorated saddles tethered along a fence at one side. People were milling around, talking loudly, gesticulating wildly.

Flora climbed down stiffly, waiting for the luggage to be unstrapped. The noise about her hurt her ears and the stench here was more profound. She stepped away from the stage and looked about her, wondering whether her uncle was come and if she would recognize him.

In one corner a knot of men in fringed jerkins and trousers were squatting about a heap of skins, smoking as they argued over what was apparently the price. A little way off a young man stood watching them, arms folded, face impassive.

Seeing the black hair that fell to his shoulders, the olive-brown skin, the high cheekbones and narrow black eyes Flora felt a leap of excitement. This was the first Indian she had ever seen except in picture books.

'Four trunks for Miss Flora Scott!' The coach-driver called out the name loudly as he deposited the last of them on the ground.

The tall Indian raised his head and sent Flora a long, considering look before he unfolded his arms, stepped across to the piled luggage and lifted a couple of the trunks without apparent effort, depositing them at the side out of the way of the main rush of hurrying feet.

'Thank you . . .' Flora began.

He had returned for the other two trunks, hoisting them up and shouldering them over to join the others without a glance in her direction. He bent over them for a moment, then straightened up and turned, black eyes scanning her briefly.

'Thank you, sir.' Flora, somewhat at a loss, began again. 'That was very kind of you.'

Did one, she wondered, give Indians tips? Uncle Frank had never mentioned Indian

Americans in any of his letters home she had seen.

The Indian gave a slight shrug.

'My dear young lady, what possesses you to address a redskin as sir?' a voice enquired in tones of the deepest disapproval.

'I beg your pardon?' She turned to look at the short, plump man who had broken off his conversation with a nearby group to speak to her.

'You're from England?' He seized her hand and shook it. 'Cornelius Frame at your service, Miss — Scott, was it? You must be Frank Scott's niece. Word that you were expected has spread and caused quite a fluttering among the dovecots. Well, you are not to be scolded for your little slip of the tongue!'

Withdrawing her hand Flora looked down at him coldly.

'The gentleman shifted my trunks for me,' she said. 'I was merely thanking him.'

She had glanced involuntarily towards the Indian and caught the edge of a fleeting smile before he turned and walked away.

'It doesn't do to let these people get above themselves,' Cornelius Frame said with a slight frown.

There was a sarcastic retort on the tip of her tongue but she was forced to swallow it as a tall man jumped down from the wagon he had just driven in and strode towards her, one sun-browned hand outstretched.

'Miss Scott?'

'Yes?'

'Brent O'Brien, your uncle's manager,' the newcomer informed her. 'Sorry if I'm late but the road's a mite crowded today. Is this your luggage?'

'I've just been explaining to the young lady that we don't refer to redskins as gentlemen, O'Brien,' Cornelius Frame said.

'Oh?' Brent O'Brien glanced at her questioningly.

'He shifted my luggage aside, that's all,' Flora said shortly.

'Oh?' Brent O'Brien's dark eyes roved round the yard.

The Indian had paused near where the horses were tethered and was regarding them with a brooding look.

'That one?' Brent O'Brien looked amused. 'You astonish me, Miss Scott. Indians aren't in the habit of acting as porters for anybody. You must've taken his fancy. Good day to you, Frame!'

He nodded curtly to the other and without further comment began to load the trunks on to the wagon.

'Do we have much further to go?' Flora

enquired.

'About fifteen miles. Your uncle has a farm and comes into town only when business requires it. I'd better give you a lift up to the passenger seat.'

'I can manage,' Flora said. She stepped up on to a spoke of the huge wheel and flopped down somewhat inelegantly.

'Right! Hold on!'

He settled himself in the driving seat, gathered up the reins and drove out of the bustling yard into the dusty street. A wooden boardwalk was raised above the road along part of the length, flanked by a number of buildings mainly of wood, some with glassed windows and others with an open frontage filled up with shelves on which various types of merchandise were displayed. In the narrow lanes leading between the gaps in the buildings Flora could see what looked like warehouses.

'I thought Chicago was a large city,' she couldn't help remarking.

'Oh, it's growing fast.' Brent O'Brien guided the horses expertly along the street. 'The population has grown by about ten times in the last seven years, and last year Chicago was granted a City Charter.'

'Does it smell like this all the time?' asked Flora.

'Pretty much all of the time,' said Brent with a rueful grin. 'That's why your uncle prefers to live on his farm.'

'He didn't come to meet me,' she couldn't help commenting.

'He had a meeting to attend. We'll be at Scott's Place in just over an hour once we're clear of the town.'

They were soon bowling along a dirt road bordered by fields of corn though Flora soon learnt that here in America it was called maize. Some had already been harvested, in others the maize stood uncut. A stream of horses and pony traps were bound in both directions and in the fields she could see workers bent over their flashing sickles. Here and there smoke plumed up from a wooden shack, or a bed of golden-hearted blossom revealed a homestead. As they drew further away from Chicago a dusty wind blew up that made her cough.

'Best cover your nose and mouth with your scarf,' Brent O'Brien advised, 'You'll find riding drag a thankless occupation.'

Flora did as he suggested, clinging fast to the side rail as the horses gathered speed. Her companion, having apparently exhausted his fund of small talk, had fallen silent, seeming not to mind the layer of white dust that covered his skin as they journeyed further into the countryside.

They slowed slightly as they passed through a tiny village, where small wattle and daub houses were set in rough circles. Washing was hanging over nearby bushes and several children squealed as they played tag.

'They're Indians!' she exclaimed in surprise as Brent O'Brien drew up sharply to avoid a couple of them.

'They are Peoria.' He nodded. 'They farm here.'

'But I thought that . . .' She paused, confused.

'You thought all Indians went hunting and scalping,' he completed, his smile wry. 'Here they do some hunting, but they live in villages and grow grain and vegetables. Provided they're left alone they don't bother much about the scalping.'

'Then the man who moved my trunk . . . ?' She looked at him, wondering whether there had been a hint of teasing in his last remark.

'In town perhaps to trade, or buy some necessary goods —'

'It almost seemed as if he was expecting me,' said Flora. 'He lifted my luggage as soon as the stagecoach driver called my name. Why was Mr Frame displeased when

I thanked him? He said I should not have called him "sir".'

'You will find that there are many citizens of this country who consider the Indians to be people of a lower order — not entitled to the normal courtesies or respect. And Cornelius Frame has a high opinion of himself. He is a speculator, like dozens of others. He makes money from other people's ill fortune.'

From his words and tone it was obvious that he, for his part, had little respect for Mr Cornelius Frame. And as they drove on Flora had the uncomfortable feeling that he also had little respect for a young woman who had arrived not knowing anything about the new country to which she had travelled.

He had fallen silent again as they left the little villages behind and entered a stretch of woodland that loomed unexpectedly and through which they were soon driving; the dust of the road was left behind them now and the branches of tall trees were splayed above their heads.

'The Scott Place isn't far now,' he said. 'You'll be glad to get there I daresay.'

After the jolting of the wagon and the hot, dust-laden air she would have been glad to get anywhere. As if sensing this he drew up and reached down into a leather bag at his feet.

'Water flavoured with a dash of whiskey to give it flavouring,' he said brusquely, handing her a leather bottle. 'Help yourself.'

Flora took a gulp and spluttered slightly as the fiery liquid coursed down her throat.

'That's a lot of flavouring,' she said, regaining her breath.

'Refreshing though.' He took back the bottle and tilted it to his own lips.

When they set off again she had to admit to herself that her mouth felt less parched though she also felt slightly dizzy. Noting his impatient glance towards her, however, she sat quietly, holding on to the rail as the wagon swerved between the trees and emerged into another small village, bereft of coppery children but with several white ones seated on a long bench with a young woman in a print gown reading aloud to them.

'The school,' Brent O'Brien said, acknowledging the young woman's smiling nod with an uplifted whip. 'Minnie Hargreaves is the regular teacher. Nice young lady. Her father is overseer on the farm. The house is half a mile further on. You can see it from the rise.'

Flora wasn't sure exactly what to expect. In the short time since she had landed nothing had been quite how she had pictured it. What she certainly had never dreamed of seeing as they drove up a long gentle slope was an English country house with terraces leading from a stone façade and, beyond, a garden bright with flowers. Beyond the garden were great fields of maize interspersed with dark patches of woodland reaching as far as the eye could see.

'All this is my uncle's?' she exclaimed.

'He's what they call a warm man round here,' Brent O'Brien said. 'Now aren't you glad you came, Miss Scott?'

His voice was silky smooth but she sensed disdain in his expression as strongly as if he had given tongue to it.

Two

They drove down the long hill on the other side, the gradient gentle, the house becoming larger as they drew nearer. Flora could see white nets at the long windows, and decorative carving below the eaves and then they had entered open gates and were bowling up a gravel drive. They came to a stop before the long stone façade in which a door was opening. A man wearing a high cravat and a suit of black broadcloth emerged, his face reminding Flora of her uncles Edward and Rupert but ruddier than theirs, the mouth tighter and the eyes heavy-lidded.

'Flora, my dear! My apologies for not coming to meet you but I had urgent business to attend to,' he explained. 'Let me help you down. No trouble?'

This last was to Brent O'Brien who shook his reddish-brown head and asked in his turn: 'How did the meeting go?'

'Not to my liking!' Her uncle's lip had

curled scornfully. 'With Washington backing it there'll be little we can do while this madness persists. I'll speak to you later. Niece, come inside! I'll have you shown to your room so that you can bathe and change and then we'll meet at dinner. Here I like to dine at six but we'll eat at five today so we can savour a long leisurely evening together. I look forward to hearing news of home.'

After twenty odd years he still thought of England as home, Flora thought, as with his hand on her arm she mounted the terraced steps between banks of rock flowers and entered a cool wide hall. A staircase of carved and polished wood wound upwards towards a skylight and doors opened to left and right. Beyond the stairs she glimpsed an arched and columned entrance framed by long velvet drapes looped up with plaited ribbons. Under her feet the carpet was richly patterned with a deep pile. Everything spoke of comfort and luxury.

'Tina, my niece is here!'

Her uncle had raised his voice slightly as a slender woman with black hair wound into a heavy chignon at the back of her head glided from the pillared room. She was, Flora estimated, in her late thirties, eyes narrow above high cheekbones, skin a pale olive. Her plain white apron and black gown were those of a parlour-maid but there was nothing servile in her bearing. When she spoke it was with a slight Spanish accent.

'Miss Flora, you are welcome. Please to follow me.'

'I'll see you at five,' Uncle Frank said. He turned and walked through a half-open door beyond which a desk and high-backed chair could be seen.

Flora followed Tina up the curving staircase and along a broad gallery to a door at the end which the woman opened before standing aside politely.

The bedchamber beyond was as elegant as everything she had seen so far, with pale nets at the windows and looped from the bedposts, furniture of polished walnut and a dark-green carpet into which her feet sank. Her trunks stood in the middle of the room, obviously having been carried up the back staircase that she had noticed at the end of the gallery.

'It's lovely!' she said warmly. 'You must've gone to a great deal of trouble.'

'Mr Scott wished everything to be in readiness for his niece,' Tina said. 'The bathroom opens out of this room and the room opposite is a parlour for your own use. I will have hot water brought up.'

'Thank you. I take it that you're the . . . ?'

Flora found herself hesitating, a trifle confused, for if Uncle Frank already employed a housekeeper what part was she supposed to play?

'I am Tina,' the dark woman said stiffly. 'The servants have taken their orders from me but they will, of course, take them now from you, Miss Flora.'

'I don't want to usurp your position,' Flora said quickly, sensing hostility behind the narrow eyes. 'For the moment I would prefer everything to remain the same.'

'As you wish, Miss Flora.'

Tina moved smoothly to the door, glancing back as she went out.

Two younger girls came in, carrying buckets of hot water which they emptied into a gleaming hip bath. Fleecy towels hung on a long rail and there were dishes of soap and bottles of oil ranged on a side table.

Flora asked the girls for their names and gave them what she hoped was a friendly smile but they merely giggled, nudged each other, said Peggy Sue in unison and hurried out.

After the long dusty journey the bath felt heavenly. Flora stayed in it until the water was cool and then dried herself vigorously, hearing from the bedroom the faint sounds

39

of someone moving around. When she emerged from the bathroom the adjoining chamber was empty but most of her garments had been hung neatly in the wardrobe that occupied one long wall and her hairbrushes and vanity case had been laid out on the kidney-shaped dressing-table.

Meals, she surmised, would be formal in this household, so she chose a dress of dark green, its bodice shawl-collared, its wide skirt patterned with a band of lighter green. There was little she could do with her unruly hair save flatten it under a bandeau and twist the rest into spirals. Nothing could be done, she thought wryly, that could improve her face, the wide mouth and high-bridged nose defying all efforts to minimize them.

'At least you look neat, dear,' her mother was in the habit of saying.

'Neat is as neat does,' Flora misquoted at her reflection and betook herself into the gallery just as a gong sounded from below. Her uncle, emerging from the opposite wing, offered his arm gallantly.

'You look charming, my dear.' He gave her an approving nod. 'I've invited O'Brien to join us. He was kind enough to meet you in my stead. Rather rough about the edges but a young man with ambition. What did you think of Chicago?'

'I expected it to be much bigger,' she answered cautiously as they went down the stairs and entered a handsomely appointed dining room.

For an instant she had the odd notion that all the things in the Scott house at home had been replicated here as if a little England had been recreated in this raw land.

'It will grow,' Uncle Frank said confidently. 'There's money there as well as wind. Not that I'd dream of actually living there! The noise and the smell would be insupportable — ah, Brent, there you are!'

The manager turned from the small table where he was pouring drinks to bow slightly in her direction. In contrast to her uncle's frilled cravat and black suit he wore dark-blue broadcloth and a plain cravat. His russet-brown hair had been slicked back but threatened not to stay like that for very long and his dark eyes betrayed nothing beyond mild indifference.

'My niece will take sherry, I think?' Uncle Frank glanced towards her. 'Whiskey for me. Shall we take our seats?'

They did so, Brent pulling out Flora's chair. The table, which could easily have accommodated a dozen, was set with china and crystal for four. Uncle Frank seated himself at the head of it. Flora, taking the chair opposite Brent O'Brien, wondered for whom the place at the foot of the table was intended.

She hadn't long to wait, the arrival of the soup being preceded by the woman Tina, who had removed her apron and came to sit down. The manager rose politely as she entered. Uncle Frank did not.

The food was being served by two women in identical sprigged gowns, their long hair plaited at the back of their heads.

Her uncle dominated what little conversation there was, mainly enquiring after the family and the state of affairs in England, though he seemed little interested in her answers.

Soup was followed by carved meats with tureens of vegetables. Flora, lifting her fork to her mouth, was arrested by her uncle's casual tones as he said:

'As you can see, my dear, the household staff are well-trained. Half-breeds!' He inclined his head briefly in the direction of the two maidservants.

Flora, laying down her fork, sent an embarrassed glance in the direction of the slim black-gowned woman who occupied the foot of the table, one olive hand curved about the stem of her wineglass.

42

'Oh,' Uncle Frank said, 'Tina's a Mestiza, of mixed blood, part Spanish, part Mexican, part Apache. She's from New Mexico where I spent some time before I came further east. The Apache part is very small — a grandmother, wasn't it, Tina? So you need not fear for your scalp!'

'Apache women,' Brent said, to nobody in particular, 'have never taken scalps, and the Chiricahua Apaches — Tina's relatives — find the practice disgusting.'

'My manager is an educated man,' Uncle Frank said, applying himself to his meal again.

His head was lowered and Flora risked a glance towards Tina, who had raised her eyes and directed such a look of burning hatred at her employer that Flora felt a cold chill run through her. Then the housekeeper dropped her gaze, lifted her wineglass slightly and nodded in Brent O'Brien's direction before she sipped composedly.

Fruit and coffee were being served. Uncle Frank was talking again, relating an anecdote from his own childhood, asking after his other nieces. On the surface all was calm but Flora, drinking her coffee, was aware of cross-currents of emotion — of which her uncle seemed to be happily unaware.

The long evening was still warm and

pleasant, the sky beyond the french windows was suffused with a rosy light.

'If you wish to take a turn around the garden to relax after the long journey here,' Uncle Frank said at last, looking at Flora, 'please feel free to explore. I have some letters to write but Brent here will be happy to escort you.'

'I've work of my own to finish,' Brent O'Brien said somewhat stiffly, 'but of course if Miss Flora wishes . . .'

It wasn't the most pressing of invitations but Flora rose at once, saying:

'A stroll would be refreshing. I'll get my cloak.'

'Of course.'

Brent rose politely as she excused herself and went upstairs to don the thin dark-green cloak with the paler lining that matched her gown. When she came down again he was waiting in the hall.

'What would you like to see?' he enquired as they went down the front steps. 'The garden, stocked at vast expense by your uncle? The stables? We have some very fine horses. Do you ride?'

'Yes, I do.'

She was glad to be able to answer so positively. So far she hadn't made a very definite or favourable impression on anyone, she thought wryly.

'We must find you a good mount,' he observed as they walked slowly down the long drive.

Which meant, she supposed, a nice placid pony for an English lady. Her voice had sharpened slightly as she said:

'I enjoy a good gallop!'

'Right! The stables, then?' Brent O'Brien glanced at her and added, 'Perhaps not in that dress, though?'

'Let's just walk,' Flora suggested. 'I'd not wish to keep you from your work.'

'I have some accounts to reckon up but they're not urgent.'

'Do you live at the house?' she enquired as they strolled towards the long slope that reached to the woodland from where she had seen her uncle's property for the first time.

'I've my own place a couple of miles off,' he said.

'And work it yourself as well as managing my uncle's farm. That must be demanding.'

'I've a mortgage to pay off,' he said briefly. 'Once it's paid I'll be my own boss.'

'Your wife . . . ?'

'No wife.' There was faint amusement in his voice. 'I've been ten years working every possible hour to establish myself. That doesn't leave a whole heap of time for anything else.'

'I suppose not,' Flora said.

Surely it was his turn, having just met her, to show some polite interest in her doings! It was obvious that his mind was on other matters as he continued along the bottom of the hill where the track curved towards a deep stream.

'I never knew my uncle had been in New Mexico,' Flora said. 'In fact I really don't know very much about him at all. He has certainly prospered.'

'He has,' her escort said.

'And never married. I daresay like yourself he never had much time.'

She could feel herself flushing uncomfortably as she heard her own words. No doubt he regarded her as a rather tiresome busybody pumping him for information, but his own taciturnity was irritating her.

'No, he's not married,' Brent O'Brien said after an appreciable pause. 'My place starts over there, just beyond the stream.'

She could see fencing and the outlines of a square wooden house, fading now as the twilight deepened.

'It looks very snug,' Flora said inadequately.

'Suits me,' he said laconically. 'Is there

anything else you want to know?'

'You must think me full of curiosity,' Flora said, her blush deepening, 'but I know so little of my uncle. He emigrated when I was a very small child and since then we've heard of him only at irregular intervals, until he invited me —'

'Ay, he said he'd had a letter from one of his brothers telling him of your father's death,' Brent O'Brien said.

She had never seen the letter sent to Frank Scott. Now, as clearly as if it was laid out before her for her to peruse, she knew that somewhere in the message acquainting him with his brother's death had been a broad hint that their poor sister-in-law was not only widowed but saddled with a plain daughter who would be almost impossible to shift on the marriage market.

'So I travelled out here for a long visit,' she said aloud, uncomfortably aware that the silence was becoming awkward. 'Living in London can be dull and —'

'And you've a spirit of adventure yourself?'

She sensed faint mockery in the lightly spoken query. Suddenly she wanted to plant both feet firmly on the ground and say very loudly:

My uncle invited me out here because it's obvious my family told him that they'd a spinster daughter on their hands who only had two hundred pounds a year and who never attracted more than a passing glance from any eligible male, so may we please turn round and walk back and you can go and add up your accounts and stop trying to hide the fact that you are as bored with this conversation as I am.

Before she could say anything, however, Brent O'Brien said:

'Excuse me, please. I see a friend over there!'

Suddenly, leaving her behind, he strode ahead, hand outstretched, towards a young woman who had emerged from a copse of birches.

She was to think many times later on how strange it was that when something important happened it often didn't seem important until long afterwards. Yet without her realizing it that particular moment imprinted itself on her memory.

The sun had almost vanished below the horizon, painting a rim of scarlet across the sky. Against the fiery brilliance were appliquéd the varying shapes of the trees, the glinting stream, the outline of the fencing around the distant house.

She turned her attention to where the two figures of Brent O'Brien and the girl now stood, he bending towards her as he took her hand, she in a dress that had no colour in it beyond grey, her long silvery hair falling unconfined to her narrow waist.

Then the image quivered and sank with the last rays of the dying sun as Brent O'Brien turned and said:

'Miss Flora Scott, may I present Miss Tessa Fontaine?'

The girl stepped forward, one slim hand outstretched in her turn.

'You are Mr Scott's niece just arrived from England?'

She had a husky voice, sounding as smoke looked when it blew over a hill. The evening had robbed her face of colour but the light, almost translucent blue of her eyes was still visible for a moment before the light darkened further.

'Yes, I arrived this afternoon,' Flora said, surprised by the strong, rough grip of the small hand. 'Are you a neighbour?'

'I live with my brother at the edge of the village,' Tessa Fontaine said. 'Brent, have you heard how the meeting went? My brother will tell me nothing.'

'Not well, from what Mr Scott told me,' Brent said. 'Some spoke out against the motion but their voices weren't heeded and those who had most stake in the matter weren't suffered to attend at all. It's a bad business altogether.'

'Very bad,' the girl said. 'Excuse me, Miss Scott. I must return to the house before I am missed. I am happy to have met you.'

She ducked her head, the silvery hair parting to fall about her face like the wings of some exotic moth, and flitted away.

He stood looking after her, his back half-turned from Flora the gloom obscuring any expression on his face, then he said abruptly:

'It's a bad business indeed. I'll walk you back to the house, Miss Flora. I think we must leave the stables for another day.'

'If you wish to walk with Miss Fontaine I am quite capable —' Flora began.

'She hasn't far to go,' he said. 'Shall we turn back? Tomorrow I'll pick out a mount on which you can have your good gallop.'

'There seems to have been an important meeting,' Flora said.

'Not something that could interest a young lady from London,' he said.

'How can you possibly know what would interest me?' Flora said, her temper starting to fray. 'English women are not all unintelligent!'

'I wasn't implying that,' Brent O'Brien said quickly. 'The fact is that you are Frank

50

Scott's niece and for that reason you might find yourself involved in a conflict of opinion were you to take too keen an interest in local affairs.'

'Which men run anyway!' Flora said impatiently. 'You had much better tell me something or I may say the wrong thing inadvertently in the course of conversation.'

'The meeting,' he said levelly, 'was, from what your uncle told me, a lively one. I'd call it damnable but then I wasn't present. I was meeting you in Chicago. The point is that the Government, in its infinite wisdom, has decided to resettle the remaining Peoria.'

'Resettle?' Flora looked at him in perplexity. 'I assumed they were already here and settled.'

'So they are,' he said shortly. 'So they have been since the start of the coming of time. Once there were many tribes in Illinois, but they were a warlike lot and their populations decreased until mostly there were only Peoria left. For a time Illinois was French territory, and during the French-American War the French attacked the Peoria because they thought they were on the side of the Americans, and later the Americans attacked them because they were Indians. But the Government passed what we call the

51

Indian Removal Act just over eight years ago, and Washington is pressing hard for its implementation — indeed, some would say more than its implementation. Most of the Peoria were forced to sell their farms and their land, and were moved to new lands west of the Mississippi. Those who remain hope, I think, that if they are peaceable they will be allowed to stay on their farms, but the outcome of the recent meeting in Chicago makes that look a bleak prospect indeed. Now those who should know better have decided to push the Peoria westward.'

'My uncle said that it hadn't been to his liking,' she remembered.

'Your uncle has many Peoria working on his land. They cause no trouble and work for lower wages than the whites would do.'

'At least he doesn't employ slaves,' Flora said.

'Slaves have to be bought, clothed and fed,' Brent O'Brien said. 'Indians are cheaper.'

'You're not very polite about my uncle,' she challenged.

'I've no reason to be,' he said shortly, then interrupted himself with an impatient exclamation. 'I ought not to trouble you with old, worn-out quarrels, Miss Flora! They happened a long time ago. Your uncle pays me good money and is respected by his fellows. If you'll excuse me I'd best be getting home. The main terraces are lamplit so you can't get lost.'

He bowed before she could lodge any objection and walked rapidly away towards the side of the big house, heading, she surmised, for the stables.

Flora grimaced slightly and walked on up to the main entrance, the night-scented stock sending a wave of perfume up as she passed. As she entered the hall through the half-open door her uncle called to her from the room on the left.

The study where he sat in a comfortable chair puffing at a large cigar wasn't a big room but it was handsomely appointed with a flat-topped desk, several bookcases and walls panelled in pine.

'Did you have a pleasant walk?' Uncle Frank enquired, gesturing towards a chair. 'Brent is a good fellow, knows his stuff, works hard and doesn't try to cheat me. I even fancy he has a certain respect for me though we don't see eye to eye on every subject.'

'He told me about the meeting you attended,' Flora said, sitting down.

'Hardly a subject to interest the ladies!'

'But I am interested!' she said quickly. 'In

a strange country it's best to learn as much as possible, surely?'

'Well, it's a bad business,' he said gloomily. 'There's no reason to resettle the Peoria. Most of them are ready enough to sell their land at below the asking price and then are willing to pay rent for the privilege of staying on it.'

'That sounds like sharp practice,' Flora said uneasily.

'Nonsense, Flora! Indians don't understand the value of the lands they sell,' he said with a faint chuckle. 'You mustn't let these matters upset you. I've no doubt they'll leave peacefully enough and settle on the plains. If there aren't enough buffalo there to satisfy them they can trek north and join their cousins the Northern Cheyenne. All these tribes are related somewhere along the line, you know.'

'And what do the Peoria think?' she enquired.

'My dear niece, they're like children,' he said soothingly. 'One doesn't ask the opinion of children! You mustn't let these matters agitate you. What bothers me is that when they do leave we might have a flock of undesirables swarming in. For that reason if nothing else I opposed the measure but progress cannot be stemmed, it seems. So what else did you and O'Brien have to talk about?'

'You don't mind if I go riding?'

'You enjoy riding?' He looked pleased, though whether at the information she had just given him or at the change of subject she wasn't certain. 'Splendid! Brent will see you well mounted. You may also like to go riding with friends. There are some very charming young ladies in the neighbourhood who will be pleased to offer friendship.'

'I met one neighbour,' Flora said. 'A Miss Tessa Fontaine.'

There was a sudden cold silence in the little study. Frank Scott put down his cigar in a large ashtray at his side and stared at her. Once again she was conscious of the tight mouth and heavy-lidded eyes, half-closed now but showing a stony glint.

'Is something wrong?' she asked.

'Nothing that is your fault, my dear.' His lips stretched into a smile though his eyes remained glacial. 'You must understand that you are, of course, perfectly entitled here to make such friends as you choose. Your own good sense will guide you as to who are desirable acquaintances but I must warn you that the Fontaine girl is not a suitable friend for a decent woman.'

'Why?' Flora asked bluntly.

A dull flush spread upwards from his neck though whether of rage or embarrassment was impossible to tell.

'My dear niece!' He rose, placing a heavy hand on her shoulder. 'There are certain topics, even here, that cannot be discussed in mixed company, far less between uncle and niece. You are of full age and may, of course, follow your own inclinations but I do request you to follow my wishes in this matter.'

Flora said nothing, some instinct warning her to remain still and silent.

'So that's settled!' he said in a satisfied tone. 'I hope you will soon come to regard this house as home, my dear. I've told Tina that in future she is to take her orders from you should you desire any alterations in the running of the household. Now I shall bid you good night. You must be weary after such a long journey.'

'Good night, Uncle.'

The heavy hand was removed from her shoulder, she rose, dropped a small curtsy and went out, glancing back to see that he had seated himself again and was knocking the glowing ash out of his cigar with such ferocity that little sparks flew about the table.

In the hall Tina stood, a black-clad figure against the dark wood of the staircase, her face expressionless under a hanging lantern.

'Did you want anything more, Miss Flora?' she asked.

'No thank you, Tina. Oh — perhaps some drinking water in my room?'

'I've already placed a carafe of water there, Miss Flora,' Tina said.

'Oh, thank you.' Flora wanted to say something warm and friendly to the woman but her demeanour was cold and stiff. Somewhat lamely she added, 'I was very sorry to hear that the Peoria are to be sent West.'

'Oh, they'll cause no trouble,' Tina said. Her lip had curled slightly but her tone was impassive. 'They've allowed themselves to be cheated so often that once more will make no difference. Goodnight, Miss Flora.'

She crossed the hall and tapped on the study door. Flora waited until the door had closed behind her and then mounted the stairs to her room.

The curtains had been drawn, the lamps lit. Flora went over to the window and pulled the curtain back a little to reveal the moonlit terrace below and the garden beyond it, which reached to the main gates. It felt as if a piece of England had been conjured up here but behind the gates the track stretched past wooded hills to the village and in the shadows uneasy forces were stirring. Her uncle's words and Brent O'Brien's scornful opinion of the meeting that had been held warned her that in this paradise, hidden in the high, waving maize and the swooping branches of the trees serpents dwelt, plants grew, conjured in men's minds, that could poison everything that lived here.

She let the curtain drop and went over to her trunks, now piled neatly against one wall. In an outer pocket in the smallest trunk she kept a pocketbook in which she had noted down details of her journey with some idea of using the notes to make her letters home more interesting.

It was time to jot down her first impressions if only to make certain later on that she had not misunderstood the situation here.

The pocketbook was there but her fingers encountered something else, evidently overlooked by whoever had unpacked her garments.

She took out the object and held it closer to the lamp, her brow furrowed as she turned the silver disc this way and that. It was jewellery of some kind with a hole bored through the metal for a chain, though no chain revealed itself on a second search inside the pocket.

Flora turned it over and saw something carved into the circle. A mouth that smiled with closed lips had been etched into the silver.

She sat down on the edge of the bed and tried to think but no answers came. Only questions whirled in her head.

THREE

All about her the harvested stooks of maize stood in ordered rows beneath the sky. Along the river the Peoria women laughed and gossiped as they did their laundry, the water foaming as they rubbed cakes of yellow tallow soap into the wet bedsheets and garments and then flapped them vigorously below the surface of the fast-flowing water. Others were wringing out the clothes and either laying them to dry over nearby bushes or taking them to the ropes stretched between poles outside their houses.

Flora checked the sturdy pony that Brent O'Brien had deemed suitable for her and watched the scene with pleasure, wishing she could capture it on canvas. Like all girls she had spent many hours painstakingly drawing and painting vases of flowers and baby cherubs with wings in the seminary she had attended daily but when she had left school and begun to paint in her free time her brush sometimes wandered away from the reality of what she was looking at and found faces in flowers, the tongue of a serpent flickering from the curved handle of a jug, and her colours were always brighter than nature had decreed, reds and oranges and purples spilling from her brush. Needless to say none of her paintings graced the walls of her home.

'They look positively savage, dear,' her mother had said apologetically.

Now she itched to capture the bold, swift movements of the women with their skirts of red and green tucked above bare brown feet, their long elaborately braided hair, and the copper bangles jangling on their wrists, giving them a vitality that was aeons away from the stuffy drawing rooms where ladies like herself and her mother endured the discomfort of tight lacing and were trained never to raise their voices or laugh without putting a polite hand before their mouths.

It was three days since she had arrived and much of that time had been spent in exploring the house and garden. Uncle Frank, setting himself to be hospitable, had accompanied her, approving his manager's choice of mount, insisting she taste the various dishes being prepared every day in a huge kitchen at the back of the house where a black cook, adorned with a frilled and towering headdress, presided over several menials who ran hither and thither at her bidding.

'Choose the right servants,' Uncle Frank said complacently, 'and a household almost runs itself.'

She had been aware as he spoke of Tina's cynical black gaze fixed on them from the corner where the housekeeper stood, hands folded at her neat waist. The older woman glided silently about the house, appeared at the evening meal where she sat mute, was glimpsed here and there in various rooms usually with a duster in her hand. What was obvious was that she needed no supervision or help and her chilly glance rebuffed friendship.

There were books in the study and more in a room behind it.

'Whenever I have occasion to go away on business I always buy a few books,' Uncle Frank told Flora. 'A well-bound book is a mark of civilized living.'

'Surely well-written would be more to the point,' Flora had answered.

Her uncle had given her a quick frowning glance as if he suspected her of levity.

The gardens contained not only flowers but vegetables and fruit trees, planted in rows as if they were on parade. They were beautiful but Flora had a sneaking fondness for the trees that grew untidily along the village track and crowded the hill above the maize fields.

Early this morning Uncle Frank had, to her secret relief, driven to town where he would spend the next few days.

'It's unfortunate, my dear Flora, but I have a series of meetings to attend which cannot be monitored by anyone save myself,' he had explained. 'I hope to be back in time to escort you to church on Sunday morning. That's when you will be formally welcomed into the community and the ladies will soon afterwards present their calling cards and issue their invitations. There is a flourishing sewing circle and a Foreign Aid Mission Society and also a choral group, I believe.'

Flora smiled faintly without answering. Sewing had never been a favourite occupation; she found it difficult to carry a tune for the length of a song and in her heart of hearts she was inclined to believe that missionaries might do better if they remained quietly at home.

Now at last with Uncle Frank safely out of the way she had donned her riding habit and ordered the pony, Bess, to be saddled up. So far she had taken only short, demure rides on her with her uncle riding alongside.

She sat now, watching the Indian women at their laundry, delighting in the bustle and colour. This was a scene she would love to paint but she doubted if she had the skill.

Away from the village the cornfields stretched apparently forever with long tracks to divide one from another. Men were loading maize stooks on to wagons while women followed the gleaming scythes of the reapers to take up the gleanings. Ahead of her the path she was on led into another copse of trees. Overhead the sun was brilliant but the edges of the leaves were tipped with flame and brown and the few clouds in the sky seemed to hang lower than before beneath the brilliant blue. Autumn was here, Flora thought, and then, according to her uncle, the weather could change overnight, bitter snow-laden winds sweeping over everything.

The trees were heavy with hazel nuts. Flora reached up from the saddle to pluck some down and fill her pocket with them but Bess suddenly shied nervously, ears laid back. Further within the copse bushes growing around a solitary oak shook unnervingly.

Flora had never regarded herself as a nervous person. Yet at that moment she had to remind herself firmly that this wasn't wild untamed country but merely a few trees in the midst of farmland where maize was now being harvested for the markets.

'Who's there?' She raised her voice slightly, half-expecting to see a child or an animal emerging from the thicket.

Instead the soft padding of feet sounded; she heard the sharp crack of a breaking twig.

Flora waited a moment and then, assuring herself she was much braver than she felt, slid from the saddle and pushed her way through the trees into the copse.

The oak tree towered over the surrounding bushes, its branches proud with kingship, but apart from a slight breeze rustling the leaves on the bushes everything was still again. Flora stopped to part the tangled creepers that wound themselves around almost everything that grew in the shelter of the oak but saw nothing more than dense vegetation behind it. A small child perhaps, though she had seen none here.

Rising, puzzled, she tilted her head to the autumn-tinted leaves and saw something there, glinting golden from a twiglet.

An instant later she held in her hand a little golden crescent, companion surely to the silver sun she had found in the outer pocket of her trunk. This hung from a thin gold chain but when she turned it over she could see the face with a smiling mouth etched there.

She pushed it into her pocket, returned to the pony and remounted. There was a mystery here which probably had a simple explanation, but some instinct warned her to be cautious whom she questioned about it.

She was riding back towards the main gates when a voice hailed her and Brent O'Brien loped towards her, shirtsleeves rolled to his elbows, a wide-brimmed hat on the back of his russet head.

'Had a pleasant ride?' He straddled the low fence that marked the boundary of the maize field.

'With my uncle being in Chicago,' Flora told him, 'I've a chance to explore a little on my own.'

'Ay, there's a meeting of the state legislature to make plans for the removal of the Peoria,' he said.

'Removal!' Flora stared at him. 'Is that what they're calling it now? It's nothing of the kind and well you know it!'

'I don't choose government jargon,' he replied coolly.

'But you could speak out against it. I'm sure my uncle will raise objections at the meeting!'

'No doubt he will for whatever reason,' Brent said with a downcurving grin. 'His is one voice and he'll not hold out for long against his fellow citizens.'

'The women washing down at the river seemed happy enough,' Flora remembered. 'Surely they don't want to leave?'

'They know other tribes have been moved by force. Part of their thinking is fatalistic — what will be will be. Part is blurred thinking,' he told her. 'They cling to the hope that it will never actually happen.'

'They ought to resist,' Flora said.

'With scythes and pitchforks?' he raised an eyebrow. 'Or bows and arrows, perhaps? Have you ever witnessed a fight between men armed with guns and men without them? Oh, they have hunting rifles but the distribution of ammunition is already controlled.'

'There must be white people who disagree with it,' Flora said, her cheeks flaming. 'They will have plenty of guns and ammunition!'

'White against white in defence of redskins? What a romantic you are!' he gibed. 'Let me tell you exactly what will happen. When the soldiers arrive a few hotheads among the Peoria will try to resist but they will be captured or killed, the rest herded westward to their reservation on the plains. There will be indignant meetings held in the church and general agreement that what's happened is wrong and shameful and it's a crying pity that nobody can do anything about it. Then a few will realize that there are some snug little farms around going cheap and others will remind themselves that the Peoria are savages when all's said and done! In a year's time we'll be collecting money to send to the Indians in their reservation and in ten, maybe twenty years, it'll be as if they never lived here at all.'

'You're saying that I don't know what I'm talking about,' Flora said slowly. 'But you're among those who will do nothing, aren't you?'

'I've my own affairs to run without taking on any other business.' He sounded cold and distant, as if her indignation irritated him.

'But you must have some notions!' she persisted.

'They don't involve standing up against the army.' He took a hip flask from his side, tilted his head for a draught, wiped the rim of the mouth and held it out. 'Miss Flora?'

'Is it flavoured with whiskey?' she demanded.

'More than somewhat.'

'Then no thank you! So you're going to do nothing?'

'Miss Flora, we can't work miracles.'

'Well, it couldn't happen in England!' she said decidedly.

'Couldn't it?' He took another swig from the bottle and replaced the lid. 'Miss Flora, it happens everywhere. When was the last time you saw a Romany caravan on the move and never wondered if those people really wanted to travel? When you light your coal fire in the winter — or pardon me! When your maidservant does so — do you think of the people crawling beneath the ground dragging carts of coal with them for low wages so the rich can keep warm? Of course you don't! There's injustice every-where and we'd all go crazy if we thought about it too often. Excuse me, but I have to get back to work!'

The curtness of his tone indicated, she thought indignantly, that he obviously regarded her as a fool brought up in the lap of luxury and ignorant of anything beyond her own small, sheltered world.

'One thing more!' she said equally sharply. 'The Indians have names for their tribes like Cherokee, Kiowa, Comanche and so on?'

'Those are some of the dominant tribes

divided into clans and then sub-clans under other names. The Sioux is a huge people but there are Teton Sioux and Brule Sioux and so on.'

'And they have personal names like our names? I ask for a reason,' she added as he frowned slightly.

'A few have adopted white surnames,' he told her. 'Most are given a secret personal name at birth which isn't spoken again until they die. They also receive a personal name when they are small children, usually something they point to or the first word they say clearly. Later still they acquire names which reflect their personalities. Some of those are translated into English or French or whatever tongue the nearest white settlers speak. Why do you ask?'

'Would you know an Indian named Moon or Sun?'

'I imagine that's a fairly common name,' he said dismissively. 'Have you any reason for —'

'Merely idle curiosity,' Flora said coldly. 'Good day, Mr O'Brien.'

Flora clucked her tongue to Bess to move her on and rode off, conscious of the manager's puzzled stare. Had he been more sympathetic she might have confided in him, but his ill manners had stunted her own attempt to be friendly. Obviously he regarded her as a snobbish white woman who had arrived convinced she knew everything about everything.

Dinner that evening was a solitary meal, since Tina absented herself from the table. Evidently the housekeeper had no wish for any closer friendship. Flora ate her soup, braised beef and apple tart in lonely state and went upstairs to the little parlour that had been provided for her use, to write to her mother and the two uncles remaining at home.

She conjured up grateful phrases describing the kindness of Uncle Frank's welcome and a long glowing account of the house and gardens.

Indeed to call it a farm gives quite the wrong impression for the house is elegant and spacious and the gardens quite beautiful even in autumn. There is too a flourishing social life in the village in which I shall participate no doubt.

Through the windows the harvest moon hung like a ball of bright molten orange in the sky. Within the solid walls sound was muted. She had written nothing of the Peoria women in their bright skirts or the

71

children who played tag along the banks. Poor Mama would very likely fret lest she was fraternizing with the natives! What her family wanted to hear was that she was a social success and that already several gentlemen had paid her compliments or engaged her in conversation. It was galling to reflect that her arrival had excited no more than the mildest stirs of interest and that the only man with whom she had had any conversation at all regarded her as a fool.

After sealing her letter and signing it she rose, drew the curtain against the too exuberant moon and retired to her bedroom.

The next morning, having eaten her breakfast, she rang the bell just as Tina was noiselessly crossing the hall.

'Yes, Miss Flora?' Hands at her waist, cold black eyes fixed on the younger woman, the housekeeper was the model of respectful attention.

'I shall go riding again this morning,' Flora said. 'There are nuts and berries in the woods. I thought of gathering some for a pie.'

'Certainly, Miss Flora. I can have a covered basket attached to the saddle,' Tina said promptly.

'I've been talking to Brent O'Brien,' Flora rushed on. 'He thinks the Peoria will soon be moved out.'

'Brent generally talks good sense,' Tina said.

'The inevitable, you mean? Tina, when you came from New Mexico . . .' She hesitated, uncertain how to continue without offending the housekeeper.

'I came to Illinois with Mr Scott of my own free will,' Tina said without a flicker of her eyes. 'He offered me a good opportunity.'

'You don't mix with the Peoria?'

'They're farmers,' Tina said with a hint of scorn. 'My grandmother's people were warriors. Nobody has forced them off their land. If you'll excuse me I have my duties to perform.'

'My uncle —' Flora began.

'He's known as a good man, Miss Flora.' Tina raised her glance briefly, fixed it on the other's flushed face and went out again.

'And that,' Flora thought wryly, 'is exactly what you deserve for trying to make a confidante of the housekeeper!'

She went upstairs to don her riding boots and the tricorn hat with the hard crown and to check the pocket of her jacket where she had put the two . . . tokens? Jewellery? What did they signify?

She seated herself by the dressing-table and looked at them again. Both were the same size, the sun of silver and the moon of gold, the smiling features sharply etched, the one missing its chain, the other with its chain. One had been left in the outer pocket of her trunk and the other had been hung on the branches of a tree.

Someone, she mused, must know what they signified. Perhaps the Peoria were planning to resist their so-called removal, but if so why put the silver sun, or was it a full moon, in her luggage? No, it was a sun, its circumference edged with tiny slivers of silver to represent rays, she surmised.

She put them back in her pocket and went downstairs to the stables at the side of the house. Bess greeted her with a whinny, though whether that was because she recognized her or at the prospect of exercise Flora couldn't tell. There were no grooms about, the pony stood ready saddled. She led her out and mounted up without difficulty.

The weather was still warm though the breeze hinted at a coming coolness and she fancied the maize fields had lost their glint.

Flora took the long gentle hill at an easy pace, then trotted along the unpaved road with the huddle of buildings along one side and on the other a smithy and a general store which appeared to sell a great variety of goods, with bags of seed potatoes and loaves of sugar mixed up with jars of candy, some tired-looking fruit and rolls of calico. At one end was the school yard that she had passed with Brent O'Brien. Today it was empty but voices chorused from the long shack beyond.

Flora dismounted, tied Bess to a hitching post and strolled along the street, occasionally impeded in her progress along the raised sidewalk by a group of bonneted, chatting women, baskets balanced on their hips. It reminded her that she'd undertaken to pick some nuts and berries, but first she hoped to find out a little more about the sun and moon that nestled in her pocket.

Whoever had placed the tiny sun in her trunk had done so secretly, risking discovery. The moon had been hung for someone, not her, to find. Perhaps it would have been wiser to leave it there.

'Excuse me, but you are Frank Scott's niece, are you not?' A good-looking man, just emerging from a grain store, had paused to doff his hat. His silvery fair hair and light-blue eyes seemed increasingly familiar as he continued:

'Forgive me for speaking to you without an introduction but my sister mentioned that she had met you. I am Charles Fontaine. I trust you'll accept my apologies for any embarrassment Tessa may have caused?'

'I was happy to meet your sister,' Flora said, somewhat nonplussed at his words. 'Indeed I thought her charming.'

'You're very kind, Miss Scott.' He allowed himself a slightly wintry smile. 'You will understand, of course, why we won't be calling. Good day.'

He bowed slightly and walked off, leaving her staring after him. She might have followed him to request an explanation but the school bell sounded and a group of small children poured out of the yard, obviously delighted to be at liberty. Flora had turned to look, retracing her steps towards the young woman whom Brent O'Brien had greeted on her arriving in the village.

'Minnie Hargreaves?'

She entered the gate and paused in front of the schoolteacher who looked up out of bright brown eyes set in a round face framed by coiled plaits of ginger hair.

'Miss Flora Scott.'

She stopped ringing the school bell and offered her hand as the echoes died away.

'You're the daughter of my uncle's

overseer,' Flora recalled, 'which is all I know of you, so please excuse my introducing myself. Is school over already?'

'The children help with the harvesting,' Minnie Hargreaves said in a faintly defeated tone. 'It's difficult enough to get them to settle in class at any season but harvesting time is the worst. My father and I had planned to call on you on Sunday. That's the custom here.'

'Oh, I hadn't realized.'

'After church, of course,' Minnie Hargreaves said.

'So until I've shown myself at church I don't exist?' Flora gave a rueful smile. 'I wondered why nobody had been to visit. I'd not expected such formality out here.'

'People regard it as important to maintain civilized standards,' Minnie said gravely. 'Otherwise we might all end up like poor Tessa Fontaine.'

'What did Tessa Fontaine do?' Flora enquired.

'Did your uncle not tell you?' Minnie looked slightly surprised, then blushed as she answered her own question. 'No, of course not! It isn't a topic to be discussed in mixed company. The truth is, Miss Scott, that Tessa Fontaine was taken by Indians when she was still a child. Three or four wagons were on their way to Pine Creek Ridge bringing families to settle here. She was with her older brother and her parents. The wagons were attacked. There'd been Indian trouble for several months. The parents were killed as well as several others in the group but Charles managed to escape. Tessa was snatched away. Abducted, Miss Scott! It was ten years before army scouts found her and brought her back and then she was — well, you may take my meaning.'

'I'm not taking it very far,' Flora said.

'She was — tainted,' Minnie said, lowering her voice. 'Of course it's not entirely her fault but any girl of spirit would have resisted unto death, don't you think? Her brother has kindly given her a home but she cannot mix in polite society and naturally her marriage chances are ruined! It's very sad.'

She didn't look particularly sad, Flora thought. Her bright brown eyes were gleaming slightly as if she found a certain relish in the tale.

'How long has she been back?' Flora asked.

'Just over a year,' Minnie said. 'She causes no trouble but then she has a forgiving brother.'

'Who wasn't killed or captured,' Flora said.

'He was scarcely more than a child himself,' Minnie told her. 'You know, over the years many attempts were made to find her but those redskins can melt into the landscape when it suits them and unfortunately many of the captive children adapt far too quickly to the native customs and become little savages themselves.'

'But why steal children anyway?'

'There'd been some kind of outbreak of fever among them, by all reports and several small girls had died. Most regrettable, of course, but that doesn't give them licence to steal other people's children to replace them.'

'No, of course not,' Flora said.

'And when she was rescued,' Minnie was continuing, 'she was most ungrateful. She kept insisting she was a white Peoria, if you please!'

'She adapted?'

'Far too readily in my opinion,' Minnie said. 'However, it's an unpleasant subject. One doesn't like to dwell upon it but it's as well that you should know the facts lest you inadvertently say something . . .'

She let her voice trail way.

'Put my foot in my mouth?' Flora said

pleasantly. 'I'm rather apt to do that on occasion. It's kind of you to give me warning.'

'And we can talk of other things when we next meet,' Minnie said comfortably. 'As I said, my father and I will call on you and your uncle after church on Sunday. In the afternoon if that's convenient?'

'I'm sure it will be,' Flora said. 'My uncle went to an important meeting, you know?'

'Oh, we ladies like to keep up with current events,' Minnie observed.

'The resettlement of the Peoria — you are in favour of it?'

'I think it very hard on them,' Minnie said, somewhat unexpectedly. 'They are peaceful, hard-working people and their babies are rather sweet, but the land is needed, my father tells me. One cannot stand in the way of progress.'

'Progress?' Flora looked at her.

'Until Sunday then?' Minnie extended her hand again. 'It will be a great pleasure to welcome another lady into our little church.'

She smiled and trotted across the yard, as complete a picture of self-satisfaction as Flora had ever beheld.

FOUR

Flora, restraining her indignation with some difficulty, waited a moment before making her way back to where Bess was tethered.

Riding back along the street and down towards the river with its border of trees, she reminded herself that people didn't change when they came into a new land. Most of them brought their customs and prejudices with them, and passed them on to the next generation. At least Minnie Hargreaves's words had provided a clue as to the meaning of the two tokens.

She had hoped to find Tessa Fontaine down by the river but there was only a scatter of Peoria children, fashioning pipes from the hollow reeds that skirted the low banks and blowing through them to produce a series of far from melodious sounds. As Flora halted Bess a woman with her skirts hoisted up emerged from a nearby dome-shaped dwelling, waving a saucepan at them and yelling in a completely unfamiliar language which Flora guessed to be one of the local Indian tongues. Giggling, the children fled.

'They drive me crazy!' the woman said, stepping closer to Flora and speaking in English. 'My own boys are the worst but it's hard to scold them.'

'I'm not married but I'd still find it hard to scold a child,' Flora admitted.

'You're Flora Scott.' From her broad, coppery face two dark eyes were staring at Flora in a frankly appraising but friendly manner.

'I am,' Flora said, 'and you are . . . ?'

'Mary Redfeather. My husband, John Redfeather, owns a small sawmill some way off. Were you looking for someone?'

'I wondered where the Fontaine house was.'

'Where the white Peoria woman lives. Folk don't call on her.'

'I'm not folk,' Flora said, meeting the questing black stare with a smiling look of her own. Mary Redfeather lowered the saucepan, gave her a keen glance, then showed her white teeth in a smile.

'Just past the bend in the river. Charles Fontaine rode out for Chicago about ten minutes since.'

She gave a brisk meaningful nod and

marched back towards the dome-shaped dwelling, clad in birch bark, outside which the small children were still tumbling before Flora had a chance to thank her.

Flora rode on along the river bank. Though the sun still shone out of a mellow sky the breeze had sharpened and leaves streaked with amber, scarlet and brown fluttered in the air like a swarm of exotic butterflies.

She found the house without difficulty. It was of fair size, its wooden walls inset with small windows at which white netting fluttered slightly. Smoke spiralled from a chimney, a picket fence surrounded a neatly planted garden with a shell-edged path from gate to front door.

As Flora dismounted and tethered Bess to the hitching rail by the gate the front door opened and the slender form of the girl she had seen by the river appeared and hurried down the front steps towards her.

'My brother isn't here, Miss Scott!' She held out her hand as if to ward her off. 'He's ridden to Chicago.'

'I came to see you,' Flora said, opening the gate and approaching.

'But your uncle —'

'Is in Chicago too.' Flora closed the gate behind her. 'Won't you ask me in?'

For a moment she thought the girl would refuse but, after a hesitation, Tessa Fontaine nodded briefly. She turned and led the way past rows of neatly planted vegetables into a narrow hallway off which a pleasant parlour opened.

'Will you have some tea?' she enquired, glancing at a kettle steaming on the hob.

'Thank you,' Flora said, taking off her hat.

'Oh, and please sit down.' Tessa indicated a chair set well away from the netted window.

Flora, having seated herself, watched her obviously reluctant hostess busying herself with cups and saucers. In broad daylight she was as mothlike as before, her plain grey dress draining what little colour remained in her lightly tanned skin. Her pale-blue eyes were dark-shadowed as if she wept often and slept little; her silvery hair was tied carelessly into a long tail that swung against her back as she moved.

'When you were with the Indians,' Flora said bluntly as Tessa set down the cups on a round table, 'did they give you another name?'

'When I was married, yes.' She handed Flora her drink and sat down herself.

'Married? I hadn't heard —'

'Nobody is likely to tell you either,' Tessa

said, sipping her tea and putting the cup down again. 'Even if people mention it they tell it wrong and gossip isn't truth. I was married three years ago to a man I freely chose.'

'Then surely —'

'You don't understand,' Tessa said with a weary air. 'It is winked at when a white man takes an Indian wife because they are regarded as good homemakers and mothers and there are fewer white women here to be shared around. It's a different matter when a brave takes a white wife.'

'And you married . . . ?'

'His name in English is Smiling Moon,' Tessa said, her voice softening. 'When we married he gave me the name of Smiling Sun because I was part of him and I was always smiling in those days. Does that answer your curiosity?'

'You didn't want to come back to your own people?'

'I was nine years old when the wagon train was ambushed,' Tessa said. 'I recall the yelling and the rush of arrows thudding into the sides of the wagons and then someone threw a blanket over me and I was pulled on to a horse. At first it was very hard and I wept so much they named me Crying River, but little by little I settled down. Children do, you know. I never forgot my own tongue but taught some of the words to the other children and learned their language and their ways in return. The Peoria are Indians, Miss Scott, but they are also people who can love and grieve. When I was sixteen I was told to choose a husband and I chose Smiling Moon, for he had made it clear that he wanted me as a wife. Then a year ago the soldiers came. I was washing clothes in the river and the soldiers seized me and gagged me and took me to their fort. Then I was brought here to live with my brother, away from the farms and the high hills and the sacred places, in a village surrounded by fields of maize. And now I am tired to talking.'

She spoke in a dispirited manner, her eyes dull.

'Do these mean anything to you?'

Flora took the little silver sun and the little golden moon out of her pocket and handed them to the younger woman.

Tessa looked down at them as they lay in the palm of her slim hand, her entire face flushing with excitement. When she looked up her eyes were sparkling.

'Where did you get these?' she whispered.

'When I arrived in Chicago,' Flora told her, 'a tall Indian stepped over and lifted my trunks to the side out of the way of the wagons and horses. I can only think that he must've slipped the sun into the outer pocket of my smallest trunk. The moon I found hanging on a tree when I was out riding. They must belong together, surely?'

'They do,' Tessa said, her voice slightly breathless as if an unbearable excitement had gripped her whole being. 'When we marry we choose tokens so when I wed Smiling Moon and he named me Smiling Sun he made the moon for himself in gold because gold is the metal of the man and the sun in silver for me because silver is for the woman. When the soldiers found me there was not time to get away but I contrived to slip off my token and leave it in the long grass by the river. I prayed he would find it but I couldn't be sure.'

'Wasn't he taking a big risk, putting it in my trunk?' Flora said.

'He must have heard your name spoken and known you were bound for this place. Word of the arrival of a newcomer spreads very fast.'

'And they mean?'

'That he is near and thinking of me.' She clutched the tokens tightly, her small face glowing. 'Even if you hadn't given them to me I would have found out about them somehow. He will come soon to fetch me away.'

'Then why the tokens?'

'You think he can simply ride into the village and knock on the door?' Tessa said, impatience creeping into her voice. 'He would be shot at once. Even to be in Chicago means a risk, for the Peoria are barely tolerated in the city.'

'Perhaps the Indians here would help you,' Flora suggested.

Tessa curled her lip slightly.

'I do not think that they would run the risk,' she said. 'If they were discovered helping me, a white woman, to return to that tribe their farms would be taken from them and they would be driven to join the others beyond the Mississippi.'

'An Indian woman directed me to this house,' Flora told her. 'Mary Redfeather . . .'

'She's well enough,' Tessa said reluctantly. 'She buys what I need from the village and I pay her when she brings it here. It's not pleasant to go into the general store and be conscious of people glancing at me out of the corners of their eyes.'

'I hadn't thought to meet such intolerance!' Flora exclaimed.

'Did you think people out here were different?' Tessa's face bore a fleeting shadow of bitter amusement. 'They are the same everywhere. Since the soldiers brought me back my brother has been very kind, though I suspect he would rather they hadn't tracked me down, and one or two people acknowledge me but the truth is that I'm an embarrassment to the rest. Why have you come to America, Miss Scott? Was it to set the world to rights?'

'My uncle invited me for a long visit,' Flora told her. 'It was a chance for me to travel and escape the confines of life at home and Uncle Frank intimated that my help was needed. But since my arrival he has been much occupied with business and Tina runs the house beautifully so there's little for me to do.'

'I have seen Tina,' Tessa said. 'She is very beautiful and very angry inside. She carries her life in her face, that one, and I think, Miss Scott, it hasn't been an easy one.'

'Flora, please. If we're to be friends it would sound better.'

She had spoken impulsively as she began to rise but Tessa remained where she was, her expression wary as she said:

'Friends?'

'Why not?' Flora said robustly. 'I choose my own companions and if I like them it matters not a jot if they're married to Peoria or anyone else.'

'Flora.' She pronounced the name carefully. 'Which bloom?'

'Probably a hollyhock!' Flora said.

'It won't help your standing here if you choose to befriend me,' Tessa said. 'Your uncle will be angry, I'm sure, and the men will put their heads together and decide that your reputation is tarnished by your friendship with me — and if they do not their wives will do it for them.'

'I don't care —' Flora began.

'You will care when nobody calls on you and you're not invited anywhere,' Tessa said, rising from her seat and looking up at her visitor. 'You will care when nobody offers for you in marriage! And you would like one day to wed, wouldn't you? And you forget, I won't be here very long. At the first opportunity I will rejoin my husband and leave Pine Creek Ridge behind me.'

'Where will you go?'

'Where Smiling Moon goes,' Tessa said, a soft note entering her voice. 'If I can get away from here my brother won't seek me a second time. The truth is that though he is kind he secretly regrets that I was ever found and brought back.'

'Then at least let me help in some way,' Flora offered. 'We need not be openly friends if that's your wish, though for my part I don't care a fig. But there must be some way in which I can help?'

'You're very kind.' Tessa bit her lip as if she was working something out in her own mind, then nodded. 'Smiling Moon must be in the neighbourhood. At least I can let him know that I have seen the tokens. I'll thread them both together with a special kind of knot that he will recognize. Then you could leave them where you found the second one, to let him know that I am aware of his being near. Will you do that for me?'

'I'll do it at once,' Flora promised. 'I promised to pick some nuts and berries so it won't look odd if anyone sees me there.'

'He came so near and I didn't know.' Her eyes brimmed suddenly with tears and she brushed her hand across them in a childlike touching gesture.

'What of Brent O'Brien?' Flora asked suddenly. 'He seems to be your friend. In fact the other evening when we were riding into the village —'

'You fancied that Brent and I . . . ?' Tessa was laughing. 'No indeed, though he's a good friend to me! He cares not a jot what other people say or think and he has no care for his reputation since everybody knows him to be honest and hardworking. But there is no love between us! He is to marry Minnie Hargreaves when he has paid off the mortgage on his farm.'

'Brent O'Brien and Minnie Hargreaves,' Flora said slowly. It seemed wrong, even grotesque. Brent's tanned, hawkish features, his russet hair, the faintly mocking gleam in his brown eyes rose up in her mind's eye, and were succeeded by the round face, the prim features and the ginger plaits of the schoolteacher.

'Their children,' she said lightly, wondering why she should care, 'will be redheaded, anyway.'

'Her father is overseer on your uncle's farm and Brent is manager,' Tessa said. 'What could be more suitable?'

'Brent O'Brien didn't mention it,' Flora said.

'Oh, he isn't one for talking about his private affairs,' Tessa said. 'He hasn't told you about . . . ?'

She paused, looking uncertain.

'About what?'

'Never mind! Clearly he hasn't. The story isn't generally known. You won't speak of the two tokens? Let that be between the two of us.'

Flora nodded, and accepted the tokens from an obviously reluctant hand. She looked at the curiously intricate knot with which Tessa had secured the cord which now held them. Then she slipped them into her pocket again.

'You will put both back where you found the second one?' Tessa queried anxiously.

'You have my word,' Flora said, shaking hands. 'No, please, I can see myself out!'

She went swiftly back to where Bess waited patiently and remounted, wishing that Tessa hadn't told her about Brent and Minnie. Not that it mattered to her in the least, she decided, but she would have chosen a different kind of mate for the farm manager.

She headed towards the curve of the river, frowning as she saw another rider approaching. For an instant she fancied it was Charles Fontaine, returned from his trip to Chicago without having reached his destination, but as the rider came nearer, jerking on the rein, she saw that the silvery hair was the result of age, there was balding at the crown and the face was ruddy and square beneath it.

'Mr Hargreaves.' She drew rein in her turn. Her uncle had introduced him when they had taken a short stroll in one of the nearer maize fields, and she recognized now the contrast between the good humour of

93

the smile and the sharpness of the small eyes under heavy brows that had retained their gingery tint.

'Good morning, Miss Scott. You've been paying a call?'

'On Miss Fontaine,' she said incautiously and saw the eyebrows shoot up.

'That was very kind of you,' he said, 'but perhaps you are not aware —'

'That Tessa Fontaine was reared for many years by the Indians and took a husband from among them. Yes, I did know.'

'Your uncle would not be very pleased to hear of it,' Hargreaves said, 'though I assure you of my own silence on the subject. He has very strong views on matters of etiquette and morality.'

'Which does not extend to more than a token protest against the plan to drive out the local Peoria.'

'You are very plain-spoken, Miss Scott,' he said.

'I'm my own mistress and speak as I find,' Flora said curtly.

'Indeed?' His smile faded slightly. 'No lady can ever claim to be entirely her own mistress, surely? The authorities would not have hunted for Tessa Fontaine for so long had they accepted that viewpoint.'

'She has a husband,' Flora said boldly.

'I understand she was wed to a Peoria according to Indian rites. That is no marriage at all!'

'But surely —'

'You must excuse me, Miss Scott, but I have some supplies to order in the village. I am happy to have met you again. Your uncle will be able to explain the way in which affairs are conducted here when he returns from Chicago.'

'You didn't go?'

'I am not on the legislative council,' he said. 'However, I have every confidence that the vote will be a fair one.'

'And nobody will say very much on behalf of the Peoria,' Flora said.

'They have no vote since they are not citizens.'

'Just like women!' Flora said wryly.

'You have a ready wit, Miss Scott.' Flora was on the point of retorting when a spatter of dust heralded a third rider and Brent O'Brien rode up, drawing rein as he reached them.

'Good morning, Miss Scott. Hargreaves!' He nodded briefly. 'I rode beyond the village to find out if anything has been decided at the meeting and met several men on their way back. Apparently it broke up early since there were so few dissenting voices and no need for a second ballot.'

'And the Peoria will be moved out I suppose?' Flora said tightly.

'Most districts will move them in the spring,' Brent said levelly. 'We here shall start moving them in a fortnight or three weeks.'

'Giving them the chance to find the best hunting grounds and settle there,' the overseer said.

'And giving them the chance to starve during the winter unless they are picked off by marauders and hostiles first,' Brent said.

'The young bloods here generally go on their annual hunt before winter sets in,' the other reminded him. 'They'll likely be provisioned.'

'Exactly what the council thought!' Brent tipped back his hat with an impatient gesture. 'The evictions will take place while the younger, fitter men are away so that women and children and the elderly can be herded away without resistance. There will be resistance whichever plan is used.'

'Will the Indians hear about the plans?' Flora asked.

'When secret arrangements are made in council,' Brent told her, 'head for your local Peoria and he'll tell you all about it!'

'I can't believe my uncle would agree to

any of it,' Flora said. 'Surely he is a man of honour!'

'You've not told her yet?' Hargreaves smiled, not altogether pleasantly. 'Maybe you should, if only to increase her understanding. We'll expect you for supper tonight. Minnie is making one of her pies. Good day, Miss Scott!'

'Tell me what?' Flora demanded as the older man rode past them. 'What am I supposed to know, or am I to be kept in ignorance?'

'There's no particular secret,' Brent said. 'I simply don't go shooting my mouth off about affairs that are over and done with, that's all. However you may as well hear. Your uncle acquired Scott Place which was not, of course, called that then some ten or twelve years ago when he was travelling in New Mexico. He won it in a poker-game and I'm sure he didn't cheat. He won it from an elderly Irishman who'd never quite conquered his addiction to whiskey and gambling. The more he lost the more he wagered, in the belief that his luck was about to change. It didn't, of course, and he lost the entire property on the turn of a card.'

'Your father?' she hazarded.

'Daniel O'Brien.' He nodded. 'A fine

upstanding figure of a man in his youth with a head of red hair and a brogue you could cut with a knife, by all accounts! He sailed steerage to America and spent some years in the fur-trapping trade, based in St Louis. He became something of an entrepreneur as a trader, made himself a nice little packet, married and drifted up into Illinois. There were a good many Peoria Indian farmers here then, and ever the entrepreneur, he made a fair deal with some of them and took up farming. But his wife died giving birth to his only son —'

'You? You were only a baby when . . .' Flora could not help interrupting.

'Yes, I never knew my mother,' answered Brent, with a look of . . . wistfulness, was it? Flora could not be sure.

'And after that he started drinking more heavily, gambling more often. Every couple of years or so he would go off to his old haunts in St Louis, mainly to buy horses, and then, by the time I was about eighteen, and he could safely leave me in charge, he'd go away for longer, pushing even further towards the west, hoping, apparently, to get to New Mexico, where he'd heard that some of the very finest-bred horseflesh could be bought from the Apache tribes. But it wasn't until the Spanish had left New

Mexico, in 1820, that he was actually able to get to Santa Fe — the trail had been opened up by an old frontier soldier called Becknell. Anyway, there was drink and gambling aplenty in Santa Fe, and he met a girl down there, much younger than he was, but there's no fool like an old fool — and the girl was a mestiza into the bargain.'

Flora sat perfectly still, staring at him.

'She needed a protector so he married her, legally in church and then went off for an hour or two to drink his bride's health with his friends. There was a poker-game going on and the rest you know.'

'He left his bride and went off to play poker?' Flora spoke so indignantly that Bess shifted restlessly beneath her.

'She was there too,' Brent said with a sour grin. 'Seated at a table with a glass of something or other in front of her, waiting for the game to end. When it ended Frank Scott owned the house and land and my father, realizing what he'd hazarded and lost, suffered a heart attack and died.'

'That's terrible,' Flora said quietly, shocked into pity.

'Hard luck,' Brent agreed, 'but perfectly fair and legal. Your uncle saw to the funeral, had the property deeds legally attested and came to Pine Creek Ridge. He'd already made a great deal of money in speculations and so was able to transform the farm and the house into what he wanted.'

'And you were disinherited,' Flora said.

'You make it sound very dramatic.' Brent looked amused. 'It was a blow at the time but my father had the right to do as he pleased with his property, and your uncle was decent enough to keep me on as manager here.'

'And the poor new bride?'

'Frank Scott offered her his protection and brought her here too.'

'Tina,' Flora breathed.

The housekeeper with her coiled black hair and hard black eyes rose up in her mind. Tina, then, was younger than she had supposed.

'Tina was working at the tavern where my father died,' Brent told her. 'She had agreed to marry him to escape from a life of drudgery. She agreed to accept Frank Scott's offer for the same reason I suppose. Tina doesn't confide readily in other people.'

'And you agreed to work for him. How could you?'

'You think I should have challenged him to a duel or something? What a romantic you are! His money pays me for the work I do, work I enjoy, and pays the mortgage on my own place. Shall we ride? The horses are getting restless.'

He spurred his mount on, leaving her to heel Bess, who had begun to crop the grass at the side of the road. He slowed as she drew level with him and sent her a smile that held a reluctant apology.

'You must excuse my bluntness,' he said.

A bluntness which possibly concealed long held resentment, she wondered?

Aloud she said: 'I prefer plain speaking. One gets little of it in London drawing rooms! But you are mistaken if you think me a romantic. I never was.'

'But you travelled to a strange continent.' He sent her a sideways glance. 'I think only romantics truly become explorers.'

'And I find myself in exactly the kind of place where I was born and reared,' she said lightly. 'Oh, the scenery is different, much more spacious than our parks and gardens, and the people are different — at least the Indians are — but manners and customs are just as confining here as they were at home.'

'Meaning none of the ladies will pay a formal call upon you until they've seen you at church?'

'And they wouldn't call on Tessa Fontaine

if she spent every day there!'

'But you have called?'

He gave her another quick glance.

'I think,' Flora said, 'that she has been treated quite shamefully. Was it her fault the Indians attacked the wagons and abducted her? And she was married to a man she freely chose! Yet they brought her back and now nobody calls upon her or invites her to places. And her brother apparently colludes with such treatment.'

'They are afraid,' Brent said and his tone was serious. 'They are afraid that if they get too close to the Indians the civilization they've brought here will crack and crumble. They prefer to believe that Tessa is an aberration, that other girls in her situation would have tried to escape or flung themselves into a river or over a cliff. The truth is that many white women taken captive have married within the tribe and apparently been quite content. When people fear something they condemn it.'

'Well, I shall continue to visit Tessa Fontaine if I choose,' Flora said.

'It's not my concern anyway.' He had slowed his horse to walking pace as they rode and his tone drawled an apparent lack of concern.

'So people will continue to avoid Tessa

Fontaine and you will continue to work for the man who won your property in a game of poker —'

'My father's property. I'm quite happy with what I have. You must ride over and take a look some time when you're not too busy taking up lost causes. There's quite a parcel of land beyond the house itself.'

'And when you're sole owner you will wed Minnie Hargreaves,' Flora said and blushed scarlet at her lack of tact.

'That's the plan. Minnie and I have been friends for a long time and she feels for the injustice that was done to me, though it's never particularly bothered me myself and I can't altogether absolve my father from blame. You have been having a nice little gossip, haven't you?'

'Tessa Fontaine happened to mention it,' Flora said stiffly. 'I met Minnie Hargreaves earlier but she said nothing.'

'The engagement isn't official yet. Minnie has her schoolteaching to occupy her and I've no intention of taking any bride to a house that isn't fully and legally mine.'

'I wish you both happiness, Mr O'Brien,' Flora said.

'Thank you, but couldn't you make that Brent?' The amusement was in his face again as he pulled up and turned in the saddle to look at her. 'We may seem very conventional to you but in general manners are becoming more free and easy.'

'And my name is Flora,' she said.

'A truce then?' He leaned to shake hands firmly.

'A truce,' Flora said and found herself smiling.

'If you'll take a bit of advice,' Brent said, 'you won't embroil yourself too deeply in our local affairs. It won't win you any friends.'

'I shall still hold to my opinion!' she flashed.

'With which I shall largely agree. Were you riding anywhere in particular?'

'I — I was going to collect some berries and nuts.'

'There are usually plenty at this spot. Give your basket to me and I'll have one of the Peoria children fill it for you and bring it up to the house,' he said. 'It's near twelve and you won't want to make Tina even more grumpy than usual by being late for dinner.'

He leaned to unhook the basket from the saddle. His thick russet hair grew almost to his collar, its strands shining against the tanned skin. With an effort Flora averted her gaze and an instant later he had straightened up into his own saddle and was riding away, taking with him the chance she had had to hang the tokens of sun and moon on the crimson-tinted tree.

FIVE

The church was crowded with worshippers
when Uncle Frank drove her there in the
pony trap on the Sunday morning following
his return from Chicago. He had arrived
late at night, looking tired but with a curi-
ous air of self-satisfaction about him as he
came into the sitting room at the back of
the house, where the windows looked out
into a narrow enclosed garden.

'Still awake, my dear Flora?' He dropped
a kiss on her cheek as she looked up from
the book she was reading. 'You don't like
your parlour upstairs?'

'I like it very much, Uncle,' Flora said
thoughtfully, 'but I meant to take a stroll in
the garden before I retired so it made sense
to read my book here.'

Her hope of making her way quietly to
the Fontaine house to explain her failure to
leave the tokens on the tree, even perhaps
to hang them there under cover of dark-

ness, was not something that she wished to reveal.

'You must get your beauty sleep,' he said playfully. 'Everybody will be looking at you tomorrow.'

They had already been observing her for days, she reflected wryly. In a small place gossip spread and it was unlikely that her visit to see Tessa Fontaine had gone entirely unremarked. Only the suspicion that the other girl might herself be further ostracized by a second visit had kept her away.

'I hope they will also be paying attention to the sermon,' she answered sharply.

'The Reverend Eliot generally preaches well,' Uncle Frank told her.

'And the meeting in Chicago?'

'My own personal preference is to allow the Peoria to remain,' he said, 'but more far-sighted minds than my own argued powerfully for the other side. It will be a less colourful place when they are gone but they are being paid for their farms, and they will be well settled again with their own people in the new territory.'

That they were being forced to leave land that had been theirs for generations was apparently of little moment. Flora bit back the retort in her throat and went up to her room.

Now, shepherded into a pew by her uncle, with Tina making a silent and black-shawled third, Flora was acutely aware of covert glances from behind prayer books and hymn sheets. At least, she consoled herself, she looked respectable and neat even if she could never be regarded as a beauty. Her dark-green dress with its high-buttoned basque was in the latest London style, her bonnet a silk coal scuttle with white feathers trimming the crown.

The interior of the church was white-washed; dark-red hassocks contrasted pleasingly with the pews of light wood. The minister was a youngish man who evidently considered it his duty to preach a sermon on the Good Samaritan, reminding the congregation how often during the past week he had been pleased to witness personally acts of kindness carried out by members of his parish.

A not so subtle way of flattering them, Flora thought cynically, and half-turning her head to conceal a smile, met the equally wry expression of Brent O'Brien who sat in the pew behind her, hat on his knee, dark suit and string tie a contrast to the shirt and breeches he wore during the working week. His dark eyes, meeting her own accidental gaze, flickered slightly and he gave a brief, almost imperceptible nod as if he had recognized and acknowledged the fact that their thoughts coincided.

Next to him Minnie Hargreaves, in a black-and-white striped dress, her bonnet trimmed with cherries, gave his arm an impatient little tap as if she called an inattentive pupil to order. On her left her father sat with head bent, his breathing too heavy for one who was entirely awake.

Flora faced the pulpit again, her lips twitching as the last hymn was announced. She had noticed several Peoria at the back of the building as she had entered, mainly women with babies strapped to them. A couple of men, their plaits confined by narrow strips of leather or cloth, lounged below the windows of unstained glass, silent and with no expression that she had been able to interpret in their faces.

The service over, the Reverend Mr Eliot, followed by his wife, stationed himself in the porch to shake hands with various members of the congregation.

'May I present my niece, Miss Flora Scott?' Uncle Frank said formally.

It was Mrs Eliot who shook hands first, her manner slightly flustered as she said:

'We are both glad to be able to welcome a new member in our little community. Your uncle is one of our regular worshippers and gives most generously to the school. Minnie Hargreaves tells me that she has had the pleasure of meeting you informally.'

'Yes indeed,' Flora said.

'You will forgive us if we are not among those who call upon you today,' Mrs Eliot continued in an anxious, flurried tone. 'My husband and I always pay our respects to the dear departed on Sunday afternoons but I hope we may see you during the week at our little sewing circle? Ah, Lucy, my dear, how fresh and charming you look.'

'That woman,' Flora muttered as she settled herself in the trap, 'must be the most boring person I've met so far.'

'Amelia Eliot lost three children to a cholera outbreak when they first settled here,' her uncle said reprovingly.

'Oh.' Suitably chastened, Flora bit her lip, conscious of Tina's gaze on her from the seat the housekeeper occupied behind.

'You must put on your prettiest dress when we get home,' Uncle Frank said. 'After our dinner we shall have a constant stream of visitors. The ladies will certainly be quizzing you inexhaustibly on the latest London fashions and will wish to ask if you have seen the new Queen. There are rumours that Victoria is very plain.'

'She's very young,' Flora said, 'but as I've never seen her I can't vouch for her plainness. As for fashion, since that subject can't occupy us for very long I'm afraid they will find me very dull and go away speedily.'

'They will wish to return home and tell their sons and brothers what you're like,' he said, laughing.

Flora was spared the necessity of answering as the trap swerved between the open gateposts and a few minutes later they were seated before an ample dinner.

'The Fontaines were not in church,' she risked saying when the baked apples had been served.

Tina, in her usual seat at the bottom of the table, sent her a quick, cold glance.

'Charles Fontaine stayed on in Chicago for a day or two,' Uncle Frank said, 'and his sister is hardly likely to come to church alone, though they do attend on most Sundays. They sit in the rear pew and leave before the final hymn. Charles is a splendid young fellow but he is somewhat hampered socially by the presence of his sister.'

'I don't see why,' Flora argued. 'It wasn't her fault that she was captured by the Indians. At least they seem to have treated her kindly.'

111

'It would've been better had they put a bullet through her,' Uncle Frank said coldly. 'At least we can be thankful there was no issue of the union. A half-breed has little place in a civilized society. I do beg you not to introduce the subject when our guests arrive, my dear Flora. It is not a matter to be discussed. Indeed I am not happy to have it alluded to at any time! You will have plenty of female companions without having to seek out those who are socially undesirable. Now, do let us talk of something more congenial! What did you think of the sermon?'

'It was very tactful,' Flora said, and was surprised by a smothered sound from the end of the table which sounded suspiciously like a giggle.

For the rest of the meal they talked trivialities and at last, the coffee having been drunk, Uncle Frank retired to his study to smoke a quiet cigar, Tina went noiselessly to the kitchen, presumably to supervise the preparation of refreshments for the guests, and Flora betook herself to her own room to run her eye over the unpacked dresses neatly ranged in her wardrobe.

In the end she picked a dress of sprigged silk in muted shades of blue, added a yellow sash and managed with fair success to confine her hair beneath a fillet of the same shade.

The problem of how to place the tokens on the tree exercised her mind during the long afternoon that followed. It was unfortunate that during the day the Peoria children seemed to enjoy playing at that spot and equally unfortunate that her own comings and goings were certainly noticed by the neighbours.

Meanwhile she greeted the ladies who, accompanied by their husbands, came in a thin but steady stream through the hall into a formal drawing room where refreshments had been laid out on a long side table and the maidservants, demurely clad, moved silently with trays of coffee, tea, lemonade and negus.

There was no sign of Minnie Hargreaves. Presumably she and Brent spent their Sunday afternoons together.

There was little opportunity for Flora to sample more than a neatly cut sandwich and half a glass of negus as it quickly became apparent that the guests, particularly the ladies, were eager to chat with the newcomer whom, according to custom, they were now welcoming formally into their midst, though many of them must have glimpsed her riding or walking in the immediate vicinity.

Flora set herself to patiently answer questions.

'No, I have never seen the new Queen though she has been described as small and youthful but with great dignity.'

'No, I was fortunate not to suffer any ill-effects during the voyage.'

'I believe shawls are still very much in fashion for the evenings but mob caps do seem to be on the way out.'

'Oh, we do indeed contribute regularly to the foreign missions . . . yes, I know there are several sewing circles in London and elsewhere . . . the theatres are generally well attended . . .'

And if someone doesn't introduce an interesting topic soon I shall go stark, raving mad!

Smiling on cue, bending her head slightly to make conversation easier for the women who were smaller than she, she ached for a strand of intelligent conversation, for someone to enquire about the latest book or to ask if the labour laws in England had been tightened. These women in their Sunday best chitchattered like a flock of birds and any question she put about what was happening in other parts of America was greeted by fluttering smiles and the inevitable remark:

'That isn't something that really impinges

114

on our lives here.'

Not one word was uttered about the Peoria who might soon be banished from the land they farmed, not one syllable spoken about the Fontaines.

Within a short space of time she noticed that while the ladies revolved about her in their full skirts and little lace-trimmed bonnets the men had drifted to the other side of the room where she caught snatches of conversation about stock prices and the increase in freight charges.

And most obvious of all was that not one gentleman had sent her an admiring glance; not one fond mamma hinted that a son might like to be introduced. Despite the rumoured shortage of eligible women Flora Scott was not anyone's dream partner.

By the time the last slippered foot had tripped out it was dusk. Uncle Frank patted her shoulder, looking pleased.

'You've made a good impression, Flora,' he said. 'They will now tell their menfolk who were not present that you are a respectable and eligible young lady. Depend upon it but you will have a string of eligible beaux riding over to make small talk or engage you for a dance at the next ball. You brought ball-gowns, I hope? If not we must send to Chicago, though the choice is sadly limited here.'

'I have everything I need,' Flora said. Either her uncle was a consummate liar or he'd attended a completely different gathering!

'Excellent!' He patted her shoulder. 'You must get Tina to arrange your hair. She is quite skilled at it. Now if you will excuse me, my dear, I have a standing commitment to meet a group of friends on Sunday evenings but you must order what you fancy.'

He patted her shoulder again and went upstairs.

He seemed to take for ever before he reappeared, gave a few brief instructions to the silently hovering Tina, then went off to get his horse.

'Did you want anything special for supper, miss?' Tina enquired.

'I'm going for a stroll,' Flora said. 'I may want something light when I return but a sandwich or some toast will do very well.'

'Yes, Miss Scott.' A quick, flickering glance glinted from the narrow black eyes and Tina moved away.

Flora went upstairs and changed into a simple, sombre dress with a basque jacket. With a plain dark bonnet on her unruly hair and a pair of stout walking-shoes she reck-

116

oned she could reach the trees on foot and so not run the risk of being questioned on her uncle's return as to why she'd suddenly decided to go riding.

Autumn was on the threshold of the season. There was a definite chill in the breeze and the dim fields around were stripped and bare now save for the dark silhouettes of the last stooks of maize. As Flora walked briskly along, the moon emerged from behind a cloud as if to remind her of the tokens nestling in her pocket.

There was nobody about. Lights gleamed here and there from nearby *asis,* as Flora had been told the Indians' wattle and daub dwellings were called. Once she heard a burst of laughter as two Peoria girls went up a path and entered one of the domed structures. Otherwise only the splashing of water where the stream widened into a river as she followed its winding course and the whispering of the rushes that grew to the water's edge accompanied her.

She paused uncertainly as she reached the house where the Fontaines lived, trying to decide whether to call on Tessa, but as she paused the front door opened and Charles Fontaine appeared on the threshold. He turned to call to his sister within.

'I'll just check on Hero, Tessa, and then join you for a coffee.'

Fortunately he went past without stopping to look about him. Flora, standing motionless in the shadow of a large bush not far from the gate, held her breath until he had disappeared round the corner. It gave her the chance to slip quietly away, rounding the curve that hid her from view until she was far enough away to slacken her pace.

She fancied that once she had reached the thicket with its dominating oak she would merely have to hang up the two tokens and then depart as swiftly as she had come, but she hadn't expected a rapidly increasing darkness as a cloud skittered across the moon and remained there. It made it impossible to pick out one particular clump of trees and bushes from another.

She walked on, away from the Fontaine house, relieved that, this section of road having no sidewalk or paving, her shoes made only a faint crunching sound as she moved forward.

And there was the great oak tree, dwarfing the slimmer trees around it!

Flora squeezed herself between a couple of beech trees whose foliage almost concealed the lower part of the oak's trunk and stood in the darkness, conscious of the swaying branches over her head and the rapid beating of her own heart. On her previous visit she'd been mounted on Bess and able to reach up for the glinting moon. Now, though her height was well above the average, there was no way she could leave sun or moon in a place inaccessible to any child who strayed by.

For the first time in her life Flora found herself wishing devoutly that she was taller!

She put her foot on a low slanting branch and hauled herself up a couple of feet, but the branch above escaped her grasp and swung upwards again. For an instant she teetered wildly and then, without warning, felt herself seized about the waist. Twigs caught in her skirt as she was pulled down and her own involuntary cry of alarm was stifled by a hand clamped over her mouth.

Never in her life had she had occasion to fight before, though she'd always flattered herself that in an emergency she would be able to defend herself, but the hand that had prevented her from crying out had, if anything, tightened and the other held her fast against the trunk of the oak.

Flora forced her muscles to slacken and grow limp and as the hand over her mouth momentarily relaxed its grip she bit down hard on the imprisoning fingers.

The grip was relaxed and she heard a grunt of pain as she looked up into a dark, savage countenance.

'Smiling Moon?' Somehow she gasped out the words and the hand was removed from her lips, its owner shaking it to relieve the pain of her bite, though with the other hand he still held her in a bruising grip.

'Who are you?' He had a deep voice, accented but not difficult to understand.

'Flora Scott,' she said gaspingly. 'Tessa is my friend. Smiling Sun is my friend.'

Her assailant thrust her even harder against the tree, his eyes searching her face. What he discerned in the darkness evidently satisfied him for he took a pace back, still holding her, lowering his voice as he said:

'You are the woman by the stagecoach. You are called Flora Scott and you are come to visit your uncle.'

'You knew who I was in Chicago?'

'People talk about those who come and go. Many families come and men alone but not often a young woman alone.'

'And you put the smiling sun in the outer pocket of my trunk,' she said, her initial fear evaporating since he obviously wasn't going to hurt her. At least that was what she silently assured herself though the curved knife thrust into the waistband of his buck-skins invited a wary glance.

He nodded.

'Why?' Flora asked.

'You thank me for my help,' he said. 'More important I know you go to Pine Creek Ridge where my wife is held. Perhaps when you find the sun you ask questions about it and then Smiling Sun hears and knows that I am close by.'

'I don't run round asking questions until I've some idea of what's going on,' Flora said crisply. 'Once I was told about Tessa — about Smiling Sun, that is, then I went to see her. By then you had left the gold moon — was that you in the bushes when I found it?'

'If I had been there you would not have heard one twig snap,' he informed her loftily. 'I gave the moon to a Peoria child to hang up. He climbed the tree, as though for a game. It was full day and too many eyes watching for me, a stranger, to come close.'

'I gave Smiling Sun the tokens,' Flora said, her breath coming more easily now that her fear was diminishing. 'She hung them both on the one cord and asked me to hang them here on the oak tree again. She is kept close by her brother and fears to venture far.'

The Indian ran the cord through his

fingers until he came to the intricate knot.
He gave a flicker of a smile.

'It is the sign that she knows I am here,'
he said.

'And soon you will take her away again.'

'Soon I will take her away,' he said, but
for the first time she discerned a note of
hesitancy in his voice. He had released her
and now leant against the trunk of the oak,
his fingers continuing to caress the twin
tokens.

'But you're not certain you can, that's it,
isn't it?' Flora said. 'If you're spotted you'll
be shot and if she runs away you'll both be
followed.'

'Perhaps I will bring a war party,' he said.

'To attack the whole village? There would
be many deaths!'

'My wife is worth many deaths,' he said.

'But would the elders among your people
agree to risk so much for one woman?'

'They too grieve my loss,' he said mood-
ily, 'but many tell me that a year has passed
and that it might be wiser to find another
wife. Their blood is cold, not hot like the
blood of a young brave.'

'Wait a little while longer,' Flora urged,
though she wasn't sure for whom she most
feared: the local people or this arrogant yet
uncertain Indian who, save for his bronzed

skin and black plaits, might have been any young man yearning for a lost love but unsure how to get her back.

'I have waited too long already,' he said. 'Why should I wait longer?'

'Because,' Flora said recklessly, 'I will help you.'

'You? Why should I trust you to help us?' His tone was suddenly sharp and suspicious.

'Because I have already taken the tokens to Tessa — to Smiling Sun,' she urged. 'I shall think of some means of getting her out of the village and back to you, but you must give me a little time to plan. You said that you're near. How near? Where?'

'I sell animal pelts in Chicago,' he said. 'It shames me, for a warrior brave does not become a trader, but for my wife I will bear a little shame.'

'You're in Chicago, then. For how long?'

'Very soon I must ride west again to join my people,' he told her. 'Winter is on its way and we must build the lodges for the women and children. I cannot wait more than a few weeks. Already the elders complain that I neglect my duties for the sake of my wife.'

'I'll think of something,' Flora said again. She had the unsettling feeling that she stood on the edge of unknown waters without a boat or a chart to help her.

'I hope so.' He spoke softly and sombrely. 'The place next to me on my panther skin is cold and empty. Smiling Sun has been away too long.'

'You spent a year in tracking her down?'

'I would spend twenty years,' he said, 'for a sight of her silver hair and the touch of her hand in the dark night and the sound of her voice whispering beneath the wind.'

A dart pierced her, whether of sympathy or envy she couldn't tell. No man, she thought suddenly, would ever be so much in love with her that he'd risk his life to track her down and leave tokens of his presence. Tessa Fontaine was a fortunate woman.

'One month's length,' he said now. 'I will wait one month and then if she is not with me I shall go to the young braves of my people and ask those who are willing to make a war party and not listen to the elders whose hearts grow as cold as their bones are weak. I shall ask them to ride with me to seize my wife. One month!'

'Very well!' Flora heard herself say weakly.

'You are a brave woman, I think,' he said abruptly. 'Not as brave as an Indian but braver than most white women.'

He turned and vanished into the darkness of the trees and the thicket, not so much as the crack of a twig betraying his route. Only the moaning of the night wind as it gained in strength accompanied his going.

Flora, leaning weakly against the tree, thought suddenly that she had just been paid the first genuine compliment since her arrival. It was ironic that it should have come from a native Indian who was passionately in love with someone else!

She waited until her breathing had resumed its normal rate. Then she pushed her way back through the tangle of creeper and regained the main track.

From the direction of the village, where lights flickered in many windows, she could hear the occasional murmur of voices and once a snatch of song issuing from a saloon bar that she had passed earlier.

The wisest action would be to return at once to the house but she hesitated. Her uncle had spoken of a meeting with friends. Did that mean more discussion of the fate of the Peoria or was he merely playing cards? It was, after all, through a card game that he had gained his property.

Even as she hesitated hoofbeats sounded along the track and a voice rang out.

'Good evening! Rather late to be admiring

the view, isn't it?'

'I took a short stroll,' Flora said defensively as Brent pulled up his mount and looked down at her.

'In the moonlight?' He glanced skywards as the pale orb re-emerged from the clouds. 'Very romantic! Excuse me.'

Leaning from the saddle he plucked a spray of leaves from the crown of her small bonnet. 'Do respectable young ladies from London go tree-climbing in the evenings, then?'

'I'm not exactly young,' Flora said stiffly. 'Twenty-seven is hardly youthful!'

'It's not exactly ancient either,' Brent said. 'You're a remarkably honest person, Flora. Most women guard the secret of their age as if it were a crime to have lived more than twenty years!'

'Well, I've no false pride,' Flora said lightly, dropping the spray he had handed to her. 'I wondered if my uncle was home yet.'

'The cards are running so strongly in his favour that I doubt if you'll see him before breakfast,' Brent told her. 'Which reminds me — have you had your supper yet?'

'No, but —'

'Then you'd best have it with me,' he said calmly.

SIX

Flora stared at him for a moment, unable to conceal the surprise in her face.

'With you?' she said at last.

'You've seen my house only from a distance. Come and see it nearer at hand and I'll escort you home afterwards.'

'I couldn't possibly,' she said. 'It would flout every convention for me to enter a gentleman's home alone and after dark.'

'You disappoint me,' Brent said. 'I fancied you came here to escape the conventions that bound you in London.'

'I've found as many conventions here,' Flora said.

'And won't defy them?' He swung himself from the saddle, bent down, and tossed the spray of oak-leaves into the ditch. 'You're a prunes and prisms miss after all then. You speak boldly but don't match action to your words.'

Flora suddenly longed to blaze out at him

127

that she had ventured out alone to aid Tessa Fontaine in achieving her desires for freedom, that she had just spent an uncomfortable and heart-jerking period arguing with a hot-tempered Indian. Instead she said drily:

'It would require some very great inducement.'

'I want to discuss something with you privately.' His tone had altered, becoming darker and heavier. 'Believe me, but it's an important matter.'

'In that case,' Flora said, realizing that his words had unlocked her own wishes, 'then of course I'll come.'

'Good!' he said briefly. He steadied his mount and turned again to assist her to the saddle as effortlessly as if she were a child.

'Nobody is likely to see you,' he remarked, taking the reins and leading the horse into a narrow path that led away from the main track. 'Neither is my house overlooked.'

They reached it in about a quarter of an hour. Flora could now see closer at hand the strongly built wooden building, its porch illuminated by a low-burning lantern. Its barn and stables stood out at one end, the wash-house at the other. The land between was given part to grazing and part to vegetable plot.

'Come along in,' he invited, helping her down. He tethered the horse to a low rail.

He ushered her into a wide living area with no entrance hall, lighting another couple of lamps as he did so; he then moved to the windows to fasten the slatted shutters.

Flora, loosening the strings of her bonnet, looked about her with interest. It was, she saw, a masculine room with no trace of feminine influence, the windows bare of curtains or even netting, the tiled floor covered here and there by rugs woven in designs of yellow, blue and red. A fire was laid but not lit in a wide hearth, and several carved wooden objects were arrayed on the high mantelshelf above.

'Gifts from some of the neighbours,' Brent said, noticing her interest. 'Small totem figures designed to bring me peace, prosperity, many children and the destruction of all my enemies. So far I've managed to avoid making too many!'

'And the books?' Her attention had moved to the long shelf of volumes against one wall, within easy reach of the sofa and two low chairs covered in cushions.

'My father's library. Pa liked his whiskey and his women and his gambling but he loved his books too,' Brent said. 'He spoke the Gaelic when he arrived in America from Ireland but he also spoke English and later he learned several of the Indian tongues. After he'd made his money in St Louis, as I told you, he brought his wife here to Illinois, found this spot, liked it and, in expectation perhaps of a family, decided for the first time in his life to settle. But then I was born and my mother died. He stayed, setting up the farm, until I was old enough to go to school —'

'And you went to school here?'

'In New York.' Brent gave her a slightly sour grin. 'A military academy which must've cost Pa a pretty penny but he wanted me to learn to read and write and figure and he was too busy amassing land to teach me. I stuck it for three years and then lit out, joined up with Pa again and settled here. By the time I was seventeen or eighteen I was running most of the place.'

'But you lived at the big house?'

'It wasn't quite as big then as it is now,' Brent told her. 'Your uncle extended it and had the luxuries shipped in. This was a shack but after word came of Pa's heart attack and the loss of the property I set to making it habitable.'

'It's comfortable,' Flora said, looking round at the far end where pans gleamed against the wall and a wood-burning stove stood glinting blackly. A high wooden counter divided what was obviously the kitchen area from the living space.

'I've eggs and corn bread,' Brent said, going through into a stone-lined larder.

'That sounds good.' For the first time she was aware of feeling hungry.

'Can you cook?' he enquired, such doubt in his tone that she felt half-indignant, half-amused.

'I can cook quite well as a matter of fact,' she informed him briskly. 'I may not be accomplished but I can make myself useful.'

'If you see to the eggs then I'll brew the coffee,' Brent said. 'The pan's there and the range is still hot.'

There was no sign of any of the tarts that Minnie Hargreaves had baked the day before. Flora took off her bonnet and jacket and pushed up her sleeves and found herself wondering whether she was expected to compete with the schoolteacher in culinary skills. It seemed unlikely but if it was so then Brent was merely displaying one of the traits that she found most irritating in men: that a female was expected to be born with a frying-pan in one hand and a feather duster in the other.

The image in her mind irritated her and

she glanced to where her host was measuring out coffee, noticing and wishing that she hadn't, that he seemed perfectly at home with his task and that his hands, long-fingered and tanned, dealt with teaspoons as adroitly as they dealt with horse's reins.

He went through into the main area and set plates, cutlery and a cellar of salt on the pine table there, indicated a chair as Flora came over with the food.

'This tastes good,' he said a few moments later. 'Having company is the best of it, though. A man gets tired of eating alone.'

'Surely you and Minnie —' Flora stopped, embarrassed.

'The conventions that you seek to escape Minnie embraces with all the passion of a young lady forced to live in a place where civilization is only skin-deep,' Brent said. 'As the schoolteacher she cannot afford to shock anybody.'

The words lost their edge of criticism since his tone sounded playful and tender, as he uttered them. Flora, eating her eggs and toast, wondered if what was true of most men was true also of her uncle's manager, that he paid lip service to female independence but saved his affection for more conventional ladies.

'Why did you go wandering into the wood

this evening?'

His sudden question caught her unawares as she was still thinking about his previous remark.

'I beg your pardon?' she said, flustered. 'I was on the road when we met.'

'Having taken to decorating your bonnet with oak-leaves?'

'There are trees in my uncle's garden.'

'Not oaks,' he returned. 'Or perhaps you thought you would climb an oak and take a closer look at the moon?'

'Was that what you wanted to discuss with me?' Flora challenged.

'No, actually it wasn't.' He set down his cup of coffee and looked at her, the teasing glint dying out of his brown eyes. 'I know you have strong feelings about the removal of the Peoria.'

'Very strong,' Flora said.

'There are those who might say that having only just arrived in America you are not yet familiar with the particular conditions existing here.'

'People may say what they like!' Flora felt her colour rising. 'Injustice is injustice wherever it's practised.'

'There's a new philosophy gaining ground,' Brent said.

'A philosophy?'

Something of what flitted across her mind must have shown in her expression because he set down his coffee cup sharply as he said:

'I suppose in England managers of farms are not expected to follow current trends of thinking or to be able to reason from the newspapers they read?'

'But you obviously do.'

'Comes of being sent away to school,' he said, good-humour returning to his face. 'There's a new theory gaining ground very rapidly. Have you heard of the Louisiana Purchase?'

'Purchase?' Flora echoed the word, wondering in what sense Brent could be using it. He grinned.

'You believe that the Indians are being cheated of their rights, paid much less than the true value of the lands and farms. Well, I can assure you that most of them are being paid more than President Jefferson paid Napoleon Bonaparte for Louisiana.'

'The President *bought* Louisiana . . . ?'

'Indeed he did, and at the stroke of a pen he doubled the size of the United States of America. And do you know how much he paid for the land?'

The notion was beyond Flora's comprehension and she shook her head.

'Fifteen million dollars. That works out at three cents an acre. A bargain, I think you'll agree. But perhaps he was following his own advice to your English writer Thomas Paine and doing with his pen what at other times was done with the sword.' Brent gave a wry grin.

'But what of the new philosophy?' Flora asked.

'Well, the lands west of the Mississippi are largely undeveloped. Some travellers have explored, to find possible routes for wagons or boats, and to assess what natural resources may be there for the exploiting. As you must have read in the English papers, there are ever-increasing numbers of immigrants coming to America. The population of Chicago has increased by ten times or more in the last ten years — it is now a city of more than four thousand souls, Flora, and it is getting larger all the time. Soon, I believe, there will be a great movement of settlers to these western territories. There is a growing belief that Divine Providence brought the settlers to this bounteous land, and it behoves all Americans, as a moral duty, to develop and bring good governance to this land for the benefit of all peoples, from the Atlantic seaboard to the Pacific coast — maybe even beyond. They see it as . . . well, perhaps destiny is the word. They see it as their God-given destiny —'

'And the Indians? How will it benefit the Indians?'

Brent's face darkened and he tapped his spoon against the side of his cup. 'In the end the Indians will be driven on to barren, stony land, decimated by the diseases the white man brought with him, cheated of their birthright, deprived even of the buffalo that roam the western plains since it is rapidly becoming the fashion for European aristocrats to visit for the sole purpose of killing buffalo for sport, leaving the carcasses to fester where they were slaughtered. This isn't a new problem, Flora. Since white men first came here many of the smaller weaker tribes have simply disappeared, their customs forgotten, their songs silent.'

'So what can be done?' she demanded.

'Openly not very much,' he admitted. 'However, over the past five years I've been quietly buying up land at rock-bottom prices from the Peoria. A condition of each sale has been that they, the original owners, are permitted to remain for only peppercorn rents on their farms, together with their heirs and descendants. I've had the agreements drawn up and ratified and copies sent to the courthouse in Bloomington, the capital of this state.'

'All discreetly done I suppose?' Flora said, a glow of admiration spreading through her.

'Very discreetly!'

'And the Peoria — your tenants? Are they all your tenants?'

'Good Lord, no! I'm still paying off my own mortgage,' he exclaimed. 'Others have bought up Peoria smallholdings but in their cases they have continued to charge full rent to the original owners for the privilege of living on them. I've secured half a dozen plots very quietly. The Peoria have only a hazy notion of ownership anyway. They regard the ground on which they build their farms, plant their crops, keep a few cows as the property of the Great Spirit just as those who hunt see the hunting grounds where they stalk the buffalo and other animals as belonging to the Great Spirit also.'

'But you bought just as other white men have done,' Flora said, puzzled.

'Because the agreements drawn up between the Peoria whose land I've bought and myself stipulate that they can continue to live on them for very low rents in perpetuity. They cannot be driven away. There are only half a dozen families, but they have vigorous young sons who will cling later to their heritage.'

'And copies of these agreements are in the courthouse? That was wise of you!'

'Deposited there according to law,' Brent told her, 'but it would make your head spin if you knew how many legal documents conveniently go missing when they are required. I kept the originals.'

'And?' She studied his face as he hesitated, seeing in his expression both doubt and hope.

'I want you to hold them safely for me,' he said at last. 'Believe me, but if it should ever become necessary for me to prove the legitimate claims of my tenants you can be sure that the papers I hold will be found and destroyed by those hell bent on enforcing the Removal Acts.'

Of course he didn't talk business or politics with Minnie. With Minnie Hargreaves he was the attentive suitor, careful to keep within the bounds of propriety but surely most affectionate in private. Flora was acutely aware of his eyes fixed upon her, his well-shaped hand still holding the restless teaspoon.

'Of course I'll keep the papers for you,' she said steadily, wrenching her thoughts from the forbidden path down which they were tempted to stray. 'Then if it becomes necessary to produce them I can do so.'

'It would be a great favour,' he said.

'But why me?' Flora questioned. '*I* know that I agree with what you say, but you don't know me well enough to be sure of that. I might start thinking as Uncle Frank does when I've been here a little while longer.'

'Not you!' Brent put down the spoon and smiled at her. 'The first day I saw you, standing in the stagecoach yard, so calm and confident. I guessed you to be a young woman with a mind of her own and the determination to back up your convictions with action. Nothing I've seen since has altered my opinion.'

'If you give me the papers I'll keep them hidden,' Flora said. 'Nobody could imagine for a moment that they would be in my uncle's house, though surely . . . He seems to have some sympathy with the Peoria?'

'Enough to appear as an enlightened human being,' Brent said rising, 'but not enough to set him at odds with his neighbours or his customers. I'll get the papers.'

He crossed to open another door beyond which she could see the carved end of a wide bed and a glass-fronted cabinet holding rifles and a couple of pistols.

'Here they are.' He emerged with a thin packet, sealed and tied.

'When you need them you may have them again,' Flora promised, laying them flat against her side. She tucked them into her sash and reached for her jacket, which she buttoned securely over them.

'Here's your bonnet!' Handing it to her he laughed suddenly.

'And the joke is — ?' She looked at him as she tied the strings of her bonnet.

'I was just thinking that the fashion for wearing coal scuttles on female heads doesn't always reflect the thoughts that go on inside those heads,' he said.

'I shall take that as a compliment,' Flora said.

'It was intended as one. Shall we go?'

Outside the darkness was triumphant, the moon no more than a faint glimmer behind a bank of cloud. Brent helped her to the saddle, his hands firm at her waist.

As he took the reins and led the horse with herself clinging somewhat awkwardly to the pommel, Flora had a sense of freedom, of as yet unexplored territory somewhere in the region of her heart. She could sense all around her the movement of small creatures in the grass and the waving branches of the trees along the side of the dirt road, could feel it in the chill breeze that tangled her hair under the prim bonnet, and was acutely conscious of the broad shoulders and slim frame of the man who walked slightly ahead, firmly treading the familiar path with no need for either lamp or moon.

As they passed through the village there were a few lamps glowing from behind the netted glass of the windows; out of the darkness voices could be heard here and there, calling their good-nights.

'This is far enough,' she raised her voice to say as they reached the walls surrounding Scott Place. 'I'll go the rest of the way on foot.'

He turned but she had already scrambled to the ground, hastily pulling out her full skirts as he stepped towards her.

'I am indebted to you,' he said.

'Will it really happen?' She looked up at him, trying to fathom his expression through the encircling gloom. 'Will the Peoria really be driven away? Surely they'll put up some kind of fight?'

'I've no doubt they will,' he said sombrely, 'but they will lose in the end. I'm not privy to any government plans for the simple reason that I've been too blunt in expressing my own opinions. Those who do agree are too timid to speak out boldly. Good-night, Flora, and thank you.'

He stepped back, not touching her or offering his hand, wheeled the horse about and mounted up.

Flora stood for a moment at the gate, watching the two shapes of horse and man melt into blackness again and then, conscious of the slim packet under her jacket, made her way up the driveway past the terraced garden.

There were lamps burning in several of the windows but the main door was closed and she turned instead to the side, making her way to the door that gave on to the back of the land.

'Good evening, Miss Flora. Did you have a pleasant walk?' Tina, lantern in hand, had emerged silently from a side door and stood, her black-clad figure faintly outlined in the rosy glow of the lantern flame.

'I walked further than I intended,' Flora said, concealing her gasp under a light laugh.

'Yes, Miss Flora. People sometimes do in these parts,' Tina said without expression in her flat, cool voice.

'And the wind is quite chilly.'

'It is windy here, it is windy in Chicago,' Tina volunteered, standing aside. 'I sometimes think the winds are whipped up by the speeches of the politicians there.' It was the first time she had made a definite statement on her own account.

Flora went past her into a narrow hallway: 'What do you think of what the politicians say?' she asked.

'I am a Mestiza,' Tina said, 'and have no opinions. Would you like some supper now, Miss Flora?'

'I think not,' Flora said, her fleeting impulse to confide swept away. 'Good-night, Tina. Is my uncle home yet?'

'No, Miss Flora. I expect him much later,' the housekeeper answered stiffly. 'Good-night, Miss Flora.'

She was still standing in the narrow hallway as Flora went through and began to ascend the main staircase, lantern in hand, eyes lowered to the polished wood of the floor.

In her bedroom the covers had been turned down on the bed and the curtains pulled closed. A small fire burned on the hearth and a lamp was lit. Flora took off her bonnet and jacket and sat down with the sheaf of papers in her hand.

Here was the proof that Peoria had the legal right to live on the farms they had sold to Brent O'Brien. She wondered whether it would ever be necessary to produce the papers as evidence.

Meanwhile, where in the world could she

hope to hide them? The servants cleaned the room every day, removed her clothes for washing and ironing, made her bed, had unpacked for her when she arrived. It was the merest chance that nobody had found the little silver sun in the outer pocket of the smallest trunk.

Under the mattress? Too obvious and the mattress was probably turned weekly. Flora looked about her, hoping for inspiration.

The wardrobe? She rose, crossed the room and opened one of the doors of the huge piece of furniture that extended along almost the entire length of a wall.

Her dresses and jackets hung limply and neatly, her bonnets were arranged on small stands on a high shelf within, her shoes were ranged on trees at the bottom. The floor of the wardrobe was composed of rectangles of wood, polished and nailed down. If only she could prise one of the rectangles loose she might be able to conceal the documents in the space beneath. Resolutely she cast her gaze about, searching for a likely object that might serve as a tool. At first it seemed a hopeless quest, then her eye lit upon a shoehorn, lying beside the row of shoes. Unusually, it was made of a silvery metal rather than of horn. Would it be stout enough to take the strain? Would it be thin enough to force open the tiny crack between the nearest rectangle and the frame of the wardrobe? Fearful of splintering the wood or warping the metal she tussled with gentle determination until, giving a sigh of relief she saw that the rectangles could be lifted up to reveal the small space below them.

It took, nevertheless, twenty minutes to coax the nails free and secrete the packet in the space below. Then she carefully replaced the wood and inserted the nails again. The agreements would be safe there and she would find an opportunity to tell Brent about the hiding-place when she next saw him alone.

Brent, she thought with sudden bitterness, would be grateful for her help. He thought her strong-minded and intelligent. If she waited a year before the chance to speak to him arose he would still regard her as a useful friend.

She put the shoehorn back where it had been lying, noticing ruefully that it showed signs of its rough treatment, and moved to the window to pull back the curtains. The moon had consented to make a brief reappearance and in the gardens below she could see the glinting of the lantern that Tina carried as she slowly paced the terrace, waiting for Frank Scott to return.

Flora closed the curtains, jerked off her outer garments and climbed into bed. Her last thought as she extinguished her own lamp was that the world was full of women waiting.

SEVEN

Frank Scott was at the breakfast table the next morning, his heavy eyes betraying a night spent at the gambling table, his beaming smile suggesting that he'd been fortunate in his cards.

'Good morning, Flora! I hope you contrived to amuse yourself last night,' he said in a pleasantly hearty tone.

Tina, then, had not mentioned her absence. Flora glanced towards the housekeeper who had so far not joined them at breakfast but was, as usual, pouring the coffee, her eyes lowered to the task, her olive face empty of expression.

'I have arranged a picnic in the garden this afternoon,' her uncle was continuing, not having waited for any reply. 'An informal alfresco affair while the good weather holds. One of the maids has gone out with invitations. Tina will ensure there is plenty of food for those who care to come along.'

Flora's heart sank slightly at his words. She had hoped to slip over to the Fontaine house to let Tessa know that she had seen Smiling Moon. Now it looked as if the morning would be spent in approving the refreshments that Tina was perfectly capable of choosing herself and in deciding which of her own dresses to wear.

'Tomorrow I must return to Chicago,' her uncle was saying as he helped himself to toast.

'Another meeting?' Flora asked.

'Life seems to be made up of them,' he said with a heavy sigh, designed, Flora guessed, to convey the heaviness of male responsibility. 'And of course, there is always other business to transact!'

'Is there,' she enquired, 'any way in which I can help?'

'My dear Flora, we may be the New World,' he said kindly, 'but I hope we retain some sense of the proprieties. A lady at a political meeting would be as out of place as a schoolmistress in a saloon bar!'

'Minnie Hargreaves doesn't frequent such places, then?' Flora said with an innocent air.

'Now you are jesting! Minnie is a most respectable young lady,' he answered, his amused expression darkened by mild disapproval. 'She could not even attend our Sunday reception since she and her father regularly visit the graves of their departed relatives on that afternoon, and O'Brien, being her intended, accompanies her and Hargreaves there, though his own father was laid to rest in New Mexico.'

'You saw to the funeral then?'

'I had no legal obligation to do so but it seemed the least gesture I could make.'

Since his good fortune had just deprived Brent of his inheritance it was, she thought, certainly the least he could have done.

'So Minnie Hargreaves will, we hope, be with us later.' He dabbed his mouth with a napkin. 'Now there is a young lady with whom you might well become intimate friends. She is educated and intelligent and she earns her living without sacrificing any of the softer traits of feminity. Now I must go. Let us hope the weather doesn't change and make it impossible for the ladies to sit out of doors!'

The rest of the morning stretched ahead of her. Flora finished her own breakfast and went upstairs to pick out a dress of pale-yellow silk sprigged with a pattern of tiny dark-green leaves, the hem ruched and tas-selled, the square-necked bodice having elbow-length sleeves with frills of cream lace. The outfit, she thought, was feminine enough to please even Uncle Frank. For the rest of the morning she sat writing a letter to her mother, saying nothing of greater events but describing the various activities in which she had been invited to participate. Her mother, safely out of sight, would be pleased to imagine her gawky daughter on the brink of social success.

The fine weather held and after a light lunch of a sandwich and coffee Flora went up to change, confining her unruly hair under a cream silk bonnet and minimizing her height as much as was possible by donning a pair of flat-heeled green sandals.

Tables had been placed below the terraces and covered silver dishes held cuts of cold beef, chicken wings, salads, various spiced dips, rolls still hot from the oven, slices of apple pie and bowls of pear compote. Another selection of tiny cakes and a huge silver punchbowl, hung about with small glasses, were in the main hall.

'You look splendid, my dear!' Her uncle, coming down the stairs, sounded faintly surprised. 'Upon my word but with that bright colour in your cheeks and that bonnet you look quite charming. You will soon have suitors for the sake of your bright eyes, not to mention —' He paused abruptly, looking as uncomfortable as a man delighted with his own success could look.

'Not to mention what, Uncle?' Flora enquired.

'Over the past twelve years I have laboured hard to improve this house and to increase my holdings in the land,' he said at last. 'This was not a subject that I intended to bring up since — well, to put it plainly, my dear niece, I have never married and have no intention of relinquishing my bachelor state, which suits me very well, but for some time I have been increasingly conscious of the fact that I have no direct heir. Continue to please me and who knows?'

He gave her an arch little bow and went past into the garden, leaving Flora with all her pleasure in her appearance sadly gone.

It was no surprise to learn that he contemplated leaving his property to her. The possibility that he might had been endlessly and annoyingly discussed at home, but it was abundantly clear that her uncle now regarded the prospective legacy as a bribe to woo any reluctant suitor who loomed on the horizon. And the house and land held out as an inducement had been won in a poker-game which had ended in the death of Brent's father and Brent's own loss of an expected estate.

There was no time to sit down quietly and remind herself that she had travelled here of her own free will and that she had never been fool enough to imagine that her looks would appeal to a man in search of a wife. Guests were already arriving, many having walked over from the village, others were on horseback or driving wagons.

The pleasure of a surprise invitation coupled with the mild afternoon had induced most of the neighbours, as far as Flora could guess, to turn up. She went dutifully to greet the minister and his anxious, fussy-looking little wife.

'Such a pleasant surprise, Miss Scott, but then your uncle always has the comfort of others in mind,' the minister was saying.

Flora smiled, shook hands, murmured the appropriate responses, all the while wondering bitterly whether the dress she had chosen, with its lace cuffs and tucks and braiding, wasn't far too lively and youthful.

'The wine is cooling,' Uncle Frank said, coming over as she turned from greeting another pair of guests. 'I hold these little affairs from time to time, hoping the weather will remain fine, the food will be eatable and the wine uncorked! Ah, here come the Belmonts. Their son is going to be a doctor, so here is one young man who won't object

152

to intelligence in a woman.'

Flora contrived a smile as she stepped to greet a couple she recalled vaguely from the Sunday visits, the mother large and florid, the husband small and dried-up, looking as if he were being turned slowly into leather. The young man with them had not been at their previous meeting and it was clear from Mrs Belmont's remarks that she regarded the tone of the picnic to be elevated by the presence of her son.

'Harold, being most religious, does not attend social gatherings on Sundays, Miss Scott, though he naturally hurries to the aid of any person unfortunate enough to be taken ill on that day. Now, Harold, why not escort our hostess about the garden for a turn, for two young people must long to be spared the tedious company of their elders for a little while!'

Harold Belmont, looking as if he would prefer to be anywhere else at that moment, dutifully trotted beside Flora as they walked the terraces with their beds of autumn blooms, carefully alerting her to the Latin names of every flower in sight.

'For the Latin gives us the root of whatever in the composition of the bloom may be regarded as healthful or otherwise — good plants or bad plants as we doctors say!'

153

'In England I learned the names —' Flora began.

'And, as we doctors say, to be knowledge-able in one of the ancient tongues is to lay a firm foundation for an educated mind which, in itself, may mitigate against certain types of nervous disease to which the fair sex is predisposed.'

Half a head shorter than herself, he peered up at Flora through gold-rimmed spectacles that gave him a resemblance to a rather talkative owl.

'Women, of course,' Flora said, 'are not encouraged to study medical matters.'

'Ladies, Miss Scott. Ladies! Indeed not, but, as we doctors say, many a woman of lower grade can under careful supervision become a most efficient nurse. Indeed on the frontier where civilization has scarcely penetrated they can prove invaluable. As we doctors say —'

'Where did you graduate, then?' Flora broke in, her patience fraying.

'I am not yet . . . a young lady would possibly not appreciate that it takes a great many years to be qualified, but as we doctors say —'

To Flora's relief Mrs Belmont, who had stationed herself within earshot, twittered up to them, skirts swaying and voice slightly shrill like that of an Amazon on the warpath.

'Harold will, of course, graduate fully in due course,' she said. 'Indeed it is a matter of wonder to all our friends and acquaintances that he has not yet received his licence to practise since there's very little a medical school has to teach him. Certainly not in Chicago, but we hope most earnestly that one of the great schools in New York, once his reputation becomes known there, will hasten to add his name to the list of students.'

'And many of the neighbours are good enough to consult me when Dr James is unavailable,' Harold piped up. 'As we doctors say, an ounce of practice is worth a pound of theory. Isn't that right, Mother?'

'Quite right,' Mrs Belmont said, her voice all sweetness.

'If you will excuse me,' Flora said, making a mental note never to fall sick unless Dr James was available, 'I see some other guests approaching.'

More people were indeed entering the garden; some had still to be introduced, others who had met her previously greeted her cordially. Many of them, she noticed with a sinking heart, had brought along obviously unmarried sons and equally obviously the said sons, some of whom were tall and personable, were more attracted by the food and drink supplied so plentifully in flower-scented and elegant surroundings than by the tall young woman whose hair was beginning to frizz beneath the brim of her cream bonnet and whose eyes were all too obviously glazing over with boredom.

It was past mid-afternoon before Minnie Hargreaves arrived, driving herself through the open gates in a smart little pony trap. She had coiled her ginger plaits into a chignon and a rather pretty straw hat was perched on her head, trimmed with spotted veiling which matched her dress and jacket. She also looked cool and fresh, unlike her escort.

Brent, still in working clothes, rode the horse on which he had led Flora the previous evening. He had acquired a coating of dust over his high boots.

'Please excuse my outfit, Flora!' He dismounted, took her hand and grimaced at his boots with one eyebrow raised in comical apology. 'Riding drag is the worst position in the world. I regret that I can't stay long but I wanted to pay my respects. Are you well?'

'Quite well, thank you,' Flora said, biting her lip as she tried not to laugh. For some reason the picture of them both cooking eggs and coffee in his comfortable house raised her spirits higher than they had been since the first guests had arrived.

'No trouble with falling oak-leaves?' he went on.

'None at all, thank you.' Her grey eyes danced with concealed merriment.

From the trap Minnie called a trifle impatiently: 'Do help me down, Brent!'

'Of course, my dear.' He was at her side in an instant, helping her over a step she could perfectly well have negotiated alone. The manner in which he helped her, his hand about her arm, his face affectionately attentive, reminded Flora that the only secret they shared was the packet of land-sale contracts now hidden under the floor of her wardrobe, and some of the laughter faded from her own eyes.

'How are you?' she forced herself to say cordially to Minnie, who, on Brent's arm, was proceeding up the path.

'Very well, though somewhat burdened by lessons to mark,' Minnie said.

'But you do good work with the children, so I'm told?' Flora said.

'I do try to give them some knowledge of reading and writing and counting,' Minnie said, 'but there are times when I wonder if I wouldn't be better employed teaching them how to dig out a bullet or cauterize a thrust from a bull's horn. The boys will forget what they learnt the moment they leave school and the girls will have little scope to use their learning.'

Flora felt a pang of sympathetic fellow-feeling for the younger woman. It was a pity, she thought, that Minnie Hargreaves should so easily accept the conventions imposed on them both.

'Ah! Minnie, my dear! How pretty you're looking!'

The indefatigable Mrs Belmont had swooped upon the newcomer. Minnie had time for a murmured excuse before she was swept away, leaving Flora to pay her respects to the Allens whom she had met and rather liked before.

'Mr Scott is celebrating your arrival in style,' Mrs Allen was commenting. 'Are you settling in happily, my dear?'

'It's a little like London in many ways,' Flora confessed.

'Only on the surface.' Mrs Allen patted her arm with a gloved, sympathetic hand. 'When my husband and I first moved here I was homesick for St Lucia which is where I was born but in time I feel that Chicago and its surrounding towns could become focuses for art and music and all the civilized things that are held to ransom by lawlessness. Excuse me, but I see Harold Belmont on his way. He makes a point of warning people off all foods that might be indigestible — as we doctors say!'

She patted Flora's arm again and moved away to join the press of people round the tables in the main hall where maids were ladling out punch and Tina, her hands folded at her waist, stood on the staircase and surveyed the throng below her out of narrow, unblinking eyes.

Flora stepped quietly away, hearing another guest say as she passed her:

'One hopes this little festivity will introduce your niece to some eligible young men but there will be little opportunity for outside entertainment with the first frosts due any day soon.'

Flora slipped through the half-open side door and wandered along the path that led to a cluster of fruit trees, their branches still heavy with apples though the grass beneath was piled with windfalls. There was a bench set here beneath the stark black branches of a cherry tree and she seated herself upon it, closing her eyes and letting the peace soak into her.

'Hiding from the neighbours?'

Brent stepped over the nearby fence and

leaned against the trunk of the cherry tree, looking down at her quizzically.

'For a few moments,' she confessed.

'You find them difficult to take?'

'It's not their fault but mine,' she admitted. 'I'm useless in company.'

'I don't count as company,' Brent said with a grin. 'And there are pleasant people here too. Good people who work hard and do what they can for others. It's unfortunate that too few of them get into power!'

'I suppose so.'

A creeper grew over one end of the bench, its tendrils, yellowing now in the autumn, twining in and out of the slats of wood. Flora pulled off a spray and shredded it between her fingers. There was a restlessness in her, which she was at a loss to explain to herself.

'Wherever you go there are people who are kind, others who are cruel,' Brent said musingly.

'And a bore is always a bore!' Flora said, tossing the remains of the spray on to the path.

'You've been talking to the Belmonts!' Brent said, teeth white in his tanned face. 'You mustn't think every young man in the district is an idiot, though. Harold may yet qualify.'

'I don't think I'll be one of the patients lining up to consult him,' Flora said.

Brent laughed again and then abruptly changed the subject.

'I saw Tessa Fontaine this morning. She asked me if I'd seen you at all. I said that I was due to ride over this afternoon. Have you a message for her?'

Flora hesitated, wondering whether confiding in him would be wise. Then she reminded herself that he had entrusted his secret to her, had trusted her.

'The oak-leaves caught in my hair last night,' she said, plunging in. 'They came from a tree where I'd been before you rode along.'

'You visit trees?'

'Smiling Moon was there.' Instinctively she lowered her voice.

'Tessa's husband? What were you about, to be meeting him?'

'I wasn't meeting him. He was there when I went to the tree.'

'Was his conversation more interesting?' he enquired.

'Don't turn everything into a jest!' Flora said impatiently. 'I thought he was going to scalp me at first. He looked savage enough even in the dark.'

'I never met him,' Brent said, seating

himself on the bench at a little distance from her. 'Are you telling me he's tracked her down?'

'He regards her as his wife whatever anybody else thinks and he's determined to get her back.'

'And how does he propose to do that?' Brent asked.

'I'm not sure.' Flora hesitated and lowered her voice still further. 'Brent, he's only a young man and he loves her. He really loves her! He looks savage but his feelings for her are very deep, as are hers for him. But he can't take her away all by himself. He can't even get up a war party to help him.'

'So you volunteered to be his first recruit, I suppose?'

'You're still laughing at me,' she said, reining in her temper with difficulty. 'You clearly think that I'm a naïve fool just landed from England and wanting to set the rest of the world to rights! Well, frankly I don't care what your opinion is! Why shouldn't I give help where it's justified? He loves her and she wants to return to the Peoria. It isn't right for them to be separated!'

'You shouldn't have made a promise you can't fulfil,' Brent said.

'I'll think of something,' she said obstinately.

'Flora, listen to me.' He shifted closer on the bench, his hand reaching to grip her shoulder. 'Don't you think I'd've helped her myself if there'd been any way? There is no way! If she tries to run her brother or one of the neighbours will bring her back, or if they can't find her Charles Fontaine will call in the army's help and she'll be brought back before she's within a hundred miles of the Peoria. Life will be hard in their new territory, you know. They will be starting to farm on virgin land, land that is quite different from what they have farmed for generations. If her husband can't raise a war party and, Lord knows, it would be a disaster with bloodshed on both sides if he did, then what chance have they got? And what chance can you possibly imagine you have to aid her or her husband?'

'I'll think of something,' Flora repeated. 'You won't say anything?'

'I don't betray confidences any more than I stick my head on the block in the sure knowledge someone is going to cut it off! If it became known that you had befriended her there would be gossip and people would turn a cold shoulder to you too.'

'Little I care for that!' Flora said, shaking herself free of his grasp.

'You ought to care,' he said, low but vehement. 'No woman can hold out for ever if the opinion of other people is against her. Life can be unbearably lonely under those circumstances.'

'Like Tessa Fontaine's life!' she flashed back.

'And all she did was get herself abducted as a child. Can you try to understand how people would react to a woman who hadn't even that excuse to offer? A woman who set herself deliberately against her peers in order to interfere in something that was none of her business?'

'So you're afraid of public opinion too,' Flora said. 'You pay lip service to the rights of others —'

'Rather more than that!' he interrupted sharply.

Flora thought of the documents hidden in her wardrobe and brushed a feather of uncertainty away as she rushed on.

'Well yes, maybe you've done more than others but this is different, can't you see that?'

'There is no way to help her. Her road back to the Peoria is closed.' Brent's tone was obdurate. 'I take no heed of those who say she was tainted by the years she spent with the Peoria or by the marriage she freely entered into, and I will stand her friend whenever it's possible but there's nothing more I can do for her.'

'But you won't say anything about —'

'About Smiling Moon hanging round here? I don't betray confidences, Flora. Lord knows but I can't think of another woman who'd even think of helping her. What I'm saying is that it simply isn't possible. Be her friend by all means, but keep it at that. Your trying to help can only bring her more pain.'

'Then if you've quite finished . . .' She made to rise, clutching her offended dignity like a shield.

'You still haven't told me,' he said, 'why you went off to the oak tree in the first place.'

'A silver sun with a smiling face etched on it was slipped into my trunk,' she said. 'I didn't understand the significance at the time. And then later on I was riding near that part of the woodland and I glimpsed something hanging up in the branches. It was a gold moon with the same face etched on it. I took both the tokens to Tessa Fontaine since I could only think of one person for whom they were meant. She told me then about the names they'd chosen and how, when the soldiers found her, she was able to drop one unseen into the grass by the river bank. She told me that they were a sign that he was near by, waiting to take her away again. She asked me to hang the moon and the sun back in the same tree but I had to wait until after dusk before I could slip out, and then I had difficulty finding the exact spot. That was when Smiling Moon grabbed me.'

'You must have been scared out of your wits!'

'Terrified for a few moments. Then he spoke to me in English and I was able to assure him that I was Tessa's friend.'

'That Indian who helped move your trunks at the stagecoach yard?' Brent said, rising and looking down at her. 'He wasn't by any chance — ?'

'I didn't know it then but I recognized him later.'

'Why in your trunk?'

'People had been talking about Frank Scott's niece arriving and he obviously saw me and guessed who I was. There don't seem to be many young women arriving alone in this part of the country.'

'Not respectable ones at any rate,' Brent said with a twitch of amusement at the side of his mouth.

'And you will say nothing? At least about his being near? Please, Brent!'

'We both have silences to keep,' he said, the amusement fading. 'Good Lord, Flora, but you'd be a handful for any husband!'

'I'm not looking for a husband,' she said flatly.

'Well, half the neighbourhood is determined to supply the lack of one for you. Not that I'd recommend our fledgling Doctor Harold — but there are decent men around who'd be grateful for a healthy young partner. Don't go spoiling your chances by clutching every lost cause you stumble across.'

'It's very kind of you to advise me,' she said sarcastically. She saw his lips twitch again with barely suppressed amusement before he straightened up as quick, tapping footsteps sounded at the other side of the wall bordering the path.

A moment later Minnie stepped briskly through a gap in the fence, her expression one of pleased surprise.

'Ah, there you are, Brent!' she said brightly. 'I supposed you gone. Didn't you have some timber to move?'

'It's waiting patiently,' Brent said.

Seen together, Flora thought, they made an incongruous pair: Brent with his thatch of russet hair, lively brown eyes, wide shoulders and long legs clad in breeches tucked into the high boots which seemed to be standard working footwear round these parts; Minnie in her spotted muslin and pert straw hat which, if slightly too summery for the season, still looked fresh and pretty, her round face with its frame of ginger plaits flushed and smooth.

'And you have not yet paid your respects properly to our host,' Minnie was continuing, her voice couched in lightly chiding tones.

'Which I will of course do at once,' Brent said with a slight lift of an eyebrow. 'It was pleasant talking to you, Flora. Good day. Minnie . . . ?'

'I shall join you in a few moments,' Minnie said.

He sauntered past them, as unselfconscious in his working clothes as if he had been clad in the spruce tweeds and twills and silk cravats sported by the other gentlemen who had accepted Frank Scott's invitation.

'Brent can be so unconventional sometimes,' Minnie said smilingly. 'You must excuse his using your Christian name so freely but his father was an Irishman, not that I ever met him. Papa and I moved here from New York after Mama passed away when the post of overseer was advertised by

168

your uncle. Of course Papa should've been manager but Mr Scott was already employing Brent in that position. A way of compensating him for the loss of his property, I daresay. Mr Scott has very pronounced views on fairness. Are you enjoying your visit here?'

'I am trying to take a great deal in at once,' Flora evaded.

'Of course you are! Still, we try to keep up a certain standard,' Minnie said with a smile. 'We have quite a pleasant little social circle among the ladies and we like to think that our example keeps our menfolk from the worst excesses of drinking and gambling.'

Flora, who doubted whether it did, maintained a discreet silence.

'Not that one can accuse Brent of such things,' Minnie was continuing. 'Indeed he is positively a slave to duty. I often tell him he works far too hard but he is eager to pay off what remains of the mortgage on his property and to save sufficient for our wedding. We think June will be a lovely month in which to hold the ceremony.'

'Yes indeed,' Flora said. 'And of course you teach.'

'I received a good education in New York before we came here,' Minnie informed her.

'The key to civilization lies in education, don't you think? Of course it is too late for many of the adults here — the men have their work to do and the women are not much interested, but I have tried to make some headway with the children. I have a mixed class, you know, boys and girls, white and red. All seated together.'

'You must work very hard too,' Flora said.

It behoved her to be polite but she wished that Minnie Hargreaves would sit down on the bench instead of standing before her rather as she must stand in front of her class.

'However, after my marriage,' Minnie said, 'I shall give up the teaching, which occupies too much time that I wish to devote to my husband and home. I must look about me for a replacement — a conscientious, intelligent woman, unlikely ever to marry, who will devote herself to the welfare of her pupils. It is rather a shame that you will be fully occupied in acting as hostess for your uncle, else I might have considered — but there! In any case you are here merely for a long visit if I understand correctly.'

'An indefinite length,' Flora said.

She hoped her face didn't reveal the indignation that was surging in her. Minnie Hargreaves was either an expert at planting little verbal darts or she was stupidly tactless.

'I shall send to New York for the materials for my wedding gown,' Minnie was saying brightly. 'I think cream lace would be very pretty, becoming to auburn hair.'

'Very becoming,' Flora said tightly.

'And one must choose a shade flattering to one's complexion.' Her eyes rested briefly on Flora's costume.

'It seems a pity,' Flora said, beginning to rise, 'to give up your school when you clearly do such valuable work there.'

'I agree,' Minnie said promptly, 'but Brent is the kind of man who will demand the uninterrupted attention of his wife, don't you agree?'

'You know him better than I do,' Flora said lightly.

'Yes, I do, don't I?' Minnie's eyes rested on her consideringly and then, as they both began to move back towards the main garden, she laughed with a little edge of triumph and said again, 'Yes, I do!'

Eight

Uncle Frank had ridden out to inspect his land, which meant he would be away most of the day. Flora was learning to think in far greater distances than she had ever known in London. Out here beyond the town farms covering hundreds of acres seem commonplace. Brent's small property was tiny in comparison but there were people who scratched a living from half an acre.

'Not that they will prosper,' her uncle had said over breakfast. 'It's essential to get in at the start and buy as much land as possible. Then if there's drought or storm one has a reserve to fall back on. What are you going to do with yourself today, my dear?'

'I thought I might take a ride on Bess,' she answered. 'I suppose it is still quite safe to ride beyond the confines of the village?'

'Why should it not be? Provided you don't go wandering off the main tracks you are quite secure,' he assured her. 'I would invite you to accompany me but you would find it all very tedious. Brent and I will check soil conditions and ascertain any shortfall in the maize field. Very dull for a young lady. And don't you have an appointment this afternoon?'

'The sewing-circle,' Flora said, her heart sinking slightly. 'It's the ladies' turn to come here.'

Since the picnic she had dutifully attended a meeting of the said circle in the neat little house where the minister and his wife lived. Mr Eliot had prudently absented himself but Mrs Eliot had flustered about, serving tea and cakes and sandwiches cut to English thinness, after which various items of clothing had been brought out and painstakingly stitched while the ladies, drawn up in a semicircle, their full skirts billowing, had talked of every unimportant subject.

And that, Flora chided herself, wasn't a fair thought for her to have entertained! The ladies had been sewing garments for the poorer children in the area, their needles flashing as rapidly as their tongues. Flora, who had taken no work with her, was given a tablecloth to hem.

'Then I shall be better out of the way,' Uncle Frank said hastily. 'Enjoy your day, my dear!'

She had waited until he had ridden out with Brent at his side and then had hurried to change into her riding habit and mount up.

Now that she was growing more familiar with Pine Creek Ridge she had found that she could reach the Fontaine house which stood a little apart from its neighbours by taking the back track that skirted the hill.

'There were mainly pines here ten years ago,' Uncle Frank had told her, 'but most of them were cut down for building purposes.'

There were still many, shedding their needles on to the rough surface of the road that curved beneath them, bordered by the stream. Flora dismounted and led her pony over the low bridge to the back of the Fontaine spread, calculating as she did so that if Tessa was to leave her home it would perhaps be better for her to slip out this way, where there were fewer prying eyes to notice.

Tessa was brewing coffee in a kitchen that opened into a yard surrounded by a high fence. As she pushed open the gate Flora saw the fair head bent over the range and called softly:

'Tessa! Tessa, are you alone?'

She wasn't sure whether her voice had

carried but Tessa glanced up at that moment and hope flashed into her face.

'Flora! I've been hoping so much that you would come!' She came out into the yard, her long tail of silvery hair swinging almost to her hips, her hands anxiously plucking the skirt of her print dress.

'Your brother . . . ?' Flora began, dismounting and tethering Bess.

'Charles has gone to check his takings and order fodder for the winter. Did you hang the token on the oak tree? Do you know if it's still there? I would go myself but Charles keeps a close eye on me and when he's not here there are always eyes to see and tongues to wag.'

'It would be possible for you to slip away in this direction,' Flora said as the young woman ushered her within.

'If I had a horse,' Tessa said, 'but the stables are kept locked and the most I can do is slip out occasionally for an evening walk, and the neighbours are always watching.'

'They ought to mind their own business!' Flora said, taking the seat by the fire that her friend indicated.

'They see me as a girl rescued from savages,' Tessa said bitterly. 'They don't admit me into their society or invite me to parties but they make it their business to see that I am well protected at all times. Do you mind sitting here in the kitchen?'

'I love kitchens,' Flora said cheerfully. Tessa's mood struck her as both nervous and subdued. 'I hung the sun and the moon on the big oak tree,' she said encouragingly, as she accepted a cup of coffee.

'I hardly dared to ask!' Hope flashed briefly into Tessa's small face. 'Have they been . . . ?'

'And met Smiling Moon,' Flora told her.

'He was there? By the oak tree? You spoke to him? Oh, please tell me everything!' Tessa set down her own untasted coffee and clasped her hands together tightly.

Flora briefly recounted the meeting, conscious of her listener's hungry blue gaze.

'He would never have scalped you!' Tessa broke in indignantly when Flora paused briefly.

'He looked savage enough,' Flora said wryly. 'At first I was sadly frightened.'

'Smiling Moon can be hot-headed,' Tessa said. 'Most young men can be like that, but in my husband those feelings are nearer the surface. He can be gentle though, and such fun to be with. When we were together we laughed a lot.'

Flora tried to imagine the dark face of the

young Peoria lit with merriment and found it difficult.

'And he took the sun and the moon, the signs of our bonding?' Tessa was questioning eagerly.

'He did.'

'And is he still near? Oh, if I could only see him!'

'He is trading skins in Chicago,' Flora said. 'I suspect he will still return to this area but he would do well to stay out of sight, surely?'

'Nobody at Pink Creek Ridge has seen him expect you,' Tessa said. 'To most people one Indian looks much like another. But a strange one, not known here, might be noticed.'

'I told Brent O'Brien,' Flora confessed.

Tessa looked worried for an instant, then her brow cleared.

'Brent will say nothing,' she said confidently.

'But he won't do anything either,' Flora said.

'Brent has a job to keep and a mortgage to pay off,' Tessa reproved. 'He would help if there was any way in which he could help.'

She sounded so prim that Flora couldn't help smiling.

'What is it?' Tessa enquired.

'I was just thinking,' Flora said, 'that if anyone who didn't know what had happened were to call they would never guess that you had lived for so long with the Peoria. You look like my uncle's notion of a demure young lady.'

'Which is what I am,' Tessa said, smiling in her turn. 'Indian wives don't usually hunt or fight, you know. They stay home and take care of the children, or help make camp as the men follow the buffalo. But when there are matters of importance to be discussed the women have an equal voice with the men.'

'Then they're more civilized than we are,' Flora said.

'Neither more nor less,' Tessa told her. 'Just different. Flora, it's been very good of you to help, to risk your own position here. Smiling Moon and I will be grateful all our lives. But if it ever came out your uncle would be furious, your own reputation would suffer and with it your chances of marriage.'

'Which were never very high anyway,' Flora said with determined cheerfulness. 'My own common sense always told me that. Even if I saw someone I truly liked the odds are that he wouldn't like me. I am completely resigned to spinsterhood, I assure you.'

Before she had left England that might have been true but it no longer was, she thought privately. This new land, for all its disadvantages, had roused something in her that was strong and free and craved fresh experiences to share with someone special.

'I think there must be a very special man for you somewhere,' Tessa said.

'And meanwhile your special man waits for my message,' Flora said, thrusting aside her own concerns. 'Smiling Moon told me he will wait for one month, and half that time has gone already. I've racked my brains trying to think up some plan and I've thought of nothing.'

'And soon he must return to his people in the new quarters,' Tessa said with a sigh.

'Will he really go?'

'Of course he will! He has a duty to his people,' Tessa said. 'They will be on the move and it will be difficult to find his own clan. You and I have never seen the great plains, but travellers who have been there speak of thousands of miles of grassland and forest and scrub with ranges of high hills and rivers that thunder over cliffs and through the ravines. They say that the sky is so huge that it frets your brain even to think about it!'

'And your brother keeps you penned up here.' Flora was sensitive to the yearning note in the other girl's voice. 'It cannot be easy for him having you here at all, surely? Would he not turn a blind eye if you were to make your escape?'

Tessa gave her a twisted little smile.

'The truth is,' she said, 'that Charles does sometimes regret that I was ever found but he knows his duty to a sister. His own life has been altered by my return, for his own prospects are somewhat blighted though he'd never be told that openly. No, he'd not actually help me in any way but I think that if I did get away he'd not have me sought and brought back a second time. And we cannot possibly let him guess that we are so friendly, for he would quickly put two and two together and know that you have been party to my leaving.'

She spoke, Flora thought in alarm, as if her escape was almost a foregone conclusion. Flora was much less certain in her own mind. There might not be bars on the windows of the Fontaine house but it was clear that Tessa's movements were strictly limited.

'I had better leave now,' Flora said aloud. 'I came by the back trail so with any luck I have not been noticed.'

'Did Smiling Moon say when he might come again?' Tessa enquired hopefully as they went out into the yard. 'His English is very good, but then I spent many hours teaching him.'

Flora shook her head. 'He was returning to Chicago. He gave me one month but said nothing more,' she replied.

'He will try to raise a war party,' Tessa said. She sounded worried but proud.

'And if he doesn't succeed?'

'The Peoria are not fools,' Tessa said. 'They will help if they can but they will not start another Indian war for the sake of one young brave. Smiling Moon must find his own solution. You see it is all rather hopeless.'

'Hopeless,' Flora said with more certainty than she was feeling, 'is not a word in my dictionary! I shall think of something, but if the land is so harsh . . . ?'

'I am stronger than I look,' Tessa said quickly. 'Life on the plains will be a hard life, but I am not afraid to face it.'

'But you can't just mount a horse and ride out of here?'

'They would bring me back and it would mean greater danger for Smiling Moon,' Tessa said.

'I shall think of something,' Flora repeated. 'Now I'd best get back. But I will work out something, I promise.'

It was, she thought, as she took the round-about way back to Scott Place, probably the most rash promise she had ever made. Yet somehow or other she was determined it would be fulfilled. The thought of Tessa virtually a prisoner and her young husband eating his heart out while he sold skins in Chicago engaged her full sympathy. Only as she turned in at the open gates of her uncle's property did it cross her mind that she was taking such a close interest because her own life was still emotionally empty.

'Miss Flora!'

Hailed by an unfamiliar voice she halted Bess and turned in the saddle as Mary Red-feather panted along the track, a thick shawl about her shoulders.

'Mrs Redfeather? Good day to you,' Flora said uncertainly.

The Indian woman reached the pony's side and laid her broad hand on the stirrup.

'You went to see Smiling Sun — Miss Tessa,' she said.

'Yes, I did, but I don't know how —'

'I see most things, Miss Flora. This is a watching kind of place,' she said.

'Spying, you mean?'

'That too!' She displayed white teeth in a

broad grin. 'Most folks don't have anything better to do with their time but there's spying and there's looking out for one another.'

'And your sort is . . . ?' Flora looked at her for a long moment, seeing nothing but friendliness in the plump face.

'I'm kept pretty busy with my brood,' Mary Redfeather said. 'But I know most of what goes on in Pine Creek. How is Smiling Sun? I'd be more friendly but I know her brother don't like it.'

'She misses her husband,' Flora said.

'She wants to return to the tribe but her brother won't let her. Folk watch her when she leaves the house, which ain't often.'

'I know,' Flora said.

'And folk watch you too, Miss Flora.'

'If you mean my uncle he will have to learn that I visit where I choose,' Flora said, annoyance bubbling up in her. 'And I ride where I please.'

'I do not speak of Mr Scott,' Mary Redfeather shook her braided black head, 'but of the schoolteacher. She watched you when you ride home on Brent O'Brien's horse.'

'That's impossible!' Colour flamed into Flora's face. 'Nobody saw —'

'My man John saw you riding home with Brent leading the horse,' Mary Redfeather broke in. 'He was out checking a snare he'd set. He saw both of you, and he saw Minnie Hargreaves standing as still as stone among the trees. John told me when he got back and told me to tell you if I got the chance. That schoolteacher holds tight to her man.'

'There was no harm in Brent bringing me home,' Flora said. 'I don't know what your John saw but he got it wrong.'

'My John don't think nothing,' Mary Redfeather said. 'He told me what he saw is all and now I've told you.'

'Well, thank you, anyway.' Flora felt completely at a loss.

'That Minnie Hargreaves is cold-eyed,' Mary Redfeather said. She stared up at Flora impassively for a moment, then turned and walked away, her full skirt swaying, her black braids bouncing against her back under the shawl.

Flora rode on up to the house, wondering why Mary Redfeather had troubled to warn her. Perhaps it was to inform her in an oblique way that not only Minnie Hargreaves kept a close eye on the newcomer from England. As for Minnie herself, she hadn't been particularly friendly, but if she had chanced to see her with Brent why not simply mention the fact?

As she changed out of her riding-habit up in her bedroom, Flora could only think that

Minnie had put entirely the wrong construction on their being together. The fact that neither she nor Brent had been aware of anyone watching made her feel uneasy.

Once changed into a day dress she went downstairs again, hearing the sounds of cheerful chatter from the kitchen. It would have been pleasant to go in and become part of the lively group but her appearance would, she knew, silence the maids and Tina would enquire in her cold, polite manner if she required anything.

Instead, after a solitary luncheon, she went into the study and took down an atlas from the shelves. America, she thought wryly, was certainly a huge country! She studied the narrow lines of blue that indicated rivers and tried to imagine them foaming in deep channels through as yet unchartered land, the brown ridges that indicated high ground, the green areas where farmland and prairie mingled. Once Tessa got clear of Pine Creek it should be possible to hide her securely among the Peoria for the rest of her life if the luck held.

A hand touched her shoulder lightly and she started violently.

'I didn't mean to give you a heart attack,' Brent said. 'The door was open so I came in.'

'Is my uncle home?' Flora asked.

'He went over to check the monthly yield and the wages bill with Hargreaves. Did you and Tessa have a pleasant talk?'

'How did you know that I — ?'

'A guess,' he said, taking the chair towards which she nodded. 'I knew you'd be riding over to see her as soon as the chance came.'

'I told her that you knew about the tokens and my meeting with Smiling Moon. She didn't mind your knowing.'

'Tessa knows that I stand her friend as far as I'm able.'

'Without doing anything practical?'

'What did you have in mind?' he enquired. 'That I should throw her across the saddle of my horse and gallop across the plains in the hope of finding her husband's tribe? Or were you thinking of going yourself? I see you've been trawling through the atlas. Your uncle had it specially hand-painted. He is a man who can afford to indulge a whim.'

'You don't like him,' Flora said levelly.

'That's not strictly true,' Brent said thoughtfully. 'My father was foolish enough to gamble away his property. Nobody twisted his arm. Nobody expected him to keel over with a heart attack when he discovered the extent of his losses. Frank Scott could have come up here and sent me

186

packing altogether. Instead he gave me a well-paid and responsible position. Soon my mortgage will be paid off and I can go into farming on my account. He treated me fair.'

'And your father's new wife?' Flora said. 'He treated her fair too?'

'She lives in the house where she would've lived had my father not sat down to a poker game,' Brent said.

'And you won't help Tessa Fontaine?'

'If I can find a way to do so then I will do what I can,' he returned. 'But any romantic notions you may have of galloping west in search of the Peoria you may forget.'

'You must think me a fool!' Flora said, colour rising in her face. 'I've no intention of doing any such thing! The furthest I shall be travelling before the winter creeps upon us is Chicago.'

'To buy skins?' he arched an eyebrow at her.

'To buy some Christmas gifts for my family at home,' she improvised rapidly. 'They may arrive a little late but I would like to send them something from America.'

'Minnie is planning a trip to Chicago in the next few days,' Brent told her. 'She wants to buy some gifts for Christmas too. If you wish I can escort you both.'

The prospect of travelling even for an hour in the company of Minnie Hargreaves was not an enticing one but since it would be impossible for her to go alone Flora nodded. At least if Brent was with his fiancée, helping her choose presents, he would find it hard to keep track of her own doings.

'That's very kind of you,' she said meekly. 'I shall tell my uncle of the proposed trip.'

'And I must get back to work!' He rose, long-legged in his breeches and high boots.

'Did you want anything in particular?' Flora asked.

'I came to pass the time of day with Tina, ask her if she required anything, that's all. Enjoy looking through the atlas!'

Flora heard his footsteps crossing the hall and a door closing. With Brent gone the study seemed suddenly emptier and she shut the atlas, returned it to the shelf and went up to her room to find some piece of sewing with which she could occupy herself during the ineffable tedious meeting that would fill up her afternoon.

Rather to her surprise Minnie Hargreaves came to the sewing circle, neat and fresh in a print dress with a blue cloak around her shoulders.

'I gave the children an afternoon off,' she

announced. 'Sometimes it's good to allow them an unexpected holiday.'

'And you will have a smaller class when the Indians have left,' Flora said.

'If they ever do. So many schemes are in operation for clearing them out of the district that they will probably be here for ages yet,' Minnie said. 'Not that I object to them. The children are among my best pupils. I shall be quite sorry to see them go.'

'I have heard of a new idea,' Mrs Eliot said in her flurried way. 'That we are born to be lords and masters over the native peoples of other lands. Mr Eliot quotes the Psalmist, "He shall have dominion from sea to sea and from the river to the ends of the earth". I said to him that that was written for Solomon, but he came to think it might be prophetic.'

'My father tells me that the idea has stirred up so much controversy that it will almost certainly lie fallow for a few more years,' Minnie told her.

'Then I am glad of it,' Mrs Eliot said quietly, as the conversation turned to the forthcoming festivals of Harvest Thanksgiving and Christmas.

The afternoon was whiled away, Tina bringing in tea and sandwiches before the members of the sewing circle arrayed themselves in cloaks and bonnets again and departed.

'In your house next week I believe, Minnie?' One of the departing ladies looked at the schoolteacher.

'Oh, heavens, I almost forgot!' Minnie looked abashed. 'Next week Brent is taking me to Chicago to buy some Christmas gifts and to look at some patterns for . . . you know.'

'You're driving alone with Mr O'Brien? My dear, is that wise?' Mrs Eliot asked.

'We are unofficially betrothed,' Minnie pointed out.

'Not that I am suggesting for one moment . . .' Mrs Eliot was becoming flustered again.

'Brent drove Flora down from Chicago,' Minnie said, not unreasonably.

'As a favour to Mr Scott,' another member of the sewing circle interposed. 'It was not as if there were any emotional ties between Mr O'Brien and our most welcome newcomer here.'

'There ought to be no difficulty,' Flora put in, feeling for once wholeheartedly on the side of Minnie Hargreaves. 'Brent O'Brien has agreed that I shall accompany him and Miss Minnie Hargreaves since I too have some shopping to do.'

'So it will all be perfectly proper,' Mrs Eliot said in a relieved tone. 'Not that any of us imagined there could ever be any impropriety on your or Mr O'Brien's part.'

Oh yes you did, Flora thought with grim amusement. *Your thoughts were so clear they were practically issuing out of your heads like balloons.*

'Of course, we shall be staying overnight,' Minnie confided to her as she saw the ladies troop down the drive. 'Shall we be bearing each other company then? I had not realized how it might look . . .'

'I shall be staying in the same hotel,' Flora said. 'If I were you I would ignore any stupid insinuations.'

'Unfortunately a schoolteacher must be above reproach in all moral issues,' Minnie said and went demurely away.

Flora closed the door and leaned against it for a moment. She felt suddenly tired and depressed for no reason. When she opened her eyes again she saw that Tina had come in her noiseless way into the hall and was looking at her.

'In this country,' Flora said impulsively, 'I thought I'd be able to leave all the old, stupid rules behind.'

'Put a dog in a pigpen, Miss Flora,' the

housekeeper said, 'and it won't turn into a pig. I heard Mr Scott arrive a few minutes ago. He went into the stables.'

'Probably avoiding the sewing circle,' Flora said wryly.

Tina gave a sudden chuckle that lightened her customary brooding expression into one of pleased amusement.

'I guess so, Miss Flora,' she said, and went away with a friendlier smile than she had so far shown.

NINE

'So O'Brien will be driving two charming ladies to Chicago?' Frank Scott said. 'Well, he can be spared for a couple of days. He can also help you arrange for the packing and transport of your purchases. And you will have the company of Minnie Hargreaves as well. Now there is an intelligent, well-educated young lady. Brent is fortunate to be courting her.'

'But not so fortunate in other ways,' Flora said, giving her uncle a long, steady look.

'Ah! You refer to his late father,' he said. 'Yes, Daniel Brent O'Brien made an unlucky choice when he sat down to play poker with me.'

'Why were you in Santa Fe?' Flora enquired.

'In those days I still had a spirit of adventure,' he told her. 'I was captivated by the heat and the vitality and — yes, the gambling too! The differences between me and O'Brien's father was that I never risked more than I could afford and I always left the table while I was in profit. These days I gamble only for small stakes with friends so your own inheritance is quite safe.'

'That wasn't on my mind,' Flora said coldly.

'Of course, this house was not up to its present standard of elegance when I first came to see it.' He was continuing as if she hadn't spoken. 'It was a large dwelling. Daniel Brent O'Brien had seen great houses in Ireland built by English landowners and wished to emulate them. It was barely furnished when I arrived and much of the land remained uncultivated.'

They were drinking their after-dinner coffee in the study, Tina having withdrawn when she had poured Frank Scott his usual measure of whiskey.

'Brent's inheritance,' Flora couldn't resist saying.

'Which his father foolishly gambled away. O'Brien bears me no grudge, my dear! He is handsomely paid and has already begun to sink his own roots on land he has bought. If he secretly hankers after this estate then the remedy's in his hands. He can always pay court to you!' His eyes were bright with mischief.

'He is to marry Minnie Hargreaves,' Flora said stiffly.

'Ay, though it's my belief it was the lady who pressed for a commitment,' her uncle said. 'However, it's probably better so because if he had begun to pay you particular attention you would never have been absolutely certain whether it was for your love or the sake of the property.'

'I hadn't considered the matter,' Flora said. 'I am not the kind of young woman whom men line up to marry and if the inducement is property then I'd rather any such stayed away.'

'Well spoken! You have an independent spirit,' he said lightly. 'But Pine Creek Ridge is a small place and it would be a pity to bury yourself here entirely. There are many places in this vast country that bear closer inspection.'

'But travel must be difficult in most places?'

'Difficult but not impossible,' he said. 'Stagecoach owners are beginning to open up routes between the largest towns, though perhaps no one would ride in them just for pleasure. But the river steamboats, now, can be very comfortable and quite entertaining.'

River steamboats? Had she not heard her uncles at home remarking, apropos of Uncle

Frank and when they thought she couldn't hear, that American river steamboats were little more than floating gambling dens? But she sipped her coffee and said nothing.

To Tessa, whom she visited the next morning when the men were all occupied away from their houses, she outlined a plan that was still vague in its details.

'You would be quickly found and brought back if you tried to leave town alone,' she said to the younger girl, 'but you are often alone all day, aren't you, when your brother is working?'

'Yes,' Tessa said with a barely suppressed sigh.

'But if two ladies were to leave together?'

'You on Bess and me having broken the locks on our stable door?' A reluctant gleam of humour showed in Tessa's blue eyes.

'Does the stagecoach ever come this far? I know that Brent met me but —'

'Once a week the stage passes by within a couple of miles. I believe it stops at a small hostelry along the route. Brent met you in Chicago because it wasn't the day for the stage.'

'And one would pay for one's fare on the coach?'

'I believe so but I don't see —'

'You said the Indians move from place to place, but there must be meeting points where the clans get together?'

'Before they were sent away to the new territory, yes. They used to meet up to exchange news, to trade with other friendly clans, to give the old and the young a few days' rest.'

'Yes, I see.' Flora reflected for a moment, then enquired, 'The same places every year?'

'There was always a big meeting which lasted about a week at the Place of Spirit Wolf when the winter began and the fall started to slide away.'

'Near the stagecoach route?'

'A few miles away from it — no, Flora! I see what's in your mind and it would never work! How could it? How could it? You and I would find it hard enough to leave the village unobserved and together and mount on the stage; and even if it were contrived when we left the coach we would still be miles from the Place of Spirit Wolf!'

'So if I see Smiling Moon in Chicago,' Flora said, exasperated, 'shall I tell him that his wife has lost her courage and intends to remain quietly in her brother's house?'

'No!' A new energy had leapt into Tessa's face.

'Then leave it to me,' Flora said, rising.

'No, I came the back way and I'll ride out to the main track without you waving goodbye and being spotted by someone or other. I've made it clear that I'm not prepared to ignore you but it would be wiser if I wasn't seen visiting regularly.'

She went out swiftly, mounted Bess and rode away, conscious of the small eager face at the kitchen window.

She had reached the now almost denuded maize field when a voice hailed her and Brent rode up. He dismounted as he reached her and gave her a helping hand to the ground with no more than a brusque greeting.

'Is something wrong?' Flora shook off Brent's hand and looked at him.

'I'm to drive you and Minnie to Chicago,' he said.

'Yes. You had already agreed I thought, but —'

'Oh, I agreed all right,' he said, giving a fleeting smile. 'Minnie wants to buy some gifts and some other bits and pieces but it was pointed out to her that it would be improper for us to drive there without any chaperon, especially as she plans to stay over, so I explained to her that there are to be three of us. Nice and cosy!'

'I too want to buy presents —'

198

'And have a few quiet words with Smiling Moon? Flora Scott, do you really think it will go unremarked if you turn up and start holding a long conversation with an Indian? Some well-meaning bystander will intervene to save your honour before you've got a sentence out!'

'You haven't mentioned to Minnie — ?'

'Good Lord, no! Minnie is privy to none of this,' he said. 'Oh, she'd likely have a certain sympathy with the plan, whatever it is that you and Tessa have cooked up together, but Minnie has her own reputation to consider and Hargreaves would sooner shoot his daughter than have her privy to any scheme that involved helping Indians!'

'Minnie knows nothing about anything of this,' Flora said. 'Neither is there any certainty that I'll see Smiling Moon. And there is no plan as you seem to suppose.'

It wasn't strictly true but she kept her eyes firmly fixed on him.

'Far be it for me,' Brent said with a sudden, sour grin, 'to accuse a lady of telling lies, but you will be very well-chaperoned in Chicago!'

All men, she thought irritably as she remounted Bess and watched him canter away, were the same under the skin. They affected to admire independence and intelligence in a female but at bottom they all had the notion that women were weak, impractical creatures!

A couple of days later Brent, with Minnie beside him, drove his wagon to the front door.

'I hope you don't mind if I take seat next to the driver,' Minnie said, leaning to shake hands with Frank Scott. 'Riding back always makes me feel a trifle unwell.'

'That's perfectly convenient,' Flora said, acknowledging Brent with a cool nod. He looked unusually smart in buckskins with a wide-brimmed hat pushed to the back of his head. 'I found out on board ship that I've a strong stomach for pitching and tossing and other slight annoyances.'

She stepped up into the buckboard and seated herself on the seat at the back, raising her hand to her uncle as Brent laid his whip across the horses.

As Flora glanced back she glimpsed her uncle's wave and the slender figure of Tina framed in the shadow of the porch.

'I have a list of things I wish to purchase,' Minnie was saying loudly above the noise of horses' hoofs and rumbling wheels. 'I hope there will be some new shops there since my father last took me to Chicago.'

'Where no doubt you'll be spending most

of your salary from the school,' Brent said teasingly.

'Some of my savings, yes.' Minnie half-turned to say with a smile, 'We don't all of us have rich uncles!'

'Fortunately,' Flora said crisply, raising her voice slightly, 'I have a small income of my own and am not dependent on a relative I hardly remember.'

She was rigid with distaste but matched her smile to Minnie's with an effort.

The trip back to Chicago was not, she decided privately, going to be as pleasant as the drive she had originally taken. Fortunately, since the weather remained mild they stopped only briefly for some water, this time innocent of any whiskey-flavouring, Flora noticed.

The stink of the swamps drifted towards them as they approached and more riders and vehicles passed in both directions. Half a dozen farm workers rode past whooping, throwing their hats into the air.

'They'll be well primed tonight,' Brent commented with a grin. 'The evenings after the stock sales are always very high-spirited.'

'And a great deal of damage is caused to local property.' Minnie frowned.

'As long as it's only property.' Brent shrugged his shoulders nonchalantly.

This was more like the land of which she had read, Flora thought, wishing suddenly that she was mounted on a horse and galloping too instead of being jolted along in the back of a buckboard. Her plain dark dress and veiled bonnet were already spattered with dirt.

'There's a good hotel at the top of the main street,' Brent said as he pulled up the horses. 'I take it you ladies will be sharing?'

To Flora's relief Minnie said:

'Two single rooms would be more convenient, don't you think so, Flora? Then we would be able to come and go without disturbing each other.'

'I'll see what can be done.' Brent handed the reins to Minnie and jumped down.

Flora amused herself by looking around her in the crowded street where varying types of people hurried up and down, occasionally impeded by groups taking up space on the raised wooden boardwalks, others dodging horses being ridden or led towards the stockyards.

'Is London as busy as this?' Minnie wanted to know.

'In the main shopping centres, but there are many quiet parks and odd little corners where one may sit or stroll,' Flora answered.

'This will be a great city one day,' Minnie

202

asserted confidently. 'Not that I would wish to live here permanently — the smells are so unpleasant! But Brent is so efficient at his job that I wish he would consider bettering himself. However, he intends to go on working for your uncle and running his own place and a wife must submit to her husband's wishes.'

'Not if she doesn't agree with them,' Flora muttered. To her relief Brent was striding back to them.

'I've managed to book three single rooms,' he informed them. 'I shall see to the horses and wagon now and join you in an hour for some lunch if that suits you, ladies?'

'I would like you to accompany me this afternoon,' Minnie said, suffering herself to be lifted down. 'I want to buy something special for Father and you have such good ideas.'

'I will get my own shopping,' Flora said firmly, 'and meet you both this evening for supper, unless you prefer —' She had been about to say, 'prefer to dine together', but Brent cut in cheerfully with:

'That will be splendid! I'll bring your valises over. They're light enough in all conscience.'

'Half-empty in readiness for the Christmas gifts,' Minnie told him, 'but I have brought a change of dress for this evening and another for our drive back tomorrow.'

'I never met a woman who didn't carry sufficient clothing for about three months,' Brent said as he resumed his place in the driving seat.

Flora, vainly attempting to brush away the dried dirt from her dark skirt, found herself wishing she had bethought herself of a change for the evening.

The hotel was unexpectedly luxurious with carpets on the floor and furnishings of dark, polished wood, dark-red drapes at the windows and bedrooms which, though small were well-appointed.

It was pleasant to rinse one's hands and face in the hot water the chambermaid carried up and to brush one's hair into a semblance of tidiness. The maid obligingly brushed her skirt and bonnet for her too, so when Flora went down into the crowded dining room for lunch she felt reasonably presentable.

'Were you thinking of buying anything particularly heavy this afternoon that will need to be sent quickly?' Brent enquired as they ate their main course. 'If so leave it in the shop and make a note of the shop's name and I'll go along and arrange for the sending before we start back tomorrow.'

'And you're going to help me with gift-buying,' Minnie reminded him. 'Not all of it, for some of the articles I wish to purchase are rather private.'

Meaning undergarments, Flora thought. Why must she be so self-consciously correct all the time!

She said aloud: 'Well, I mean to start my shopping as soon as we have had coffee. I shall enjoy looking round by myself.'

Catching Brent's swift glance in her direction she hastily bent her head and applied herself to the rest of her dinner.

The crowds hadn't abated during the afternoon. As inconspicuous as a tall woman could be in her dark cape and bonnet, Flora walked down the main street looking for the turning to the stable yard where she had first seen the skins being sold. She found the yard but though it was still a bustle of noise and movement there were no signs of any skins and the only Indian leaned against the wall and stared at her with complete indifference.

'Skins?' Flora approached him, awkward under his blank stare. 'I wish to buy skins from Smiling Moon. Smiling Moon?'

The Indian shrugged and turned away, hunching a shoulder against her, but there was a tense quality in the way he stood, his head raised.

'Tonight after dark,' she said quickly, praying he understood at least some English. 'Smiling Moon.'

She thought he nodded slightly but he gave no other indication that he had heard as he moved away without looking back.

For the moment there was nothing more she could do. She made her way back to the main street and began her purchases. For her mother and her female cousins she chose prettily bound almanacs showing on their covers the various flowers that grew here, and for her uncles and brother she selected pocketbooks of calfskin. They were modest enough gifts but since it wasn't likely they would reach England in time for the festival it probably didn't matter.

Her further purchases were made down a side street, bagged up securely and handed to her by a bored assistant.

For the rest she whiled away an hour buying a couple of sketchbooks and some paints. If the ladies of Pine Creek Ridge enjoyed forming societies she might suggest a painting and drawing circle. The desire to splash vivid colour on to paper or canvas was growing steadily in her. Colours were brighter here, or perhaps her own senses were heightened by new experiences, by the contrast between corn-yellow fields and dark woodland against a background of dusty white roads and skies that spread their tints of blue and grey over immeasurable distances with no very high buildings to interrupt them.

By the time she had returned to the hotel, packed away what she had bought and spent more time brushing off dirt from her skirts the day was well advanced. When she went down to the dining room it was to find Minnie, attractive in a fresh sprigged dress, seated alone.

'Brent went off to the cattle auction,' she said in a tone that hinted at vague disapproval. 'However, it gave me time to choose some very pretty cream lace and a charming print in silver-and-blue flowers with silk for a sash and a bertha collar. Did you — ?'

'A few gifts for my family,' Flora said.

'And here comes Brent!' Minnie said, her expression brightening.

'Apologies for my lateness, ladies.' He bowed politely, including Flora in his smile. 'I spent longer at the auction than I intended and had to wash the odours off myself before I was fit for company for anybody!'

'Were you buying for Mr Scott?' Minnie

enquired, wrinkling up her nose slightly. 'You said you had an entirely free couple of days.'

'Mr Scott keeps only a string of cattle since his main income comes from crops,' he returned. 'No, I bought half a dozen steer for friends.'

'Friends?' Minnie said sharply. 'Oh, Brent, you've been buying for the Peoria to see them through the winter! That was kind of you but hardly necessary.'

'It will become necessary if they are driven on to the plains before winter sets in,' he returned.

'Brent is always so generous,' Minnie said. 'For my own part I doubt whether anything will happen at all! Men hold meetings and talk and decide first one thing and then another and in the end everything stays exactly the same!'

'Probably,' Brent said with a shrug. 'Now, if you ladies would like to order. The menu gives us fried steak, boiled steak, roast steak and stewed steak. Which variety would you prefer?'

The meal progressed amiably enough. Flora, eating her boiled steak, which she would have called 'grilled' in England, was conscious of Brent's eyes resting upon her thoughtfully from time to time, though she kept her own gaze fixed firmly on her plate.

'There is a concert of classical music in the City Hall here,' Minnie said as they drank their coffee. 'I saw a large advertisement for it pasted up on a hoarding. Would it be possible to obtain tickets at this late hour?'

'Probably. We can always try,' Brent began.

'Not for me.' Flora seized the opportunity. 'To be honest I am more tired than I would have believed possible. I shall have an early night in readiness for the drive back tomorrow.'

'And there can be no objection to Brent's escorting me in a public place,' Minnie said, looking pleased.

'None at all,' Brent said, 'though I fancy there will be fewer men than ladies in the City Hall this evening. Most cow farmers' tastes run to the saloon bars and the er — gaming houses.'

'But you like classical music, Brent. You know you do!' Minnie protested.

'Very much.' His eyes were teasing as he glanced briefly towards Flora. 'It gives me the perfect opportunity to doze in public without offending anybody.'

'He is funning,' Minnie said quickly. 'Brent is always funning.'

'Of course. We shall see you later perhaps?'

He looked again at Flora.

'I am so weary,' she said apologetically, 'that I intend to sleep through until the morning.'

After the meal was finished she endured another half-hour of Minnie's bright conversation during which that lady discoursed upon her own impatience with Brent's generosity, her dislike of people who held endless meetings at which nothing particular was decided, her view that sooner or later a prospective suitor would arrive on the Scott doorstep for Flora.

It was odd, Flora mused as she watched her companion run trippingly down the hotel stairs, that even on the many occasions when she agreed with Minnie's point of view she found herself ready to grit her teeth with impatience.

At least she wouldn't be disturbed until morning. She went into the single bedroom and donned the breeches, checked shirt and boots she had secretly purchased during the afternoon. With her hair pinned flat against her head and a wide-brimmed hat crammed on top, and a buckskin jacket, another purchase, hiding any hint of femininity she looked in the mirror with some satisfaction and saw a youth with rather delicate features staring back at her.

She made rather an attractive young man, she decided, though her skin was too smooth and her lips a trifle too full. But, since she had no intention of allowing anyone more than a passing glance at her, she thrust aside any niggling doubts and went out to the landing, carefully locking the bedroom door behind her.

The hotel was filling up with people bent on a late dinner and the clerk at the reception desk was registering some newcomers. Flora tilted her hat over her eyes and went into the street.

Chicago was a livelier place after dark than Pink Creek Ridge. Lanterns hung in the porches of many of the saloon bars; though womenfolk seemed to have departed to their homes and most of the shops had drawn down their shutters, noise, laughter and the tinkling of a pianoforte sounded from several nearby saloons and horses tethered in line along the rails gave evidence of the presence of numerous farmers and others here sampling whatever delights were on offer.

A couple of girls in bright dresses with skirts scarcely covering their knees were leaning against one porch, talking and laughing and the sound of applause greeted what sounded like the end of a song sung in a loud but tuneful female voice.

Flora reached a passageway which was wide enough for the stagecoach to pass along it, and walked swiftly into the yard, now apparently deserted save for a few unsaddled ponies and a couple of carts piled with bales of what she guessed must be hay. If the Indian she had seen earlier had been more alert than he had appeared, which she had suspected, then Smiling Moon would be there waiting.

She paced across the yard, conscious that the surrounding walls diminished the noises from the street, then a flicker of movement from a corner of the yard caught her eye.

'Smiling Moon?' Forgetting caution in her relief she hurried towards the movement, then stopped again, brought up short by the wall in front of her. Still the faint street-noise echoed in the empty yard.

What happened next seemed to occur in the space between one heartbeat and the next. Her arms were grasped and held tightly behind her back and what felt like a sack was flung over her head, knocking her hat sideways. Her startled gasp was muffled in dense folds of sacking, then she was being hoisted up and flung down again.

For some moments she must have lost consciousness because the next thing of which she was aware was the pounding of hoofs beneath her, the jangling of harness and the heavy, suffocating darkness that swirled about her.

If she panicked now, she told herself, summoning reason to her aid, she might well die, either by using up the little air she had or by being hit hard with something. She fought back her almost overwhelming desire to scream and concentrated on taking small regular gulps of air which was already becoming dangerously stale.

It seemed an eternity but was probably no longer than a few minutes before the horse beneath her slowed and stopped. She blinked into the musty darkness, felt a rush of air and saw the shiny blade of a large knife slicing through the sacking, bringing with it air and a glimpse of a sinewy brown hand.

Then the jolting began again and she closed her eyes in terror as the gradient clearly became steeper, herself slipping and sliding on the back of the animal, harsh voices issuing commands in a strange clacking tongue of which she understood nothing.

Whether she fainted or slept she had no idea but darkness closed down upon her. Her next sensation was of being dragged down on to hard ground and of the slashing knife once more admitting air.

Then somehow or other she was struggling free from her bonds and scrambling to her feet, blinking as the dancing lights of flaring torches surrounded her. She could see dark faces, braided hair and the glint of knives.

The odd thought passed through her mind that if she had been taken as a hostage or, worse, taken to be killed in order to discourage white settlers from bringing their wives into hostile country, there would be sadness and grief in her family but there would not be one man who would mourn a lost love.

Instinctively she flung back her head and stood motionless as the torchbearers circled and surrounded her.

TEN

These were not the friendly, broad-faced Peorias whose children played by the stream or along the banks of the river. These had darker complexions and sharper features though it was hard to note details, partly because the flaring torches cast a lurid light over the scene, partly because the Indians had paint smeared on their faces and most of all because Flora was more terrified than she had ever been in her entire life.

Instinct told her that to show fear would be not only useless but dangerous. She took a long quivering breath and said loudly:

'Where is Smiling Moon?'

One, taller than the rest, stepped forward and spoke, his voice slow and heavily accented:

'He come pretty quick. Pretty quick already. We waiting.'

Another, moving forward and tapping her arm, indicated the pile of discarded sacking and made a sitting gesture.

Flora, obeying, tried to console herself with the thought that they clearly intended no real hurt to her person and that when Smiling Moon arrived he, thanks to Tessa's teaching, would speak English well.

They were also seating themselves on the ground, others stood still, rifles in their hands. A woman, clad like the men in buckskins with long heavily greased hair streaked with grey, brought water and some slices of hard dry meat which resisted Flora's attempts to bite into it until the woman, suddenly laughing, took it from her and dipped it into the water.

'Jerky,' she said in English. 'Dried meat.'

The soon-softened meat was at least edible, and perhaps they would not bother to feed her if they were thinking of killing her.

The woman had remained near her and now began to reach out and unpin Flora's hair, her own face revealing puzzlement. She said something sharply to one of the surrounding men and he too came and bent to tug at one of the brown, curling strands.

'Do you speak English?' Flora asked, fighting back terror. 'Are you Peoria?'

'Kickapoo.' The woman pointed to herself. 'Kickapoo. Them Peoria.'

Her uncle had mentioned during the

course of a conversation that the Kickapoo were a tribe who had inhabited various places, and during the previous century some had settled in central Illinois. She recalled with a little tremor of apprehension that he had said that they were particularly warlike, and had driven many other tribes away from their lands.

'Before they were relocated the tribes would frequently join up together or hold powwows, as they called their meetings,' Uncle Frank had said. 'There was intermarriage between the various clans too. There was a time when one lot would fight another lot but in recent years they seemed to be joining together more frequently. It was worrying!'

But very natural, Flora had thought, that faced with so many whites coming in and taking over their lands, they would band together for greater security. She had said nothing to her uncle since it was clear he would be unwilling to agree with that point of view and they had gone on to talk of other things.

Something was happening. She felt a stirring among the watching men, the click of a rifle being cocked, and then to her immense relief Smiling Moon rode up to the group, raising his hand and obviously identifying himself.

'Smiling Moon! Will you please tell me what's going on!'

Flora scrambled to her feet, watching as he swung himself from his horse and came towards her.

If she had expected some kind of civil greeting she was disappointed. He stared hard at her for a moment, then turning, burst into a flood of what sounded like angry recriminations in the unintelligible clacking tongue she had already heard.

When he turned back to her his expression, illuminated by the flames of the torches, was still wrathful.

'They bring the wrong woman!' he said. 'Why you? Where is Smiling Sun? Where is my wife?'

'Back in Pine Creek Ridge,' Flora said. 'You weren't expecting . . .'

But of course, she realized, the arrival of Tessa was what he had been expecting.

'But you told Panther —' he was continuing.

'Panther?'

'My friend Panther,' Smiling Moon said, speaking with almost insulting slowness as if he addressed an idiot. 'Men in Chicago make things hard for me, say I am no trader but one who comes to spy for cattle rustlers.

I leave and my friend Panther comes to wait for Smiling Sun to come. I gave you one month. Panther agrees to bring Smiling Sun to me.'

'But surely he realized —' Flora began.

'Panther does not know Smiling Sun,' Smiling Moon said. 'He comes into my clan four moons since to seek wife and I tell him of my wife carried off by soldiers.'

'But Tessa — I mean Smiling Sun has fair hair. Didn't you describe her?'

'I told him she is white woman,' Smiling Moon said.

'Did you tell him to grab me and throw a sack over my head and frighten me half to death?' she demanded.

A faint unwilling grin appeared at the side of the young Indian's mouth.

'Panther,' he said, 'thinks it best to take all wives back in that manner for some have left with soldiers of their own will. So he seizes wrong woman. Where is my wife?'

'I told you! In her brother's house. She is watched and cannot go beyond the village.'

'Then you lie to me.'

'No, I did not!' Flora spoke rapidly, conscious that his hand had moved to his knife. 'I have a plan — well, the beginnings of one. You know where you used to gather with the other clans before the winter quarters were set up?'

'At Spirit Wolf Place, yes. Sit!'

He gave her a slight push and seated himself before her, leaning forward slightly.

'The stage passes close to Pine Creek Ridge,' Flora told him. 'It might be possible for two women, both veiled, to buy tickets, board it, and —'

'You think people will not see two women in veils leaving the village?'

'Not if we take the back roads very early in the morning. A woman alone getting on the stage would be suspicious but two women, perhaps going to a funeral . . . ?'

She broke off, seeing him shaking his head vigorously.

'The stagecoach passes near to Spirit Wolf Place,' he said, 'but it makes no stop there. The drivers go fast because they fear a hold up. Two women getting off the stage would not be let — let?'

'Allowed,' Flora supplied.

'Allowed,' he nodded. 'My English dies a little since Smiling Sun was taken away from me. My heart too but we will not speak of that!'

'We could leave the stage at a — a trading post or a hostelry?'

'Trading post? Hostelry? No Indians can come to white man's hostelry, and there are no trading posts on the route. You have very foolish ideas,' he said.

'Right then, you think of something better!' Flora said impatiently.

'It is best Smiling Sun goes to Bloomington on the stage,' he said promptly.

'So you admit that catching the stage is a good idea?'

'If you can leave the village, if nobody asks to see your faces — it is possible you can board,' he said reluctantly. 'And many do ride to Bloomington.'

'How far is Bloomington?'

'One hundred, one hundred, one hundred miles perhaps more, perhaps less,' he said. 'Indians do not run over the land measuring it.'

'How long does it take to get there then?'

'Two, three days.' His white teeth flashed in a sudden grin. 'When we attack it don't get there at all!'

'Make sure it isn't attacked,' Flora said sharply. 'I will buy two tickets for Bloomington for next week's stage. And when we get there what then?'

'I have friends there,' he said promptly. 'Little Tree —' He indicated the Kickapoo woman who sat, a blanket wrapped about her, at a little distance. 'She has relations there who will help us.'

'She rides with the men?'

'She was warrior woman once,' he said with a note of pride in his voice, 'but she is old now — past forty and more peaceful in her ways but she likes still to ride. Her heart is restless though none know why.'

'Does she know Smiling Sun?'

'No. And nobody knows Little Tree,' he said. 'Sometimes she goes into the dream-time and brings back messages but only for others. For herself she sees nothing.'

'And now I have to get back to Chicago,' Flora said. 'How far . . . ?'

'One hour, one hour, maybe two hours' ride. You will be back by dawn.'

'Then someone will have to escort me to at least within sight of the town,' Flora began.

'Wait!' He rose, folding his legs in a graceful motion and rising.

He made his way to where the others still sat or stood, the flares from the torches burning lower.

He was talking earnestly to the one who had been in the stagecoach yard, their heads bent together.

'My friend,' he said, returning to her side and squatting on his heels, 'wishes to know if you have a husband.'

'No, I haven't,' Flora said, caught un-

222

awares by the question.

'Panther,' Smiling Moon said, 'has no wife.'

'Oh.' Flora stared at him.

'He thinks that you are a brave woman,' Smiling Moon continued.

'Oh,' Flora said again.

She felt utterly foolish and her earlier terror was rushing back albeit in a slightly different form.

'You would,' Smiling Moon said, having evidently decided on persuasion, 'be a friend too for Smiling Sun. Two friends to be together. No loneliness.'

Flora had a sudden grotesque image of herself penning a letter home by the campfire while around her the Peoria planned their next raid.

My husband's name is Panther and he has just erected a very nice winter lodge for me . . .

'He will give you many children,' Smiling Moon was urging.

'I — need to return to Chicago before I am missed,' she began desperately. 'Smiling Sun cannot leave the village alone or buy tickets for Bloomington.'

'But you can give your word before you leave? We need strong women in all the clans.'

He stopped abruptly, his hand flying to

223

his knife, his head raised in a listening attitude. All about them the dying flares were being rapidly extinguished and the men were cocking their rifles.

Flora found herself holding her breath as the sound of galloping hoofs could be heard approaching through the tense and waiting darkness.

'Smiling Moon! Is Smiling Moon here?'

It was Brent's voice, calling out the question, and then Brent himself, mounted on one of the horses that had pulled the wagon on their way to Chicago, hove into indistinct view.

'Smiling Moon!' he called again.

'Brent?' Finding breath and voice Flora scrambled to her feet just as a warning bullet zinged past Brent's head. Instinctively he dived to the ground, then came up rapidly into a kneeling position, pistol in hand.

'Brent! Smiling Moon is here and I'm unharmed!'

Somehow or other Flora found herself by his side as he rose, putting his gun back in its holster and turning on her a face so filled with fury that she could sense it even before one of the Indians ignited a torch and held it aloft.

Smiling Moon had stepped out of the circle and was staring at Brent doubtfully, his own gun still in his hand. When he spoke in his heavily accented English he sounded no more friendly.

'You are friend to white woman here?'

'Friend to Tessa, to your wife,' Brent answered. 'You are Smiling Moon?'

The young brave nodded, his expression still wary as more torches were kindled.

'Tessa is in Pine Creek Ridge,' Brent said. 'You have the wrong woman.'

'This one came of her own free will,' Smiling Moon said.

'I did not!' Flora interposed furiously. 'Brent, I was seized, had a sack thrust over my head and was then flung over the back of a horse and almost suffocated, not to mention —'

'The less you mention the better at the moment,' Brent said coldly. 'Smiling Moon, don't you know your own wife?'

'My friend was in the place where I was selling skins before,' Smiling Moon told him. 'The traders in Chicago begin to look sideways at me because I stay in town too long. So Panther goes in my place to wait for Smiling Sun to come.'

'But Tessa would have been there of her own free will!' Flora put in. 'Why would they need to take her by force?'

'Peoria sense of honour,' Brent said, his

expression having relaxed slightly. 'You don't know much about Indians, do you?'

'I know,' said Flora darkly, 'quite sufficient!'

'My friend Panther did not meet Smiling Sun,' Smiling Moon hastened to explain. 'He was then with another tribe and joined us after the soldiers had stolen her away.'

'And your friend thought it a great jest to take her by force and then present her to you as a happy surprise for her,' Brent said.

'But surely you told Panther what Tessa — Smiling Sun — looked like?' Flora put in, her senses reeling slightly.

'Peoria husbands,' Smiling Moon said haughtily, 'do not gossip about their women.'

'And it was highly unlikely that a white woman who wasn't Smiling Moon's wife would be coming after dark to the meeting place.' Brent nodded, and stepped forward to shake hands with the two Indians. 'Well, a mistake was made, so . . .'

'I too look for a wife,' Panther said.

There was a moment's tension. Then Brent gave a chuckle.

'Panther wants this woman,' he said, 'he is welcome to her. She is a scolding woman who has been refused by many men because she refuses to cook or sew or mend the fire when it burns low. Take her if you will but your lodge will be a cold place and your heart unsatisfied.'

There was general laughter which Flora, burning with a new indignation, was certain was at her expense. Angrily she turned on her heel and had gone only a few steps when the Kickapoo woman whom Smiling Moon had called Little Tree caught her by the hand, whispering urgently:

'When you find true love give true love this. Most secret. Hide!'

Something was thrust into Flora's hand and swiftly she thrust the object into her pocket.

'I will look,' Panther said loudly, 'for another wife.'

'And we must return before dawn breaks and the stupid woman is missed,' Brent was saying in a tone that brought the angry flush into Flora's cheeks.

Little Tree had melted into the darkness again before Flora had the chance to speak. Brent turned from where he stood with several Indians and said loudly:

'This woman ought to walk back into town for her stupidity but I have a kind heart and she will ride behind me.'

'Why not point out that I'm also wearing breeches?' Flora taunted, 'and let them all see how thoroughly unladylike I am?'

'Indian women often wear buckskins when the clan's on the move,' Brent said. 'We'd best be on our way for dawn's not far behind us.'

'How far out of town are we?' she enquired, stifling her indignation.

'No more than seven or eight miles north of Chicago,' Brent told her.

'It seemed like hours being in that sack,' she muttered.

Brent gave an impatient exclamation and went over to his horse, leaving Smiling Moon to move to her side, his voice a whisper as he asked:

'This man, Brent, he knows of the plan for you and Smiling Sun?'

Flora shook her head. 'I have told him nothing,' she said, her voice low and hurried. 'He is a good man and treats Smiling Sun as a friend but he will not help her leave the village.'

'Then say nothing,' Smiling Moon said and moved away.

'Right! Up you get!' Brent, already mounted, leaned from the saddle to help her with his hand to mount up behind him.

The last she heard was Panther's somewhat regretful remark:

'The white woman is strong.'

Brent rode out and within a few minutes they were trotting more or less sedately along the track.

'We will go faster when the clouds lighten,' Brent said over his shoulder. 'I don't want to risk this horse stumbling into a pothole. Hold on tightly for if you slide off I'm not sure I'll bother stopping to pick you up!'

Flora hung on tightly, trembling with anger and fatigue.

'We'd better stop for ten minutes,' she heard Brent say just as she found herself slipping into sleep with her cheek against his broad back.

'Very well!' Flora slid to the ground and pushed back her disordered hair with her fingers. The hat she had worn was nowhere to be seen and she knew without looking that her breeches would be dusty and in tatters.

'Best have some water,' Brent said shortly, handing her a leather bottle.

'Thank you,' she said equally curtly. She drank thirstily as he tethered his mount to a bush within grazing reach of a patch of lush grass.

'I take it that you and Tessa Fontaine hatched up some crazy scheme to meet Smiling Moon,' he said when he had quenched his own thirst. 'You slipped out to the stagecoach yard in the hope of seeing him and the one who grabbed you was under the impression you were she.'

'Evidently!' Flora said.

'And Tessa is still in her brother's house? She hasn't gone haring off in another direction with another completely impractical scheme in mind?'

'She's still in Pine Creek Ridge,' Flora said sullenly.

'It never occurred to you that Smiling Moon was starting to attract attention by continuing to hang about in Chicago? It didn't enter your head that sneaking out after dark in a frontier town packed with gamblers, dropouts not to mention habitual drinkers and other types of lowlife that you risked being spotted before you'd got anywhere near where Smiling Moon might be?'

'I wasn't spotted!' Flora flared. 'As you may have noticed I was careful to buy some male garments.'

'As I found out when I went to collect some of Minnie's purchases,' Brent said. 'I left during the concert interval for ten minutes and checked that Minnie's purchases were all packed and ready to pick up. She'd bought some garments for her father and the shop assistant enquired if I wished anything else for the lady who'd bought the hat and boots and the check shirt and breeches. Apparently these are not usually bought or tried on by respectable women.'

'You had no business —'

'The assistant merely mentioned the circumstance to me. Chicago is a fast-growing town but there aren't that many places where one can buy clothes ready-made. I'm only astonished you didn't buy a gun while you were about it! Of the dam-fool things an inexperienced female has ever done!'

'Oh, do stop lecturing me!' Flora's patience snapped. In another moment, she thought, she would have to burst into humiliating tears or lose her temper and relieve her feelings in that manner. Temper at least gave her some dignity.

'And how could you possibly count on getting any sort of message — ?' Brent was starting again.

'And how did you discover that I'd left the hotel?' she snapped.

'I had to wait until the concert was finished.' He was obviously controlling his own fury with an effort. 'I said nothing to Minnie since I didn't want to alarm her un-necessarily and when we reached the hotel she requested a cup of coffee before

231

retiring.'

'And you waited until she was safely tucked up and then went to your own room, just tapping on my door along the way?'

'My room's out at the back,' he told her. 'I went up by means of the fire escape at the side of the building — a very modern convenience in a town where most of the buildings are of wood. Your window was unlocked and your bed empty. That was really when I understood that you had some hare-brained scheme in your mind! I spent the next hour making discreet enquiries in the neighbouring saloon bars and eventually hit your trail. An unshod horse going north and others joining its tracks a little further on. It took some time because the moon was erratic and I needed to keep lighting flares and I'd also to get one of our horses out of the stable.'

'You have been busy!' Flora nodded. 'And it was all for nothing because I wasn't hurt in the least.'

'But manhandled and frightened out of your wits?' Brent said. 'Or does that kind of thing go on all the time in London?'

'That's ridiculous! I —'

'Took an entirely unjustified risk simply in order to get a message to a young Peoria who's pining for his wife! Oh, I'm aware you won't tell me of any message Tessa might have forwarded to her husband! I'm not asking you to betray any confidences, but you had better make it clear that that was the last message you'll be delivering!'

'How dare you lecture me?' Flora had felt herself stiffen under the verbal onslaught and now she spoke low and bitingly. 'Of course I feel sympathy for Tessa Fontaine! Of course I would help her in any way I could! You claim to be sympathetic to the Indian plight but you don't do much to prevent it, do you? I suppose keeping your job as manager to my uncle and paying off your mortgage is more important! Or perhaps you're afraid that Minnie Hargreaves will disapprove? Is that it? Once you're married then you'll truly be a member of the local establishment, able to play at cards with my uncle and his friends and escort your wife to parties!'

'And yet I came riding after you,' Brent said as she paused for breath. 'Now that was a very stupid thing to do! By now you might've been on your way to a Peoria wedding ceremony with yourself as bride. Next time you go adventuring I'll leave you to fend for yourself. Now mount up! Dawn's on the way and I don't want to soil your reputation by riding in with you after a night in the open!'

He had hoisted her up to the saddle before she could reply, mounted up himself and set off at a faster pace than they had come so far.

Streaks of light were appearing towards the east and the stink of the swamps upon which Chicago was built was becoming more potent. In the half-light the landscape looked bleak with piles of timber to prove where trees had been felled for the building of shops and houses as more and more people crowded into the city.

The street was almost deserted except for a few late drinkers who sat or sprawled on the boardwalk, their horses tethered along the rails nearby. Shutters shielded the fronts of the shops and here and there a lamp still burned in the windows of adjoining houses.

'You'd best go up the fire escape,' Brent told her, dismounting and leading the horse round to the side of the hotel. 'You can get in through the window before anyone stirs. Oh, and treat yourself to a good wash! You look like something left out for salvage.'

He had turned and swung her to the ground, his brown eyes suddenly teasing.

'I can manage,' Flora said icily.

'Good!' He loosened his grip about her waist and stood back. 'Oh, by the by, you do make quite a handsome young blade you know. See you at breakfast!'

He was gone before she could retort, leading the horse away, not glancing back.

Flora climbed the narrow iron rungs, hanging on to the guarding rail as the ache in her back and arms intensified. Her window was open a few inches; she pushed it up and made her entrance in less than dignified fashion, misjudging the height of the sill and landing in an ungainly heap on the floor of the passageway to her room. She made her way along it.

At the door of her room she fumbled in the pocket of her shirt for the door-key which she then recalled was in the pocket of her buckskin jacket. Indeed she admitted to herself reluctantly she was so tired that she might be forgiven for forgetting everything.

The key was there and with it came the small, glittering object that she had thrust there when the old Kickapoo woman had given it to her.

'Give it to your true love. Most secret. Hide.' Little Tree had said that, or words to that effect. Flora sat down wearily on the edge of the bed and opened her hand. On her palm in the growing light of dawn that slanted palely through the window glinted a golden star.

ELEVEN

There had been no time to sit and speculate as to the meaning of the little star. Flora slipped it into her purse, reflecting wryly that if it was destined for her true love it would be nestling in there for a very long time. She washed in cold water, unwilling to send for hot lest the arrival of the servant should disturb Minnie before Flora had completed her tasks, put on the plain, dark dress and bundled the male outfit, together with her nightgown, into her case.

Then, with her hair smoothed back demurely and secured in a net, she opened her door with caution and went down to the reception desk where a sleepy clerk was checking the register.

'Two tickets for Bloomington?' He looked up as she enquired. 'Yes, ma'am, you can surely buy them here. Any particular day? The stage goes once a week. But you can use the tickets any time provided there's room aboard. End of autumn not too many folk set out further south.'

'No particular day,' Flora said.

'Right! I can reserve seats for a month ahead?'

'Yes, that will do very well!'

The lobby was beginning to fill up as people emerged from their rooms for breakfast. She hadn't the faintest desire to be interrupted by Brent or Minnie as she booked advance seats on the stage going south.

'There we are, ma'am!' He finished writing out the tickets and slid them across the counter towards her.

'Do I have to come into Chicago to board?' she enquired, fishing money out of her purse.

'You're from — Pine Creek Ridge, wasn't it, ma'am? The river that runs through — there's a hostelry by the second bend once you're clear of the town. The stage stops there for a few minutes provided you can get there by seven in the morning?'

'Yes, we can certainly do that,' Flora said, more confidently than she felt.

'It's a fairly clear run unless the snows come early.' The clerk, now inconveniently disposed to chat, leaned on the counter. 'Not much redskin trouble this end of the year either. Most of the tribes are headed for winter quarters or hunting for last minute game. Two ladies travelling inside. Thank you, ma'am!'

'One more thing,' Flora said quickly. 'Don't mention it to my two companions who arrived with me. The trip is in the nature of a surprise for them.'

'Not one word,' he promised solemnly.

She had just reached the door of the dining room when Brent and Minnie appeared, the one emerging through a door at the back of the lobby, the other tripping down the stairs and looking fresh and wide awake in a blue dress and cloak. Flora, mentally comparing her own dull outfit, pinned a smile firmly to her mouth and greeted Minnie pleasantly.

'I slept exceedingly well,' Minnie said, availing herself of Brent's offered arm. 'You look rather tired, Flora dear.'

'I had rather a restless night,' Flora evaded. 'Good morning, Brent.'

'Everything's taken care of,' Brent said with a smiling nod. 'Your gifts for your family will be on their way in a couple of days. I suggest we have the full breakfast. Juicy steaks, wild mushrooms, eggs sunny side up, chilli sauce, hot bread.'

'You sound,' Flora said as they took their

seats, 'as if you have shares in the place.'

'No, I put what money I can save into my farm. Waiter!'

'Just toast and coffee, please,' Minnie said firmly.

'Flora, you're a good trencherwoman, aren't you?' He gave her a challenging look.

'I'll have what you have but only half a portion,' she compromised.

When it arrived it still filled a large plate. Flora, discovering she was hungry, fell to with some enthusiasm, feeling her energy return as she ate. Across the table Minnie, nibbling toast, said sweetly:

'I always imagined that English ladies ate very little.'

'And real English women have hearty appetites,' Brent said. 'I like to see people eat well. Minnie, have an egg?'

'Just toast,' Minnie demurred. 'Being small I don't need as much as a — taller woman.'

Which, Flora thought ruefully, put her neatly in the category of tall females who tucked into steaks first thing in the morning in a most unfeminine way.

When they had finished their meal Brent brought the wagon to the door of the hotel. As the two women stepped outside Flora half-expected to see one or two of the

Indians hanging around, but there was no sign of them.

Not until they were on the road again did she raise her voice to enquire, 'Used all the Indians to go into winter quarters?'

'Some tribes did. The Peoria farm and so stay in their houses,' Brent answered. 'They all go off hunting though, for a while, but usually the men get together. Even the farmers have hunting blood in them.'

'Interesting,' Flora commented. 'In England one is apt to imagine they are all bloodthirsty and too busy taking scalps to go planting crops. I know better now.'

'So your voyage hasn't been in vain then?' He threw her a comradely smile over his shoulder.

'Brent, do be careful!' Minnie exclaimed. 'You'll have us in the ditch if you keep on swerving in that fashion!'

'The horses know the road,' he returned equably but from then on conversation lapsed.

Flora, wedged more or less comfortably among the luggage, amused herself by speculating just how comradely his smile would be if she announced that she and Tessa would be on the stage to Bloomington within the month.

'I'll drop you and your purchases off at

241

your house first,' Brent said to Minnie as they drove into the village.

'But you will call later for coffee? Father will be there.'

'Yes, of course.'

They drew up outside the overseer's house. Brent helped Minnie down and carried most of the luggage to the door. He went inside, and came out again a few minutes later.

'You can sit up front if you've a mind,' he said to Flora as he clambered up to the driving seat again.

'It's really not worth it for such a short distance,' answered Flora. 'Anyway, you will only lecture me again.'

'Very probably,' he said shortly, 'so you're wise to stay where you are! Giddy up!'

The horses giddied up, setting the wagon swaying. Flora, holding on to the side rail, decided crossly that riding in the back of a buckboard had nothing to recommend it.

Tina came to the door as they stopped at the top of the drive. The Mestiza woman was her usual unsmiling self as she summoned the other servants to carry in the luggage but her expression softened slightly as she turned to greet Brent.

'Did you have a good time in Chicago?' she enquired.

'More tiring than I expected,' Brent said. 'If you ever drive up to town make sure you don't have two chattering females in tow!'

'It was then a change for you,' Tina said. 'Usually it is the men who chatter while the women are working! That will change next week. There is a big meeting in Chicago —'

'Another meeting! When will they be done talking?' Brent said impatiently.

'So long as they are talking things stay as they are,' Tina said. 'The next day Mr Scott will be entertaining many guests. A dance for Miss Flora.'

Brent, in the act of helping her down, raised an eyebrow.

'Social activities are gaining on us since Flora arrived,' he said. 'I never knew Frank Scott to entertain so much before.'

'It's called the marriage market,' Flora said ironically. 'I did hope things might be different here!'

'Flora arrived with set notions,' Brent said with a grin. 'All Indians ran round taking scalps; women were considered equal with men and all Americans chew tobacco and say Howdy!'

'I thought nothing of the kind!' Flora said indignantly. 'I did think manners would be freer here and in some ways they are but in other ways they're as hidebound as if we were all living in England.'

'A veneer of politeness to make us believe we are all civilized now,' Brent said. 'Am I invited to this dance, then?'

'I believe everybody is, together with some friends of Mr Scott from Chicago,' Tina said. 'They will be mostly gentlemen so the spare bedrooms must be prepared.'

'Which means more work for you, Tina.' Brent spoke sympathetically, lowering his voice slightly as he continued, 'How the devil do you stand it?'

'Oh, I enjoy company,' Tina said serenely. 'Miss Flora?'

She stood aside invitingly.

'Thank you for your company,' Flora said politely to Brent who bowed gravely in reply. The bow, she thought indignantly, was just a trifle too low to qualify as genuine politeness. It was clear that he still regarded her as a fool for venturing out to meet Smiling Moon and had no intention of allowing her to forget the fact.

Happily the servants hadn't yet unpacked for her. There would surely have been gossip at the male attire in her baggage. She locked the case securely and thrust it in the bottom of the wardrobe, thinking as she did so of the land-ownership documents concealed beneath the floor panels. At least

Brent had entrusted her with those, though he had no idea at that time that she would try to help Tessa reunite with Smiling Moon. He now clearly regarded her as hotheaded and impulsive instead of sensible and dependable.

'Not,' she told her reflection in the mirror silently, 'that I care one jot what he thinks!'

Shaking off the sudden lowering of spirits that afflicted her she rang for hot water and concentrated on rendering herself ladylike and decent for her uncle. He rode up soon after she had seated herself in the dining room, to greet her so jovially that the thought that he had been hatching some matrimonial plot for her brushed her mind.

'And how did you find Chicago?' he enquired genially, taking his own seat at the table.

'Brent knew the way,' she answered lightly and saw him frown slightly before he smiled.

'You have a ready wit, Flora dear,' he said. 'I can appreciate it but wit in young ladies is not on the whole as highly valued as it could be. I meant to ask, of course, whether you enjoyed your trip.'

'I bought the gifts I wanted for the family and Brent kindly saw to their dispatch,' she said. 'The hotel was comfortable and I had an uneventful trip there and back.'

Which, strictly speaking, was no more than the truth!

'Has Tina mentioned to you,' he continued as the maids began bringing in the food, 'that next week I have arranged a small party for you — a dance, no less! It really is time you began to meet more people than our small society here can offer.'

'Single gentlemen you mean?' Flora said, accepting a small portion of vegetables and waving away the steak.

'My dear, you speak very frankly!' He looked as if he didn't quite approve.

'Uncle Frank, we both know that my family is eager to see me settled,' she said earnestly. 'Unfortunately I'm not the sort of feminine, pretty woman who attracts suitors. If the men of England were not lining up at my door I fail to see how you can expect the Americans to come calling!'

'My dear niece, you do yourself an injustice!' he protested. 'There are many gentlemen who appreciate a strong, healthy young woman.'

Panther for one, Flora thought and almost choked on a piece of carrot.

'I have already made it clear,' her uncle was continuing somewhat pompously, 'that whether you wed or not my fortune will eventually pass to you, provided you con-

246

tinue to please me.'

'And that should eventually bring me a couple of offers,' she said wryly. 'Forgive me, Uncle! I know you mean to be kind but the truth is that I have no particular wish to wed any man. I shall be quite contented as a spinster.'

She had spoken what she thought was the truth. Later that day, however, having found it impossible to slip over to the Fontaine house and tell Tessa what had happened, since her uncle chose to devote the afternoon to keeping her company, she sat down by the window in her bedroom and gazed out pensively. Twilight was gathering in the sky as the day sank and the garden, with its flowered terraces, became a place of strange shapes and whispering leaves.

She had never felt more than the mildest friendship for any man in her life. For men like Harold Belmont she had only mockery and for men like her uncle a kind of weary contempt, for the Harolds of the world were stupid puppies and the Frank Scotts were men who might rise high but forgot their scruples along the way.

Brent, she thought impatiently, was like all the rest. He was more free and easy in his manner but he was in the end someone who looked out for his own interests, who might be sympathetic towards the Indians and pity Tessa's plight but would risk very little. The very fact that he was moving casually into marriage with Minnie Hargreaves told her that. No man could hope for a better match than the little schoolteacher whose father worked in conjunction with him and who was as demure and ladylike as any schoolteacher in creation.

'And I do not know,' she said aloud, 'why Brent O'Brien came into my mind at all!'

She leaned to close the window against the evening chill and paused. A slim figure had come out on to the terrace, holding her arms wide, taking a few dancing steps. Between her hands she held a silvery scarf patterned with pearly, moonlight colours that shimmered as the pale crescent rose to combat the last of the day and glittered as she twisted it between her long fingers, swaying with it now to left and now to right.

Tina was dancing, slowly, sensuously, invitingly. Flora watched, fascinated, sensing in the languid movements some echo of what her own heart craved. Then, as suddenly as she had begun, Tina let the scarf flutter about her shoulders. She turned and walked sedately back into the house.

That night, though she had expected to sleep like a log after the events of the previous night, Flora found herself half-wakeful, the scarf with its flickering silver-lit shades threading its way through her mind, the dance that had its own silent rhythm pulsing at her heart's core.

'You look tired, my dear,' Uncle Frank greeted her when she went down for breakfast. 'Perhaps you are not as hardy as you look?'

'I've always been pale and very slender,' she said firmly. 'Apart from measles when I was about eight I've never suffered from anything save a cold in my life.'

'And what plans have you for today?' he enquired genially.

'I thought I might paint something,' she said thoughtfully. 'I brought my painting materials with me and the day seems fine.'

'An excellent idea!' He beamed at her kindly. 'Culture is so important when one is trying to lead a civilized existence. I shall see you later. Charles Fontaine had promised to drop by but his sister has a slight indisposition so he sends word that he will stay home.'

Which meant there was no chance of slipping over to acquaint Tessa with what had taken place in Chicago. Flora applied herself to her breakfast, happy to find bacon instead of beef on her plate, and went upstairs to collect her sketchbook and watercolours.

She would paint the garden, she decided, and keep the painting simple and pretty so that it might be displayed to the ladies of the sewing circle.

It was cool but the wind had dropped. She stationed herself below the terraces and began to sketch the outlines rapidly in pencil.

Painting was supposed to relax one. Sketching the delicate outlines of the last of the late-summer blooms, mixing her watercolours and applying them thinly Flora felt restless and vaguely dissatisfied. The painting lacked something but what it lacked eluded her.

It would, she thought with a slight grimace, certainly please Mrs Eliot and the rest of the women she had met. A step behind interrupted her brush and she turned to see Brent standing there, clad in his working clothes, shirt open at the neck, hat pushed to the back of his russet head.

'Do you always sneak up on people?' she demanded crossly.

'Sorry! I didn't want to disturb the artist at work.' His brown eyes focused on the painting with some concentration.

'Well?' she enquired.

'It's . . . pretty.'

'And dull! At least you're honest!'

'Why choose to paint dull?' he asked.

'Because the ladies in the sewing circle might be persuaded to start a sketching group if they approve of it.'

'Oh, they'll approve all right,' he said dismissively. 'Are you really so anxious for their approval?'

'It's nice to fit in,' Flora said. 'Anyway, you are the one who keeps trying to curb my independent way of going on.'

'There's independence and there's stupidity,' Brent said. 'Why didn't you tell me that you were planning to see Smiling Moon? Do you trust me so little that you had to hare off by yourself and get grabbed by someone who didn't realize you weren't Tessa Fontaine?'

'I merely wanted to let him know she was well,' Flora hedged.

'Not strictly true!' He gave her a down-curving grin. 'You wouldn't've gone to such elaborate lengths merely to let him know that. Anyway she has a chill it seems, so it'll be a day or two before Charles leaves the house. He takes good care of her even if he does disapprove of her.'

'Takes good care she doesn't leave Pine Creek Ridge, you mean.'

'For the sake of his own reputation. You

251

know what's wrong with your painting?'

'No, but as an art expert I'm sure you're going to tell me,' she said.

'No people in it,' he said.

'I was painting flowers, not people!'

'If you want to look at flowers you can come see them growing, smell their perfume. But if you paint people you can show what they're like inside. You can read their characters in their faces and capture it for all time if you've the skill.'

'And you can look at paintings of flowers when winter comes and they've all died,' she retorted.

'Every season has its flowers,' Brent said. 'Even in the depths of the snow you can find a tiny bloom struggling through to the air. You've painted a lonely picture, Flora. Pale flowers looking bored with themselves, vague outlines, wishy-washy colours.'

'How dare you suggest that I'm lonely?' she flashed.

'Oh, were we talking about you?' He gave her one of his slightly sour grins. 'You've not put anything of yourself in that picture, Flora. And if you are lonely then you're pretty hard to please! Half the county is arriving next week after the Chicago meeting to look you over as a prospective wife. Harold Belmont too! Now there's someone who shows his inner self in his face! You could spend half your married life painting him, as we doctors say!'

He laughed suddenly, laid his hand briefly on her shoulder and went towards the house, not looking back, the feeble sunlight darkening his hair to red.

Flora felt so indignant that she half-rose, determined not to allow him the last word, but Tina had appeared in the doorway and was greeting him. Flora sank back into her seat again and stared at her pretty, pallid flowers with something like disgust.

It simply wasn't fair that every time Brent O'Brien appeared she felt conflicting emotions struggling within her. It wasn't fair that his presence should make her conscious that she had such emotions at all!

She seized a crayon and began adding to the picture, working rapidly, feeling the emotion within her spill into her hand as she drew rapidly, smudging the flower petals.

When she had finished she let her hand with the half-used black crayon drop into her lap as she looked at her painting.

There, surrounded by a few smudged flowers, blotting the others out, stood the black figure of Brent O'Brien, his features suggested by a few incisive strokes, head slightly tilted, one hand raised, the long fingers slightly spread, dominating the original. Not merely dominating, she thought irritably, but effectively cancelling out the rest!

She unpinned the stiff paper from her easel and tore it across, wondering as she did so why it was necessary to destroy something that had more life and vitality than anything she had ever done.

A covered bin stood near the door, ready for whatever trash couldn't be fed to the animals. She lifted the lid, dropped the torn pieces into the bin, shut the lid down again with unnecessary firmness and went back into the garden to collect her chair and easel.

Tina appeared from another door. She took the chair from her and enquired in her usual flat, accented tones whether she required anything more before her uncle returned.

'He's gone to see Charles Fontaine to make arrangements for the big meeting next week,' she said by way of explanation.

'And there's the dance the evening afterwards. I'm afraid it will mean a lot of extra work for you,' Flora apologized.

The narrow black eyes glanced at her momentarily.

'I'm used to hard work,' Tina said. 'Not that I do much in the way of real work since I came to live here. Cooking for special occasions and light dusting and sewing and keeping the other girls in order.'

'And taking care of my uncle's needs,' Flora said.

She hadn't meant to imply anything but the implication was there, nevertheless.

'As you say,' Tina said without expression. 'Taking care of Frank Scott's needs.'

'Because Daniel O'Brien died on your wedding day?'

'He was a kind man,' Tina said. A slightly softer note had come into her voice. 'Older than me and a bit of a drinker and gambler, but a kind man. He was proud of his son too, sent him to school when he was a boy to educate him. I was eager to meet Brent when I came up to Pine Creek Ridge with Frank Scott, and Brent was a kind young man. We've been friends since we first met. He doesn't have it so easy, Miss Flora. Managing a spread that should've been his, working to pay off his mortgage and —'

'Support a future wife,' Flora said.

'Minnie Hargreaves, yes.' Tina hesitated and then said rapidly. 'I guess that Brent's own good nature betrayed him there. Minnie's a nice young lady and she works hard at the school, takes good care of the Indian children too, and helps her father a lot since her mother died, but she lacks something, Miss Flora. Can't tell what it is exactly but she lacks something. You know she and Charles Fontaine were courting up until last year?'

'Minnie Hargreaves and Tessa's brother? No, no I didn't.'

'He was real sweet on her,' Tina said. 'Everybody expected them to get engaged but then the soldiers brought Tessa Fontaine back. Charles'd given her up as long dead. And when it came out that Tessa was calling herself a white Peoria and hankering to be back with her redskin buck, well, Charles saw that his own chances of making a respectable match were spoilt. He and Minnie parted company by mutual consent and the next thing she's on with Brent O'Brien who took it into his head to pay her some attention out of kindness and now they're going to be married next year though he hasn't got around to buying her a ring yet. But she'll make him a nice little wife. Unless something gets in the way?'

Her glance was suddenly sharp.

'Nothing will,' Flora said.

'When you're feeling low,' Tina said abruptly, 'you ought to settle to doing

something that comes from the heart, Miss
Flora, something that makes you feel better
about yourself.'

'Like — dancing?' Flora ventured.

'Next time,' Tina said, 'don't just watch
from the window. Come down and join me
if you've a mind. I'd best be getting on, Miss
Flora.'

She turned and walked, sedate in her
black dress, into the house.

TWELVE

A couple of days passed before Flora judged it worthwhile to attempt visiting Tessa Fontaine who, she hoped, was safely over her cold by now.

Instead of riding as usual, she walked, feeling the need for some exercise in the cool, crisp air. There were still patches of unharvested maize but the fields were, on the whole, denuded of their grain and many of the stocks had been moved into the long sheds that served as warehouses along the way. At this hour the children were in school save for the very young ones and she heard a steady chanting of multiplication tables issuing from the open windows of the schoolhouse as she walked by.

The sound of a trotting horse behind her caused her to step aside just as Brent drew to a halt and greeted her as pleasantly as if their previous argument had never happened.

'If you're strolling over to call on Tessa,' he said, 'Charles has gone to buy supplies today so you will be unlikely to have to make a speedy exit through the back door.'

'And her chill is better?'

'I don't know. I haven't asked. I was thinking of going to see her myself . . .'

He paused, the corners of his mouth twitching with amusement as he took in the hastily concealed dismay on her face.

'Give her my regards,' Flora said stiffly.

'On the other hand, I'm sure you have more interesting information for her than I could muster,' he said lightly. 'Give her *my* regards! Good day, Flora!'

If he knew of the plan she had decided upon, Flora thought as she walked on, leaving Brent to overtake her and trot ahead, he would most certainly disapprove. Whatever his sympathy for the white Peoria he would never risk his own future by actively helping her.

She reached the Fontaine house and saw Tessa seated at the window, one edge of the net curtain held aside. Her face brightened perceptibly as Flora opened the gate and walked up the path and the net curtain was dropped into place.

'Nobody saw you turn in here?' was Tessa's first anxious question as she opened the door.

'I don't think so,' Flora said, allowing herself to be ushered into the sitting room, 'but frankly I don't care if they did!'

'If you are too openly friendly,' Tessa said, resuming her seat by the window, 'your reputation will surely suffer.'

'Much I care about that!' Flora said stoutly. 'Brent O'Brien is your friend and I don't see his reputation diminished.'

'Brent is a man,' Tessa said with a resigned shrug. 'Men have more liberty. Flora, you went to Chicago! Was Smiling Moon there still? Did you manage to speak with him?'

'He is now outside the town lest his continued presence attract too much attention,' Flora said carefully. 'I was able to meet with him. Minnie Hargreaves knows nothing of it but Brent interrupted the conversation.'

'Brent will say nothing,' Tessa said, looking relieved. 'Now if Minnie had seen you the news would be all over Pine Creek Ridge by now! Oh, I ought not to talk like that for she has many good points and Charles is still very fond of her, but she irritates me! Flora, was Smiling Moon well? Have you a plan that will really work?'

'He seemed very well,' Flora said. 'He was with a few of his tribe.'

'And does he believe we can be reunited?'

'He knows he cannot just ride up to your door and whisk you away,' Flora said. 'But he is confident you will be together soon.'

'And the plan?'

'I have two tickets for Bloomington valid for the next four trips by stage there.'

'Two tickets, but how — ?'

'Two veiled and shrouded ladies in dark clothes going to visit relatives down there. The stage halts at the hostelry by the second bend in the river —'

'And Charles will find us by the time the stage reaches the third bend,' she broke in. 'As soon as he finds me gone he will use every means to bring me back.'

'Not,' said Flora, 'if you've already been missing for a few days.'

'But how can I — ?'

'Because you will hide over at my uncle's house for a couple of days,' Flora lowered her voice to say. 'Nobody, once your absence is discovered, will imagine you are anywhere near Pink Creek Ridge! They will assume you are well away and nobody will dream of looking for you at Scott's Place!'

'Does Smiling Moon know of this?' Tessa was looking extremely doubtful.

'He doesn't know the details,' Flora admitted, 'but he trusts me to have you on the stage for Bloomington during this coming month. He trusts me so well that he was quite willing for his friend Panther to offer marriage to me.'

'I don't know anyone of that name,' Tessa said, 'but if he is a friend of Smiling Moon then it's likely he would make you an excellent husband. Oh, Flora! It's a hard life with the Peoria. Once they were hunters and warriors, now those few who are left are tenants on what were their own farms. Soon Smiling Moon and our people will have to leave our lands, and go across the Mississippi to what they call the Indian territory. But we will make a new life there. You say you want more freedom so you could do worse than come with me.'

'Panther and I,' Flora said, stifling a laugh, 'didn't really take to each other. I am not so desperate to be wed that I'd snatch at any offer.'

'Then don't marry but come anyway. You say you want more freedom.'

'I'm coming as far as Bloomington,' Flora said, banishing from her imagination thoughts of life on a Peoria farm. 'Then I'll come back and try to persuade your brother to give up the search for you.'

'My brother,' Tessa said, 'will be secretly relieved to be rid of me though he'd never admit it. Oh, he's done his duty by me since the army found and brought me back but my return has been a source of personal disappointment for him. He and Minnie Hargreaves had begun to walk out together, you see, and my return as a tainted white woman meant that her father swiftly put an end to their friendship.'

'Tainted!' Flora repeated the word with some heat. 'You're a married woman, not a tainted one.'

'I'm a white squaw,' Tessa said with quiet bitterness. 'Nobody cares that I have known Smiling Moon half my life and that we love each other. He's a Red Indian to them, nothing more. Someone to be written about in stories or pointed out as an example of a noble savage. But to wed? No, the local ladies won't stomach that for a moment!'

'Then they're narrow-minded and prejudiced,' Flora said decidedly, 'and I suppose that most of the men are the same.'

'Brent isn't,' Tessa said, 'and Minnie tries not to be. From the first day of my return he's been friendly towards me. Does he know anything at all of your plan?'

'I thought it fairer not to confide in him.'

'He would never say anything but he would think it a wild idea,' Tessa said. 'How will you possibly contrive . . . ?'

'Does your brother go to the big meeting in Chicago next week?'

'Yes, but the stables remain firmly locked and there are always watching eyes.'

'There's a dance at my uncle's house when the men return from Chicago,' Flora told her.

'I heard about that. I have not, of course, received an invitation,' Tessa said wryly.

'But it will be dark, the servants will be occupied with preparing food and it might be possible — no, I'm convinced it *will* be possible for you to slip out through your back door and make your way to Scott's Place unseen. The ladies will be dressing themselves for the dance and the men will not yet be returned. I will meet you in the garden and take you in through the side door.'

'And then?' Tessa was looking more and more doubtful.

'There's a back staircase and I have a small sitting room opposite my bedroom which I have seldom used. I have a key to the door. You can stay there out of sight of the windows for a day or two. Meanwhile after the dance your absence will be discovered and a search begun.'

'There will be posses riding in all directions,' Tessa warned.

'But not up the back stairs into my sitting room.'

'But the house will be full of guests,' Tessa said worriedly. 'Surely it will look odd if one room is locked?'

'If the house is full of people all the more reason for me to lock the door of my private sitting room,' Flora said.

She wished she felt as confident as she sounded. To smuggle Tessa Fontaine up to her room and to smuggle her out again and on to the Bloomington-bound coach was, at the least, a very risky undertaking.

'And you will get into trouble on my account,' Tessa said contritely.

'I shall return when you are reunited with your husband,' Flora said, 'and face the music. It isn't actually illegal to help husband and wife be together, is it?'

'I don't think so.'

'My uncle will be angry but I can't bring myself to worry about it,' Flora said.

'They have been saying that you are his heir,' Tessa ventured. 'My brother told me that several men were talking about it. You might lose a husband on my account.'

'And that,' Flora said truthfully, 'doesn't bother me one little bit! I told Uncle Frank that I don't want anyone to offer for me on account of my expectations from him. The truth is that I don't really care about owning a large house won in a poker game by a man who didn't scruple to take advantage of another man's weakness and bad luck! My uncle is not my guardian so he may get as angry as he pleases.'

'He may insist on your returning to England,' Tessa warned.

'Then I shall leave with very few regrets,' Flora said.

'Your friendship,' Tessa said softly, 'is something that I shall never forget.'

'I won't call again since the time is getting short before the dance,' Flora said, rising to her feet. 'Wait until your brother has left for Chicago and then make your way to the back garden of Scott's Place. Wait until dusk and use the back roads. Wear something dark. I will meet you and get you upstairs into the sitting room. And when your absence is discovered, which it will be as soon as the dance is over and your brother returns home, then you can remain quietly there while the search goes on in all directions, and we'll slip away together and board the coach.'

'You make it sound as if it might really succeed,' Tessa said wistfully.

'It will. Now I must go. Tessa, your brother — will he be very upset?'

266

Tessa thought for a moment and then shook her fair head.

'No,' she said. 'As I told you he will be secretly relieved, for deep down he has no wish to act as my jailer here and I have never promised to forget my husband.'

'Until the night of the dance then. I'll leave by the back door if I may. The less people notice of my visits here the better. Goodbye, Tessa.'

Going through the kitchen into the back yard with its locked stables she couldn't avoid a feeling of impatience. Had she been in Tessa's place she would have forced the door open, led out a horse and made her escape, probably under cover of darkness, months before. Tessa, despite her sojourn among the Peoria, was basically timid. On the other hand Tessa had a young man pining for her, which was more than she herself could ever expect.

She had almost reached the place where the great oak grew when she saw Mary Redfeather coming towards her, a large bundle of wool under her arm and a couple of large-eyed toddlers clinging to her skirt.

'Good day, Miss Flora!' She gave her wide smile as Flora paused.

'Let me help you with that,' Flora offered.

'Bless you but this ain't no heavy burden,'

Mary said genially. 'If you could pick up a few more of them branches laying idle under the trees then that'd be a help.'

'Of course!' Flora went over to the spot indicated and began to gather up the fallen branches with their remnants of dead and dying leaves.

'Snow moon's coming,' Mary said, shifting her own bundle which was roughly secured with twine under her other arm.

'I'm told the winters are long and hard,' Flora looked up to say.

'Not when we've fires and buffalo for the eating,' Mary said. 'Our men are off hunting in a few days.'

'Could they not buy beef in Chicago?' Flora enquired.

Mary shot her a pitying look. 'Prices rise sky high when the Indians try to buy supplies,' she said with a little snort at the other's ignorance. 'Anyways as my John says, why buy beef when the Great Spirit set buffalo free to roam for us to catch? Food's for the taking, Miss Flora.'

'And your men like to practise their skills,' Flora said, pulling a ribbon from her hair to tie up her own bundle of small branches and twigs.

Mary laughed, teeth white in her broad brown face.

'Practise their drinking and their boasting too,' she said. 'Well, it gives them a chance to get away from the womenfolk and it gives the women a chance to gather wood and pot fruit against the winter moons. My John now! He finds it hard to hit the side of our barn with any weapon at all but to hear him talk you'd think he was the greatest hunter the Peoria tribe ever knew!'

'But you're happy with him?' Flora said.

'Happy? Miss Flora, first time I laid eyes on him I knew he was the only one! We went to the big powwow over at Spirit Wolf Place and the girls were all quick-eyed for husbands and the young braves all painted up ready for the courtship, and there was John Redfeather, not as handsome as the others and kinda shy, and I knew right off that I'd never want another man to warm my bed. Lucky for me he felt the same way and we were wed as soon as the powwow was over and he brought me to Pine Creek Ridge and didn't he have a little house all built and some land of his own and a good job too, for there were whites moving in from the East and half of them had never sawn up a log or planted a crop in their lives. It was real nice here then with folk mingling together, helping one another out, and red and white real friendly, but then the big

269

houses were built and more land taken for crops and money talks big when you have it and nags at your heart when you don't. But we're settled here now and John's a man I'd choose all over again if I had to. You need to catch yourself a man like that, Miss Flora!'

'Any man I looked at,' Flora said, 'would almost certainly run fast in the other direction — not that I'm looking. You know there's a big meeting in Chicago in a few days?'

'Talk of moving us out come spring,' Mary laughed again. 'Well, time enough to fret about that when spring comes. We Peoria ain't so easy to move, and most of us have papers that prove we own our land legal.'

'I really hope you can stay,' Flora said as they began walking on, wood bundles under their arms, the two children still hanging on to Mary's voluminous skirts.

'You're a good woman,' the Indian woman said. 'There's truth in your mouth. Truth in Brent's mouth too. He treats us like neighbours same as he treats the white people.'

'Tessa Fontaine wishes you well too?' asked Flora.

Mary's expression became impassive as she said:

'Miss Tessa had no call to let the soldiers

bring her back. If she took a husband then she should've put a bullet in her heart before she let them bring her back. That's what a wife should do!'

'Perhaps she hoped to escape later on?'

'And how far ahead is later on?' Mary was scornful. 'Been over a year now with her penned up in that house and her brother keeping watch to see that she don't venture out of the village! And I've heard rumour of a young Peoria hanging around, though much good it'll do him! The Peoria ain't patient people. No, I reckon Miss Tessa won't stir until she's pushed.'

Flora longed to say that Tessa was even now preparing to make her bid for freedom, but she held her tongue. The fewer people who knew what was planned the better. Instead she merely nodded towards the toddlers, saying:

'Well you're a good wife for certain, Mary Redfeather, and a good mother too.'

'Eight younglings and five of them boys,' Mary said with satisfaction. 'Oh, these two ain't my born children. There was a skirmish with the army a couple of years back on a settlement east of here and these two were found wandering afterwards. They're not from our clan but their families were killed and when my John heard he rode over and brought 'em back for me. Here's my turning. Thank you kindly for your help.'

She relieved Flora of her burden and went off, her full skirts dragged on by the children who had begun to grizzle. Flora continued on her way until she came to the stream. There was no bridge; she would have to cross it carefully.

There were large flat stones laid across and sunk into the bed of the stream, which gushed from its source down the hillside, until here, in a little valley, it flowed with some force.

'Been visiting the trees again?' Brent was dismounting from his horse and holding out his hand to her as she teetered on the stepping stones.

'I felt like a walk,' Flora said primly, accepting his help.

'How did you find Tessa?' he enquired when she stood in the road again.

'Downcast,' Flora said cautiously. 'It seems so unfair that she should be debarred from all the social activities here. Not being invited anywhere cannot be conducive to her happiness!'

'And hardly anyone calls,' Brent said. 'Mary Redfeather looks out for her when she can but Mary's hardly in the first rank of society. What Charles ought to do is

take her north where her history's not
known and maybe she'd meet someone
there who'd drive Smiling Moon out of her
head!'

'She still loves him,' Flora said.

'And love's a peculiar thing.' Brent looked
thoughtful. 'Comes at you fast like a bullet
sometimes, and sometimes just creeps up
on you when you're not looking. Ever
noticed that?'

His glance was suddenly teasing. Flora
said as primly as before:

'I really cannot say as to that. I've been
helping Mary Redfeather collect wood for
her winter fires, so there wasn't much time
for philosophizing.'

'She's a fine woman,' Brent told her. 'Her
husband's a fine man too, works hard and
only gets drunk once or twice a year. Any
oftener and Mary'd likely kill him.'

'And in spring they might have to leave?
Brent, it's so unfair!'

'So's life,' he said. 'Anyway the meeting's
not been held yet and it won't be the last
time a group of citizens with nothing better
to do get together to reorder the world. You
still have the documents safe?'

He had lowered his voice as he asked the
question.

Flora nodded.

'Good, I knew that I could rely on you,' he said.

'How could you know that?' she asked impulsively. 'You don't know me at all!'

'Some people show their characters in their faces,' he told her. 'Some hide what they're really like. I've come across a lot of dead wood making out its polished walnut or carved pine. Now you're pine, Flora Scott, tall and straight and bending slightly with every wind that blows. You don't make yourself out to be something you're not.'

'Thank you.' Flora looked at him doubtfully, uncertain whether he intended a compliment or not.

'And next week,' he said with a sudden impish grin, 'you'll be paraded before the finest gentlemen in the county, all of whom will have been told in confidence that you're your uncle's heir.'

'My uncle told you that?' Looking at him she had a sudden sinking feeling that rendered suspect all his friendly words. She would inherit the house and land that would have been his had his father not lost the lot in a poker game.

'I'd best get back,' she said abruptly. 'Will you be going to the Chicago meeting?'

'Nope! I'm not on any committees, thank the Lord! No, I shall be getting the accounts straight and promising Minnie that I'll come dressed up like a dog's dinner to the dance. Nice talking to you, Flora. I'm sure your company did Tessa a power of good!'

He clasped her hand briefly and remounted his horse, riding off in the direction of the village. Flora stayed where she was, staring after him with a troubled frown on her face.

If he ever made an offer for her she would never be sure whether it was for the property, and if he made no offer then she would never know whether he had held back out of delicacy.

Not that it mattered since he was going to marry Minnie Hargreaves anyway.

Feeling at odds with the world she walked back swiftly to Scott's Place seeing with a little sinking of the heart that Minnie's smart little pony trap stood in the drive and that Minnie herself was just emerging from the front door.

'There you are! I called to see you,' she greeted Flora. 'Rather unconventional of me to send no warning but I wished to discuss something with you. Brent escorted me from school but he had other business to attend.'

'I met him in the road,' Flora said. 'Won't you come back inside?'

'Well, just for a few moments then!'

Minnie tripped after her through the hall into the drawing room.

'Will you have something?' Flora glanced towards Tina who had taken up her usual position at the foot of the stairs.

'Thank you, no. I had a cup of coffee while I was waiting for you. You went for a walk?'

'Yes, I enjoy walking,' Flora said blandly.

'An unusual activity for a young lady,' Minnie said with equal blandness.

'Even in the evenings,' Flora said. 'In fact I met Brent one evening and he seemed quite shocked that I should be wandering about alone and insisted on seeing me home.' *And you knew that already,* she added silently, *because you were watching.*

'Brent has very nice manners for all that he's Irish,' Minnie said. 'No, what I wanted to discuss is the possibility of your filling in for me at the school until a permanent replacement can be found.'

'You're leaving so soon?'

'Not until after Christmas but the pupils get a holiday then anyway. No, I have been of the opinion for some time that it's rather pointless to wait until next June before marrying. I am considering whether or not the New Year might not be a more convenient time, with not so much work to do in the fields and even when it's thick snow people can usually manage to travel short distances to attend a ceremony.'

'I don't see what your plans have to do with me,' Flora said in puzzlement.

'Only that if the wedding is brought forward I shall feel I'm letting down the pupils if I just close the school and leave them without a teacher,' Minnie said.

'What does Brent say?'

'Oh, you know men!' Minnie gave a light little laugh like a spoon tinkling in a saucer. 'He hasn't even given me the engagement ring yet, though I suspect he intends it to be a Christmas gift.'

'If you marry in the New Year,' Flora said, 'you won't be able to wear lace.'

'Oh, I shall ask my father to bring some velvet back from Chicago,' Minnie said airily. 'The lace can always be used later, if you'll forgive the indelicacy, for a christening gown if I am blessed in that way.'

'And you want me to teach at the school until a new teacher can be found?'

'After Christmas the children go back to school,' Minnie told her. 'Flora, it's very important that they be properly educated, Indians and whites, learn to read and write and cipher so they can make something of themselves when they grow up.'

'If your wedding is brought forward,' Flora said reluctantly, 'then I will certainly think about it.'

'Thank you.' Minnie rose. 'Who knows but you may be engaged yourself before the end of the year? Your uncle is bringing friends of his from Chicago for the dance. There are bound to be several eligible gentlemen here.'

'My uncle,' Flora said drily, 'pays great heed to my comfort.'

'And I must take my leave. I'm expecting Brent to call on his way back. Oh, I believe these are yours?'

She brought out of her reticule several rolled and torn pieces of paper and handed them over.

Flora looked down at the fragments of her discarded painting, the delicate colours almost obliterated by the figure of Brent O'Brien, recognizable despite the mutilation.

'Have you taken to rummaging through the rubbish now?' Flora enquired.

'Tina came in with them in her hand and I asked her what they were,' Minnie said. 'You draw very well, Flora. I do hope one of your uncle's guests has a liking for art.'

'If I find such a man,' Flora said, 'I shall

ask for your advice. You seem to be quite expert at catching your quarry. Good day, Minnie!'

THIRTEEN

It had been a stupid jibe, unworthy of anyone who fancied herself as a well brought-up young lady. Flora scolded herself inwardly as she went upstairs. Minnie, after all, had some right to be irritated if another young woman was sketching her betrothed.

And why I put him in the painting I simply don't know, Flora told herself as she changed her dress, for actually I don't have a high opinion of him anyway.

Over the next few days she occupied herself with writing long letters to her mother and uncles filled with the kind of domestic detail she knew they appreciated. She kept Brent O'Brien firmly out of them. He was, she told herself, a man who was willing to do what he could for Tessa and the Indians provided it didn't endanger his own job. He was someone reluctant to become too closely involved. Why, he was drifting towards his marriage with Minnie Hargreaves without having troubled to buy her a ring yet!

Her uncle would see that her letters were posted in Chicago and with this request in mind she went downstairs to the study where, dinner being over, he had retired to prepare his speech at the meeting.

'My sympathies are with the Indians of course,' he had told her during dinner, 'but one must move with the times and throughout history civilizations have risen and fallen, not that one can exactly equate the Indian tribes with Greece and Rome! But certainly those few who remain here will, if I have my way, be treated fairly! Now let us leave the vexed question of politics alone for a while! You are looking forward to the dance, I hope?'

'Very much,' she had assured him.

'I ask because my conscience troubles me slightly. Since you came there's been scant amusement for you, I fear. I had hoped to be able to send more cheering news to the family myself and I do hope your mama doesn't blame me for not introducing you somewhat sooner to a wider circle of acquaintances, but we are rather insular here! And you are not a girl to leap at the first offer you receive.'

'I don't know how you can say that, Uncle,' Flora had said, 'since I've not received any offers at all!'

'Harold Belmont referred to you most flatteringly the other day as a most intelligent young lady.'

'If the only admirer I can muster is Harold Belmont,' Flora had retorted with spirit, 'may the Lord keep me a spinster for ever!'

'I am convinced,' her uncle had answered unruffled, 'that we can do better than him for you. My associates in Chicago are many of them gentlemen still in their thirties who are ready to offer the right lady a home and security and, of course, your own future expectations are not negligible.' With that he had risen from the table.

So that any marriage offer would mean nothing, Flora had thought. Perhaps she was being foolishly romantic. In England many marriages were made and proved successful based on property and class. Something wild and untamed within her craved something more.

The study door was partly open and the lamplight spilled out into the hall. Flora put her hand to the door and froze, seeing suddenly the hem of a long black skirt just above the patent-leather shoes of her uncle, hearing a voice murmur.

'Amante mio! Querido!'

Somehow or other she backed away silently, her slippered soles making no noise as she retreated hastily up the staircase again.

Tina and Uncle Frank? But of course! And she had been naïvely blind not to realize it before.

Tina had married Daniel O'Brien because he had offered her a life away from the taverna. But O'Brien had died on the wedding day and Tina had accepted the protection of Frank Scott and come east to the United States with him, ostensibly as housekeeper but obviously, from the scene she had just witnessed, to provide other comforts for him.

It was small wonder that Tina had greeted her sullenly on her arrival. She must have feared that her official position as housekeeper was about to be usurped and that Frank Scott might grow weary of her altogether.

An unwilling sympathy for the older woman crept through Flora. She had after all no real knowledge of the kind of life from which Tina had been plucked. Who could blame her for taking the path she had taken? But Uncle Frank had cared little for the feelings of either his niece or his lady-love.

She put the letters away and slipped on cloak and bonnet. What she needed was a brisk walk round the garden to clear her head and give the other two time to separate.

She went out through the side door, closing it softly behind her, and made for the path that led to the stables.

Mary Redfeather had said a snow moon was coming. Perhaps not quite that yet but the wind tore at her skirts and her bonnet and she was glad to seek the shelter of the stables where the horses stood, either feeding or with their sleek heads over the half-doors of their stalls as if they stood in a line passing on snippets of conversation.

A lantern swung in the wind from the main door as Flora went in and from the darker end of the long wooden building a voice called irritably:

'Close the door! I've a mare here in foal with a spavined — oh! Flora!'

Brent finished his admonition on a note of surprise as he straightened up from a horse lying on her side on a pile of hay. His sleeves were rolled up and he had apparently just applied embrocation since he stepped to a bucket, plunged his hands into it and then wiped them vigorously on a towel.

'I didn't know you worked with the horses as well,' Flora said awkwardly, going towards him.

'Once the accounts are done and supplies ordered and delivered I lend a hand wherever it may be needed,' he told her. 'Come on, girl! *Arriba!*'

The mare reluctantly rolled over and stood up somewhat shakily.

'Her foal's due in a few days,' Brent said, 'so I want to keep her on her feet for as long as possible. Sorry I was sharp with you just now but horses catch cold too, especially when they're in an interesting condition! Were you planning on taking a moonlight stroll or has Harold Belmont called to urge his suit?'

'Neither,' Flora said, deciding rapidly that as Frank Scott's niece she could hardly gossip about his private goings on. 'I felt like a breath of air, that's all.'

'And were rewarded by a near gale! Your bonnet is crooked.'

'Actually hanging by its strings,' Flora said tartly, cramming it on to her head again.

'I imagined you'd be trying on all your fine dresses in preparation for the dance,' Brent observed.

'I think my uncle is planning a very grand affair,' Flora admitted. 'Very important men, business associates of his, are coming from Chicago when the meeting's done. Will you be . . . ?' Her question lingered on the air.

'Minnie would kill me if I suggested staying home,' Brent said with a grin. 'Even Charles Fontaine will be there.'

'And Tessa hasn't been invited,' Flora said.

'It is unfair, isn't it?' He looked at her with sympathy in his face. 'I do what I can but so far I've been unable to talk Minnie into visiting Tessa though she too feels that the situation is cruel.'

And Minnie would naturally avoid Tessa Fontaine since Charles Fontaine, as a point of honour after his sister's recapture, had ended his courtship of her.

'I do wish,' Flora said impulsively, 'that people would stop making rules and regulations for everybody else and just accept people as they are without trying to force them into one mould! Why should women be meek and subservient and not have a say in affairs and why is it taken for granted that a man can take an Indian wife but a woman who takes an Indian husband is disgraced?'

'The children of such unions are not accepted fully in white society whether the mother or father be Indian,' Brent said.

'And you accept that too instead of railing against it! I am beginning to be out of all patience with everybody here!'

'Only just beginning?' Brent laughed suddenly and stepped towards her, his hands reaching to straighten her bonnet further. 'Flora Scott, you arrived among us like a whirlwind and sent all the surface fragments of our civilized little community flying all over the place. You left England determined to shake off all convention and arrived to find the same rules applied here and even more stringently because polite society here is only skin-deep! You can no more reform the world than you can keep your bonnet on!'

His hands were at each side of her face. She could feel the slight roughness of his fingers as he stood looking at her, and then he bent his head and kissed her on the mouth so quickly that she had not time to protest or respond before he had moved away again, saying over his shoulder:

'My apologies. That was not intended.'

'One unintended kiss,' Flora said, 'is hardly the end of the world. Good evening!'

She felt as if someone had just dashed a pail of water in her face but she held her head high as she left the stables.

At least Minnie Hargreaves hadn't been

around to witness the swift embrace. Flora walked rapidly back to the house, her lips tingling from more than the cold and let herself in through the side door. Brent O'Brien, she decided, had no manners. To be unconventional was one thing, but for a man to seize a kiss from one woman when he was betrothed to another was a different matter. It was graceless, she thought indignantly, even if he hadn't meant to do it. She reminded herself that Brent was Irish and grimaced slightly, recalling sundry remarks that had passed between her uncles in England regarding the race.

'A savage, half-pagan people, with no breeding. Many are leaving Ireland for the Americas, no doubt with an eye to the main chance, as always.'

'If they worked harder on their farms and didn't idle their lives away in drinking and telling long tales of their glorious past they might thrive, but most of them are bone idle.'

In her room again, taking off cloak and bonnet and smoothing down her hair she realized with a little shock that she was actually allying herself with opinions that had annoyed her when she'd lived in London. Perhaps under the skin all people had their prejudices.

Brent hadn't kissed her because he was Irish. He'd kissed her on impulse, probably because he was bored or had had a tiff with Minnie or something! Flora took up her journal and prepared to write a brief, heavily edited account of the day's events.

I will not, she told herself severely, give another thought to a kiss that was both unexpected and undesired.

She went on thinking about it for the rest of the evening, remembering the tender roughness of his hands at each side of her face, his mouth pressing her lips into startled surrender, the long, lean muscles of his breeched and booted leg touching — angrily she blotted her journal and thrust it back in the drawer.

The account of her days was dull anyway, since she had omitted everything of importance.

A tap on the door brought Tina, skirts now demurely smoothed down but her expression wary.

'Do you need anything before I retire, Miss Flora?' she asked formally.

She knows, Flora guessed. A Mestiza would probably always be aware of an unseen watcher.

'Nothing really, thank you,' she answered carefully. 'Oh, I have been wondering how to do my hair for the dance. It refuses to stay tidy whatever style I choose.'

'It's heavy hair,' Tina said, unbending a little. 'Brown with a chestnut sheen. If I were you, Miss Flora, I would draw it back in two bands and plait it behind into a coronet. It would look queenly then.'

'Queenly.' Flora tasted the word, wondering if she really wanted to look queenly when she was becoming aware of a wild being inside her struggling for expression.

'I can dress it for you myself,' Tina offered.

'Thank you, yes, that is kind of you.'

'I'm here to give service,' the other said expressionlessly.

'One other thing!' Remembering a question she hadn't yet had the opportunity to ask, Flora took out her purse and fished out the tiny golden star. 'Would this mean anything to an Indian?'

'Where did you get this?' Tina asked sharply.

'I acquired it,' Flora hedged. 'I merely wondered —'

'It's just a trinket,' Tina said. 'Nothing more! Good-night.'

It had not been, Flora reflected when she woke the next morning, a very good night at all. She had tossed and turned, conscious of a thought at the back of her mind, the faint first glimmerings of an idea that eluded her as she sank into a troubled doze only to wake with a start from a cloudy dream in which she had been riding a russet-hued stallion that was carrying her away from Pine Creek Ridge into an unknown future.

Wearily she dressed. Scraping back her heavy hair as she gazed at the pale, heavy-eyed face in the mirror, she decided wryly that if her first kiss had this effect on her looks she had better avoid inviting a second!

At breakfast her uncle's manner was so normal that she guessed at once that Tina hadn't mentioned to him the fact their intimate embrace had been observed. When the meal was over Flora went out to the stables. She was relieved to see no sign of Brent and asked one of the farm hands to saddle up one of the bigger horses. Today she wanted to ride fast and not jog on a pony.

'There's Moonlight, Miss Flora.' The man shifted the straw he was chewing from one side of his mouth to the other. 'He's pretty spry and needs a firm hand.'

'Fine! Moonlight will suit me very well,' Flora said firmly.

Mounted up and feeling the tugging on the reins she experienced a moment's disquiet but as the farm hand opened the gate and stood aside her confidence returned and she touched her mount into a trot, increased her speed to a canter and, as they came to the place where the stream widened into a river, gave the stallion his head as they thundered down the track.

There was a blur of movement before her and a warning shout. Something hurtled and as she pulled frantically on the reins Moonlight reluctantly slowed, then stopped and turned his head with an almost human expression of disappointment on his face.

'Who the hell put you up on Moonlight?' Brent demanded, picking himself up gingerly from the bank where he had flung himself and brushing himself down with both hands.

'I asked for a spirited horse!' she retorted, dismounting with some difficulty.

'Stand still for heaven's sake!' Brent ordered. 'Your skirt is caught up on the pommel! There! Now you look fit to face your neighbours again. Do tell me! Were you deliberately trying to ride me down? I suppose if I'd really kissed you last night you'd have demanded my scalp as well!'

'That remark,' she said icily, 'was in the worst possible taste, Brent O'Brien! And what do you mean "really"?'

'Deep and slow and savouring the moment,' he replied.

Flora glanced at him, then suddenly found herself smiling.

'This is silly,' she said, holding out her hand. 'Last night is best forgotten. I hope we can continue to be friends even if we disagree about so many things.'

'Of course we can.' His hand grasped hers firmly.

'And I wasn't trying to ride you down,' she added. 'I hope I'm not so stupidly reckless. Why are you on foot anyway?'

'Sometimes I do get down and use my own legs and feet,' Brent told her. 'I'm taking a message to Minnie. I've not long left the stables myself.'

'How is the mare?' she asked.

'Coming along splendidly!' He looked pleased as he spoke.

'Are you invited to the dance?'

'Of course!' He grinned at her companionably. 'Minnie has decided to wear one of the new dresses she has just had made up so she's in high spirits.'

'And you're to be married sooner than was planned. I wish you both happiness.'

'Sooner?' His voice had sharpened. 'We're to wed in June.'

'Oh? Maybe I misunderstood,' Flora said

in confusion. 'But Minnie definitely said that the wedding was brought forward. She asked me if I would deputize for her at the school until a replacement can be found.'

'And the bridegroom is the last to know.' He spoke lightly but his smile held sourness.

'Perhaps she just forgot to mention it,' Flora said awkwardly.

'I'll talk to her. If the wedding's to be earlier the honeymoon will have to be rearranged too.'

'Where are you going — or is it a secret?'

'No secret,' he said briskly. 'Minnie longs for the sights and excitement of New York, so New York it is! Are you going to stand in at the school?'

'I'm not a schoolteacher,' Flora said stiffly.

'And Minnie won't be for much longer. I think she will miss her work. She's very good with the children.'

'Yes.'

They looked at each other for a moment. Then Brent said:

'I'd best get on. Do you mean to remount Moonlight?'

'Yes.'

'Then do me a favour and don't give him his head! I don't want to have to explain to your uncle why you broke your neck!'

'Fortunately looking after my personal safety,' Flora said tartly, 'is no concern of yours! Neither, I would've thought, was doctoring the horses. Surely a manager —'

'Sits in an office with account books spread out around him? I spend a lot of time doing just that,' he assured her, looking amused. 'But, as I told you, I lend a hand any place where I'm needed, and I happen to like horses!'

'Yes.' She spoke quietly as she remounted, placing a foot on his linked hands and remembering almost reluctantly how tenderly he had put his hands on the sick mare, gentling her with murmured reassurance.

'Were you riding to any place in particular?' he still handed her the reins as he looked up at her.

'Away from the house,' she confessed. 'It oppresses me.'

'It's a fine big mansion,' Brent said.

'Full of beautiful things imported from other countries! Won in a game of chance! I'm sorry, Brent, but I cannot help thinking that my uncle took a most unfair advantage of your father and his offering you the position of manager wasn't particularly generous! And his bringing your father's widow up here to act as his housekeeper wasn't done out of the kindness of his heart either!

I am only surprised that she accepted!'

'Tina had a hard life before she met my father.' Brent frowned slightly. 'She was only too glad to be offered your uncle's protection. And she's always been friendly towards me.'

'I wasn't condemning her —' Flora began.

'Best not to condemn anyone until you know all the facts,' he said brusquely. 'Don't let Moonlight gallop!'

He dropped the rein and walked on, the set of his shoulders tense with displeasure. Flora bit her lip at her indiscretion, then abruptly swerved her mount about and set off at an obedient trot in the opposition direction. Soon, though, Moonlight was going at a canter, and then at a gallop.

They had galloped as far as the gates of Scott's Place before Flora remembered Brent's order not to give Moonlight his head. But the stallion, though he had enjoyed his freedom from constraint, slowed obediently as she tugged at the reins.

Tina was in the garden, dead-heading late-flowering shrubs, her black hair covered by a black shawl so that she looked for a moment, as she half-turned, like a carbon silhouette against the fading greens and reds and yellows.

'Tina, would you allow me to paint you

sometime?' Flora asked impulsively as she slid from the saddle.

'Paint me? Tina looked at her for a moment and then smiled briefly. 'As the house-keeper, you mean?'

'As whatever you please,' Flora said. 'In costume?'

'Ah! Perhaps with a feather in my hair, like an Apache,' Tina said, some of the pleasure draining from her face. 'Or in a mantilla with a brocaded and hooped skirt to denote my Spanish blood or in a sombrero, which is what Mexicans wear?'

'I only meant —' Flora began.

'You want to make a series of paintings of characters you met while you were out here.'

'You don't like me, do you?' Flora said bluntly. 'When I first came you were cold and sullen but I hoped you were beginning to feel more friendly. I'm sorry it isn't so.'

'I don't dislike you.' Tina twisted a handful of dead flowers in her fingers, shredding the petals on to the fading grass. 'I feared you might want to take over the running of the house but you haven't done that, nor have you interfered with the way I carry out my duties. But I wish you were not so . . . hidebound in your ways! I wish you didn't try to put people in boxes and keep them there!'

'I don't! I despise convention,' Flora protested indignantly.

'You make us all characters in your own private play,' Tina said. 'I am the Mestiza who worked in a tavern and your uncle is the man who cheated another man out of his home and Charles Fontaine is a villain for keeping his sister close to home and . . . Miss Flora, I was educated in Santa Fe and might have made a good marriage but my father died leaving debts and I couldn't get employment as a governess or a teacher. I took the job at a taverna in order not to starve and I married Daniel O'Brien not only because I wanted a home but because he was a kindly man, and I accepted Frank Scott's offer because I still needed that home and I wanted very much to meet Daniel's son.'

'Brent . . .'

'Is a good man too,' Tina said. 'He's not a hothead who rushes around trumpeting his opinion of the way the Indians have been treated, though he does everything in his power to help them as much as he can — Charles Fontaine could have rejected his sister altogether but he took her in even though it meant his courtship of Minnie Hargreaves was cut short. And Minnie herself might be irritating and spiteful sometimes but she works hard for the school and all her pupils. People aren't all black and white, Miss Flora, but mixtures and trying to fit them into the pictures you've made in your head won't work!'

'Have you finished?' Flora said tightly.

'Yes, and I ask pardon for being so frank,' Tina said. 'You've every right to complain of me to your uncle. I spoke my mind is all! And I don't dislike you. You've got grit and a lot of energy, Miss Flora and that's a rare thing in a young woman. And I'll tell you something else. I think you deserve a husband with more in him than any you've been pushed at so far! I mean Harold Belmont who's the biggest fool east of Santa Fe.'

'As we doctors say,' Flora commented.

Suddenly she found herself laughing in sheer amusement at the ridiculous situation in which she found herself, being scolded for the very faults she condemned in others by a woman who was far more than a housekeeper to her uncle.

'Are we then friends?' she enquired, holding out her hand, 'and will you sit for me in any costume you choose? I would like to have a record of the people I have met here.'

'Meaning you're not staying? That'll be a

disappointment to your uncle,' the house-keeper said. 'Maybe you'll change your mind when you meet one of the gentlemen he's bringing back with him from Chicago.'

'Having assured them all that he intends to name me as his heir?' Flora shook her head ruefully. 'The kind of man I might approve will back off for fear of being thought a fortune hunter and the wrong sort will smell money and not see me at all. Tina, even if I do go back to England I doubt if I'll ever get married. I am not the sort of woman men fall in love with. I might as well make up my mind to the fact.'

'Oh, you never know how things might turn out,' Tina said vaguely.

'I think I've a shrewd idea how they will,' Flora said. 'Thank you for the scolding. No, I mean that! I was making uninformed judgements about people and maybe getting some of them wrong! What is it?'

The older woman had frowned slightly, then nodded her head as if she had just resolved something in her own mind.

'I was just realizing,' Tina said, 'why Minnie Hargreaves has brought her wedding forward. It was on account of those pieces of the painting you did that she took from me when I fished them out from amongst the garbage. Jealousy's a powerful strong feeling, Miss Flora. Powerful strong and sometimes dangerous too!'

FOURTEEN

At least she and Tina had established some kind of understanding! Flora felt happier about that but the other problems remained. It was all very well to realize that people were a mixture of qualities but it didn't help her to like Minnie Hargreaves more or to feel the most intense irritation with Brent, whose thoughts chimed with hers in so many ways but who remained careful and cautious when it came to action.

The house was being prepared for the dance that would follow the Chicago meeting. She was amused and surprised by the thorough sweeping, polishing and dusting that went on in rooms that were already immaculate.

The last of the garden blooms were being cut and placed in cold water to refresh them and bunches of berried stems were being arranged in tubs. The kitchen was aclatter with the washing of already clean china and the polishing of cutlery in which it was already possible to see one's face. More servants had been drafted in to help, and in the long wing that adjoined the main house and held extra chambers, bedrooms were being prepared.

'Though in time to come,' Uncle Frank told her at dinner on the day before the meeting was due to take place, 'we may hope to build an hotel here. People on their way further south or coming north would appreciate a comfortable night's stop.'

He looked quietly pleased with himself as he presided at the head of the table. On his right Flora toyed with a piece of steak and hoped fervently that there would be a wider selection of meats when the guests arrived. At the end of the table Tina, who seemed to have withdrawn into her shell again, sipped her wine.

'With Chicago so near,' Flora said, 'would travellers not stay overnight there and then head in whatever direction they were going?'

'As they do,' he nodded, 'but for those willing to travel an extra couple of hours a more genteel establishment might please them greatly. It might well be profitable for anyone who had an interest in such a place.'

'Meaning yourself?' Flora gave him a questioning look. 'Surely you have sufficient money already, Uncle?'

'My dear niece, one can never have sufficient money,' he smilingly said. 'The whole object of having any at all is to increase it as rapidly as possible. My brothers unfortunately are of a different opinion. They are unwilling to risk their capital on any but the most risk-free enterprises, whereas I like to speculate — not recklessly; I'd not have you think that! But I study the markets, invest where I see possibilities for expansion. And so today I am what may be called a prosperous man while my brothers are in the middle ranks of affluence.'

'But they don't have cheap Indian — or slave — labour to help them,' Flora said.

'You must learn, my dear,' he said after a second's cold silence, 'to refrain from making what in a man might be construed as provocative remarks and in a woman are, to say the least, unbecoming.'

'Why should what is said in all sincerity be more unbecoming in a woman than in a man?' Flora enquired.

'Now you are teasing me, my dear niece!' He shook his finger at her in heavy-handed playfulness. 'There will always be higher standards of conduct expected from the weaker sex.'

'Who, because of their so-called weakness,

ought surely to be judged by lower standards?' Flora objected.

'Ah, I don't deny you have a pretty wit!' he said, breaking a bread roll in half with a little snapping sound, dropping both pieces on to his plate.

'Thank you, Uncle.'

She was wasting her time, she reflected, as she continued with her own meal. He had no respect for anyone or anything save profit. In a huge country full of exciting possibilities he had devoted himself entirely to the accumulating of wealth and, no doubt, with the promise of that wealth eventually being inherited by her there would soon be an offer of marriage from someone or other. Flora laid down her knife and fork and forced a smile.

'I understand that various dainties are being delivered from Chicago for the supper during the dance,' she said.

'Certainly! Some preserved fruits, excellent French wine, meringues filled with cream, the treats one seldom sees here.' He nodded, looking gratified. 'Tina will be overseeing the culinary side of the evening but she will heed any advice you wish to impart.'

'I think Tina will manage anything she does splendidly,' Flora said.

'Yes, she's a useful creature,' he said carelessly. 'Come into the study when you are quite finished, Flora. I have something for you.'

He crumpled his napkin and left the table. On Tina's face as she looked after him was an expression of such naked hatred that Flora felt a cold shiver caress her spine.

'If you will excuse me,' the housekeeper said in a tightly controlled voice, 'I have other duties to attend.'

'Tina, my uncle spoke unkindly and without thought,' Flora began.

'Unkindly? Yes. Without thought, no! Your uncle never speaks without most careful thought,' the housekeeper said, 'but he is better-natured at other times than you might think.'

She gave her stiff little bow and went away, leaving Flora to sip her coffee alone and muse on the odd responses people had to the behaviour of others.

When she tapped on the study door Brent opened it, standing aside to allow her entrance with a polite smile on his tanned face.

'My manager has a habit of wandering in through the back door,' Uncle Frank said from the depths of the armchair where he was seated. 'And helps himself to my whiskey,' he added a moment later as Flora too sat down.

'Interrupting a meal to which one hasn't been invited is hardly polite,' Brent said, lifting his glass in salute and leaning nonchalantly against the wall. 'I've been telling your uncle, Flora, that you are a good rider and would find a more spirited mount to your taste.'

'Brent suggests Moonlight, but he can be difficult,' Uncle Frank said.

'I have actually been on his back,' Flora said cautiously, guessing that Brent wouldn't have acquainted her uncle with the full story. 'Provided one holds him to a trot he is really quite biddable.'

'If you think you can handle him, my dear, then by all means ride him,' her uncle said, 'but for safety's sake let Brent accompany you for the first couple of times until Moonlight is accustomed to your style of riding. You could escort my niece tomorrow morning for a brisk canter but pray don't allow her to tire herself. She has a dance to attend in the evening.'

'You're not going to the meeting?' Flora looked at the manager.

'I am not on any committees,' he returned.

'Your voice would be a valuable addition to any discussion,' Uncle Frank said. 'You are known to be sympathetic to the Indian plight and not to mince your words, but you are also reasonable and —'

'Hardly likely to sway opinion one way or the other,' Brent returned somewhat harshly. 'No, I'll remain clear of public meetings and cabals and mind my own affairs.'

'But you will be escorting Minnie to the dance?'

'Of course. She's looking forward to it immensely. Do you want to ride tomorrow morning, Flora?'

'Yes,' Flora said without hesitation.

'The Peoria are setting out on a ceremonial hunting expedition. They make quite a display of it which will be interesting for you to see,' he told her.

'Would they mind if I took some quick sketches?'

'Provided you ask first I daresay that most of them would be delighted,' Brent told her.

He obviously knew nothing of the sketch of himself that she had painted so impulsively into her drawing of the flower garden. Minnie had clearly not told him about it for the sensible reason that any man, if told that another woman was taking some interest in him, would naturally look with more attention at the said woman. Tina would have said nothing because the Mestiza kept her own counsel.

'I'll call for you after breakfast,' he said, taking her hand again. 'The accounts are up to date and we're well over the profit margin, Mr Scott. Good evening.'

'We indeed!' Her uncle lifted his brows in amusement. '*My* profit and one day to be *yours,* my dear!'

Flora said nothing, only relieved that Brent had already left the study, closing the door behind him.

'And now, my dear, I have something to give you,' Uncle Frank said genially.

He rose, crossed to a tall cupboard in the corner of the room and unlocked it.

Flora watched as he drew out a flat leather case, clicked open the lid and returned to where she was seated. He held the case open before her, keeping his eyes on her face.

On white velvet the necklace and earbobs gleamed richly, their reddish-gold settings enhanced by square-cut garnets, each stone flashing fire.

'I bought them a long time ago, my dear,' he said, 'with the profit from my first maize yield. I knew I would find a wearer for them one day.'

'They're beautiful, Uncle,' Flora said, her breath catching in her throat, 'but surely —'

'Had I ever married they would've graced my bride,' he told her. 'However, as I find life much more comfortable as a bachelor, it is a condition I have no intention of altering. The workmanship is Mexican. Very skilled.'

Her fingers itched to touch them, to feel the weight of the garnets against her flesh, to caress the finely carved gold in which the stones were set.

'You see, my dear,' Uncle Frank said, 'I give you a small part of your inheritance now even though you and I do not always readily agree. They impose no obligation upon you.'

Which meant of course that they did! She could hardly continue to argue against her uncle's views when she had accepted what was, in effect, a bribe to persuade her to follow his wishes.

'You ought to give them to Tina,' she said abruptly, clenching her hands against temptation.

'Why in the world would I want to give them to my housekeeper?'

There was amusement as well as mild disapproval in his face.

'Because — Uncle Frank, I'm not a child and I do thank you for such a kind and generous offer,' she blurted miserably, 'but

I'm not a fool either. Tina is far more than a housekeeper to you and . . . I mean, she runs your home, provides all the comforts a wife could provide and she's —'

'Assuredly not my wife,' he said.

The amusement had vanished. She looked up into a face of stone, the lips thinned into a narrow line.

'You brought her to this house when Daniel O'Brien died of a heart attack, just after their wedding ceremony,' she said a little desperately. 'You'd just won all his property, in which she would've shared had he not . . . and she's a Mexican . . .'

'So must be hung round with Mexican gold and garnets?' He took a step back, still holding the open case. 'By that reckoning the blacks who mine diamonds should be decked out like princes! And Tina is a Mestiza, not even a half-breed but a jumble of three races at least!'

'She's a human being!' Flora snapped, her temper rising, 'and she deserves some reward for her years of loyalty! She must've given up a great deal to come here with you.'

'She left a taverna where she danced for the customers, played a guitar and was run off her feet the rest of the time serving drinks and washing up from what I can gather. I was not a regular visitor to the establishment.'

'Only for the occasional poker game when you won an entire estate?'

'You should not have said that, Flora!' He took a step back, his fists clenched as if he feared he might strike her.

'I'm being honest!' she flared.

'Daniel O'Brien was a fool and a bit of a drunkard.' Her uncle sounded suddenly weary. 'He had just married a good-looking girl and he came with her into the taverna, declaring it was his lucky day and drank a couple of tequilas and sat down to play while Tina, like a good, dutiful bride, sat in the corner. He gambled recklessly and the more he lost the more he gambled until there was only his land and his house left. How was I supposed to know it was more than a shack in a field? He mentioned he had a son who was looking after the place while he was in New Mexico. When he died suddenly, right there on the floor of the taverna, having just lost everything, was I supposed to hand the lot to a young woman — a Mestiza — whom I'd barely noticed? I paid for the funeral and I offered to bring Tina up here with me and she accepted. She was grateful enough at the time! When she arrived I met the son, Brent, who impressed me as a youth with good sense and education. I offered him a position as manager which he accepted. He wanted to make his own way and bought land and built a house and I let him take what he wanted of his father's things. There'd been a shack there of sorts, where they'd spent most of their time while clearing the land. The main house, this house, was a shell with hardly anything in it at all.'

'And Tina helped you make it into a beautiful home.'

'And took an interest in Brent who was, still is, legally her stepson. But the notion that I might marry her or treat her like a real lady never entered my head or hers. Tina knows her place. She's a convenience, nothing more!'

'And the rest?' Flora demanded.

'The rest is not a subject for a lady, particularly a spinster lady, to think about, let alone mention in conversation. You will wear the jewels at the dance tomorrow night when I return from Chicago with my guests and you will never again so far forget your upbringing or your position in society as to hint at your knowledge of such unsavoury matters. And that is all, my dear niece!'

He thrust the case back into her hands and stepped to open the door for her.

Flora resisted the temptation to fling the

gift back at him, rose from her chair, gave him a stiff and formal little bow and walked into the shadowed hall where she stood for a moment, fighting against a sudden ridiculous urge to burst into humiliating tears.

From the direction of the kitchen she could hear the maids chatting and laughing as they prepared the various dainties that had been arriving during the day.

Then she walked slowly up the elegant staircase to her own room where she splashed cold water on her face and tried to calm herself.

It had done her no good at all to answer her uncle in such a fashion. His opinions were shared by most of the people whom she had met, assuming that Tina's position in her uncle's life was known. They were the opinions of most of the men certainly, she reasoned, seating herself on the edge of her bed, her hands still trembling with suppressed rage, and no doubt some of the men gossiped with their wives. Nobody as far as she knew condemned Frank Scott for his irregular relationship with a Mestiza, but poor Tessa Fontaine was shunned because she had made a marriage with a Peoria man who loved her so truly that he would risk his life to get her back.

She wondered suddenly if Tina had heard

the outburst. If so how had she felt about it? Perhaps she, Flora, was wrong to be indignant on the other woman's behalf when Tina had, after all, stayed here for twelve years.

Few women in Tina's position as the penniless widow of a gambler could have been lucky enough to be offered a place in the very building they had expected to call home. Or had Tina bitterly resented her position here? If so why stay for twelve years, giving up chances of remarriage and motherhood for herself?

Had she ever hoped that Frank Scott would make her his legal wife? From what she had heard other men out here had wed Indian women and not been ostracized like Tessa Fontaine.

Or had the venomous looks that Tina occasionally darted in Frank Scott's direction been the outward signs of her inward hatred and loathing for the man?

She looked down at the jewels again, seeing them gleaming in the lamplight. There was no doubt they were beautiful and she could at least wear them knowing they hadn't been won in a poker game! But what to wear with them?

She opened the doors of the huge wardrobe and surveyed the dresses hanging on their rail, the skirts long and limp without the stiff petticoats that held them out and helped minimize the waist. So far she had not had the chance to wear any of the half-dozen grand frocks she had brought with her from London. She had worn her dark riding-costume and the simple figured gowns that were for mornings in the parlour and afternoons spent sewing or sipping tea with female friends.

The ballgowns were more elaborate, low-necked with tiny puffed sleeves, the skirts embroidered and beribboned.

None of them pleased her. With her tall slender frame and long legs she was apt, she decided gloomily, to resemble a horse got up for the Lord Mayor's show.

There was one dress she had insisted on having made up for herself, at the sight of which her mother had pulled a disapproving face.

'It's very plain, darling! It really needs some lavish embroidery to set it off if it's ever worn at all.'

It was of heavy silk in a dull ivory shade that was really no shade at all until one held the garment under a lamp and saw how the ivory glowed subtly into palest beige and the merest hint of gold. Its deep, round neckline showed her shoulders and the long tight sleeves ended at the wrists with neither frill nor flower bracelet to detract from their simplicity.

Its only decoration was a narrow gold sash that emphasized the simple lines of the dress. A narrower gold ribbon would bind securely the chignon in which she intended to ask Tina to dress her hair.

'This one!' she said aloud and laid it over a chair for the maids to freshen and iron in the morning.

Moving to the window to draw the curtains closer she looked down at the garden. It was almost denuded of blossom now but along the terraces tall grasses waved in the briskly increasing wind and sent shadows dancing under the rising moon.

The figure of the housekeeper was silhouetted briefly against a wall lit by a hanging lantern. Tina was dancing again, not with wild abandon but slowly and sadly as if she wove a lament for something long lost and gone.

She had once invited Flora to join her, though whether seriously or not Flora had no idea. It was clear, however, from her slow movements and the elegiac fall of her long tail of black hair as she bent almost to the ground, hands open as if she waited to receive some lost happiness that this evening she wished to dance alone.

Flora prepared to withdraw into the centre of the bedroom again and leave the housekeeper to her private ritual, but then another figure joined her.

Brent O'Brien came from a darkened quarter of the garden where trees still overshadowed the paths and newly raked flower-beds. He held out his hand and Tina floated like a dark cloud to her new partner and circled with him slowly.

As Flora sat down on the bed, out of sight of those below and herself now unable to see them, she heard through the narrowest of apertures in her window the sound of them both laughing.

FIFTEEN

It was stupid to mind! Flora told herself that firmly, several times, as she sat in her room with the curtains still open a little and the lamp spreading a pool of honey on the carpet. If her uncle's manager was amusing himself with his uncle's quasi-mistress and deceiving the young woman he was going to marry it was none of her affair.

When at last she rose and ventured to look out of the window again the two had gone and the moon shone fitfully down on the deserted garden.

She reminded herself that she needed a long night's sleep in readiness for the next night's dance which, she suspected, would last until dawn, especially if the Chicago meeting broke up later than was expected. She undressed and climbed wearily into bed. After she had extinguished the lamp she lay motionless between the chilly sheets as her thoughts ran in directions she didn't want to follow.

In the end she slept and if she dreamed her mind cancelled the dreaming as she woke the next morning.

'Brent's here,' Tina informed her, following the maid who brought in hot water, bringing a tray in her own hands.

'Already? What time is it?' Flora demanded.

'Just gone seven, Miss Flora. I'll lay out your riding clothes, shall I? Brent said you were going riding.'

'He'll have to wait a while then.'

'He's in the kitchen having another breakfast,' Tina said. 'How that man stays slim considering the amount of food he puts into himself is a cause for wonder.'

There was affection in her voice, a softness in her expression. But even as Flora glanced at her in surprise she said quickly:

'He is legally my stepson still, even though I was only wed to his father for a couple of hours. We . . . look out for each other from time to time.'

Flora made no comment but went through into the small bathroom where the hip-bath stood, its interior now half-full of hot water. Fresh towels were laid ready nearby.

Twenty minutes later, having drunk the coffee and eaten the hot rolls on the tray, she made her way down the stairs.

Her uncle, emerging from the dining room, gestured her to follow him into the study.

'Good morning, Flora,' he began stiffly but was clearly determined to be forgiving as he went on: 'I hope that we understand each other a little better this morning than we did last night and that you will wear the garnets. The truth is that apart from your tendency to be unconventional I have been pleased with you since you came here. Your heart is in the right place even if your head is filled with rather impractical ideas. I start early for the meeting and hope the business will be discussed and voted upon in a very short time. You are going riding with Brent this morning?'

'On Moonlight, yes.'

'He's an excellent rider himself and will look to your safety as well as his own. I will see you this evening, then.'

He patted her shoulder as he went out, and she heard him call out a cheerful good-bye in the direction of the kitchen.

When she went through into the hall Brent was standing there, hat in hand.

'Good morning.' For the life of her she couldn't infuse any warmth into her tone.

'Good morning!' he answered cheerfully,

apparently oblivious to the coolness in her manner. 'I thought it better to get our ride over early so you can rest before the dance starts. And the men from the village will be setting out on their hunting trip quite soon too.'

'The Peoria?'

'They hunt in spring as well but the last hunt before winter is a more exciting affair. It is harder to find game and the weather may worsen. There's frost on the ground already.'

It felt indeed very cold as she went out with him to the stables.

'You sound,' she couldn't help remarking, 'as if you envied the hunters.'

'In a way I do. I ride out sometimes to do a little shooting but today is a strictly Indian affair. I'd advise you to keep a tight rein. Moonlight needs to be curbed.'

'As you say,' Flora nodded, allowing herself to be helped into the saddle.

'I've offended you?' He glanced at her as he remounted his own horse.

'Not in the least,' Flora said quickly. 'The trouble is that last evening after you left I had something of a small disagreement with my uncle. He insists on my dressing up in jewels — garnets — for the dance tonight. I know he means it kindly but I loathe being manipulated as if I were a — a slave girl in the marketplace.'

'Offer for my niece and I'll throw in an entire estate as well? Yes, I can see your objections. Your uncle is hidebound in his views, however, so it would be a waste of time for you to argue.'

'It's still highly irritating!' she answered shortly.

They rode on in silence towards the village, passing the school which was barred and shuttered. They reined in their mounts as they arrived at the clusters of shacks and small houses where the Peoria dwelt. Here all was awake and astir, children running about perilously near to the horses' hoofs, men issuing forth with their wives clinging to their arms.

Flora watched with interest. Until now she had seen little of the men save as distant figures in the fields or hunched over fishing rods by the river. Today they wore thick tunics with fringed hems, wide trousers tucked into high boots and feather head-dresses of amazing size and colour. Some of the elaborately mounted feathers swung from the crown of the head almost to the hips. A few had donned huge curving horns that reminded her of pictures she had seen of ancient Vikings.

Every man bore a bow and a quiver of arrows in addition to a shotgun, and Flora noticed that long-bladed, curved knives were thrust into every belt.

Their faces were painted in stripes of broad red and black and their hair was either plaited or blew out behind them, fluttering with ribbons as the cold wind blew.

'A fine-looking bunch, don't you think?' Brent said. 'It's not often they get the chance to put on their ceremonial paint.'

'They look savage,' Flora said uneasily.

'Oh, the Peoria dwelt in reasonable harmony with the whites for a long time,' Brent said easily. 'There was the occasional hiccup, of course, when tempers flared, but the whole nation took up farming a couple of generations ago. Before that they were often at war with other tribes. But they still prize the chance to obtain meat for their winter larders without having to pay inflated Chicago prices. Hey, John Redfeather! Will you bring down a buck today?'

He broke off to hail a tall thin Indian in the act of mounting a shaggy, unsaddled mare.

'If not today then tomorrow or tomorrow or tomorrow!' the Indian answered cheerfully. 'Good day, Miss Flora, my wife tells me you are a good friend to her.'

'Which is more than that well stuffed bedroll will be to you, John!'

As Flora dismounted Mary Redfeather, as plump as her husband was thin, and with the usual train of children behind her, bustled up.

'Our eldest boy rides out on the hunt with me today,' John Redfeather said proudly.

'I'm not talking about our Charlie!' his wife exclaimed. 'I'm talking about them two bottles of whiskey in your bedroll. One's enough! You can't shoot straight when you're sober so is it likely you'll be bringing down anything worth the skinning and the eating when you're drunk?'

She was half-laughing as she spoke and her husband grinned sheepishly as he listened.

A young boy of twelve or thirteen, only one feather in his headband, had just ridden up on his pony and was watching his parents with a look of amused tolerance on his face.

'They're raising the totem,' Brent interrupted.

John Redfeather stopped his wife's remonstrances with a kiss, slapped her on the rump and mounted his horse, signalling his son to follow him as the hunters mounted up and began to circle round a tall brightly painted and grotesquely carved post being raised in their midst. The women had fallen back, clustering in two groups and raising their voices in a chorus of unintelligible sounds, long drawn out, high-pitched and then dying into a soft, crooning sound.

'They are asking the Great Spirit to send them good hunting and fine weather.'

Brent had come to stand beside her.

Glancing at him she saw that his brown eyes followed the circling riders with something wistful in their gaze.

'You'd like to be riding with them,' she said on impulse.

'Yes,' he answered. 'There's more action and interest in what they're going to be doing than in finishing calculating last month's feed supply and getting myself togged up for tonight.'

'You should go to the meeting in Chicago,' Flora said, 'and speak up for them!'

'To deaf ears and men who believe that providence has given them this land to govern at the back of their minds, behind their smiling faces? It would be a waste of effort,' he said. 'Excuse me, I see Minnie is standing over there. I wasn't aware she was coming to watch. Usually she doesn't.'

He saluted her briefly and walked away just as Mary Redfeather came over to where

Flora stood.

'Well, that's my John and my Charlie gone for the winter rations!' Mary said. 'Mind you, even if they brung nothing down Brent sees us all right and your uncle too, Miss Flora, he ain't ungenerous. Thinks of us as poor ignorant children no doubt!'

'Mary!' Grasping her opportunity Flora plucked the other's sleeve. 'I've a private question for you if you'll answer it?'

'Depends on the question. I ain't educated,' Mary said.

'Why would a Kickapoo woman be travelling with Peoria?'

'She might be a shaman,' said Mary, looking puzzled.

'A what?'

'A woman that can go into the dreamtime and bring back news from the years ahead. Most of them are men but I've heard tell of women shamans too though I ain't ever met one.'

Her look was suddenly sharp and questioning.

'I believe I read about it somewhere,' Flora said vaguely.

'What's written is better than what's spoken,' Mary told her. 'Spoken words blow away on the wind and change the shapes of the thoughts behind them but once a word is written it's there for all time whether it be a truth or a lie. I'm proud my children go to school sometimes for in years to come what's written will stand and can be proved one way or the other. I can read a few words myself, Miss Flora, and my John's proud of me for that.'

'He doesn't . . .' Flora paused, embarrassed.

'Read?' Mary threw back her black head and laughed, every tooth glinting. 'My John is the most uneducated man you will ever meet, and the worst shot, but he's the warmest and the most tender under the blankets! I pray you'll catch yourself a man like that real quick!'

'My uncle would agree with you,' Flora said, smiling despite herself. 'He's bringing friends back tonight for the dance after the meeting, especially to look me over.'

'And you take your time in choosing,' Mary advised. 'Best to be alone than pick the wrong man! You mind my words now, Miss Flora.'

She had turned her head and was staring somewhat pointedly at Minnie who was still talking to Brent, one mittened hand laid on his sleeve, her lips moving rapidly.

Before Flora could frame a reply Brent said something to Minnie, kissed her cheek and came back towards them.

'Show's over, folks!' His joviality sounded somewhat forced. 'Shall we ride back, Flora? I daresay you'll be expected to approve the decorations!'

'I daresay Tina will be managing them very skilfully all by herself,' Flora said.

'Fine! Let's ride! Good day to you, Mary!'

She had been on the verge of taking the Peoria woman into her confidence regarding the plans for Tessa's escape but Brent's arrival had forestalled her.

As he helped her mount she glanced over to where Minnie still stood and met a cold, stony glance before the schoolteacher turned away.

'What did you think of the ceremony?'

'I thought it was beautiful,' Flora told him, 'and I am mentally shaking myself because I meant to make some sketches today and I left my materials in the house!'

'There'll be other occasions,' he said easily as he remounted.

'Where I will always be an observer,' she said wryly.

'Maybe it's no bad thing if we have a record of what once was for our grandchildren to see,' he observed thoughtfully.

'Surely the old ways won't die?' Flora queried.

'It would be nice to think so, but in reality I believe they might unless we protect them now,' he returned. 'The documents are safe?'

'Yes.' She gave him a smile and saw the slight frown on his face vanish.

'You've told Minnie where they are?'

'No,' he said shortly.

'But surely she's to be trusted?'

'Of course, but what's private between us remains private,' Brent said.

'I'm surprised you didn't ask Tina . . .' She hesitated, remembering the two figures swaying together in the dark garden.

'No. Tina has her position to think about,' he said. 'She married my father so I look out for her.'

'I thought my uncle did that,' Flora said.

'In his own way. How Tina chooses to live her life is not my concern. And soon how you live your life won't be my concern either.'

'You seem very sure that my uncle will arrive with the perfect bridegroom in tow,' Flora said sarcastically. 'But as you just told me, only our own affairs are of any interest!'

She had raised her voice slightly as they came within sight of the gates and under her she felt the surge of muscular power as Moonlight attempted to break into a headlong gallop.

'Ari! Ari!' Brent shouted the warning, unsuccessfully grabbing at the reins and as they slipped through his fingers seizing her instead as she kicked her feet free of the stirrups.

The next moment she stood shivering within the circle of his arms.

'You're fine. Not even a twisted ankle to stop you dancing for your prospective bridegroom tonight,' he said.

'I do wish,' Flora gasped, 'that you would stop going on about bridegrooms!'

'You don't wish to marry at all?'

He had raised an eyebrow as he looked down into her face.

'You may let me go now,' Flora summoned breath to say, 'since thanks to your quick thinking I am unhurt. Moonlight, I see, is headed for the stables! As for marrying, I've had small hope of a husband since I realized that I am without beauty or feminine charm! Of course a widower may fancy me, or a poor man who looks beyond me to the great house and farming land that my uncle informs everybody will be mine one day! But the truth is that until I meet a man who loves me for myself — and there's small risk of that — then I am happy to be solitary!'

'As mistress of Scott Place?'

'That gives me little pleasure to think about,' she said stonily. 'You may be resigned to the fact that you are only manager of a spread that you ought to have inherited, but I still feel the unfairness of it. Were the place mine now I would certainly offer it back to you!'

'And I would as certainly refuse!' He gripped her shoulders and shook her gently. 'Flora, you may not have any feminine charm but you're as romantic as any novel-reading young lady! I want something more than a settled life in a small place. I want to travel and see other places. I don't grudge your uncle his ownership or his success in making it the finest house and the biggest farm in the county! I enjoy managing the place and I like my own small spread but one day I mean to travel and see more of this land! And as for your being without beauty! You may not look like a china doll but I have the most intense delight in looking at you!'

Before she could frame any answer at all he had let her go, mounted up again and was cantering away towards the village.

Flora leaned limply against the fence and watched his figure diminish into the distance until it vanished around a bend in the road.

She put both hands up to her face and waited until the hectic flush on her cheeks had cooled before she walked sedately up the drive in time to meet Tina who came hurrying out.

'Moonlight just arrived in the stables! Are you alright, Miss Flora?'

She spoke with what seemed like genuine concern.

'I'm fine,' Flora said.

'You'd best come in and sit down,' Tina said. 'You'll be wanting your hair dressed for this evening and you ought to take a rest too. Have you chosen your dress? I noticed a real classy ivory silk laid over the chair.'

'To attract a husband,' Flora said bitterly.

'Yes,' Tina said without expression. 'And you will wish to look over the arrangements for tonight before you have something to eat and then rest.'

'I'm sure you're perfectly capable . . .' Flora began uncomfortably.

'The other servants will be glad to have the approval of the mistress,' Tina said.

'I am not mistress here yet,' Flora said.

'But it is your uncle's intention to make you so,' Tina returned.

'Will you leave here — ?' Her words were cut short as Tina's eyes suddenly blazed with scorn.

'And where would I go?' the housekeeper asked. 'I have no family living that I could trace! My relations are all scattered now and I have no money. Your uncle is kind in his own way and Brent is very kind for he comes over to see me from time to time.'

'To dance in the garden,' Flora couldn't stop herself from saying.

'Ah! I thought you might have seen us.' Unexpectedly Tina smiled. 'Brent is my stepson though I was married to his father for such a little time, and he understands my need to move freely sometimes as if I were a girl again. He accepts me for what I am.'

'But to stay here — what about pride?' Flora asked bluntly.

'Pride?' Tina gave a hard little smile. 'You were not too proud to come here and let your uncle seek a husband for you. We are women, Miss Flora, and pride's a starvation diet!'

'Perhaps we both lack the courage to break away, then,' Flora said.

'Like the white Peoria who lives with her brother and frets for her brave, but if he came riding to her door she'd choose safety instead.'

'You're wrong!' Her patience snapping, Flora spoke heatedly. 'Tessa is in touch with

Smiling Moon and we plan —'

'She is going to him?' Tina stared at her. 'How will she manage this?'

'I never meant to say anything,' Flora muttered. 'Please, don't tell —'

'Last night I heard something of what you said to your uncle,' Tina told her. 'You spoke up for me and so I will say nothing, but what is this plan? Perhaps I can tell you how to carry it out. Perhaps you can trust me to say nothing.'

Flora sat down on the edge of the bed and looked at the older woman.

'This evening, before the men return from Chicago,' she said at last, 'Tessa will slip away from her house and come here by the back road. I will slip upstairs with her while the rest of the household is still busy in the kitchen. Her brother will discover her absence at once but he will assume she has already fled from Pine Creek Ridge. Instead she will be in my private sitting room, which I will keep locked for a couple of days.'

'And then?'

'I have tickets for the Bloomington stage and the two of us will make our way very early in the morning to the second bend in the river —'

'I'm real glad you told me all this, Miss Flora,' Tina said with heavy irony. 'So you

335

might just be able to smuggle Miss Tessa up to your sitting room. And then? The other servants will want to know why the door is locked. How long are you going to keep her there? Two, three days? Carrying basins of food up for her I daresay?'

'Then you think of something better!' Flora said.

'I believe I can,' the housekeeper said. Her voice was suddenly quietly determined.

'And?'

'You've not told Brent of this?'

'No. He wouldn't say anything but I know he doesn't want to be involved. Brent seldom seems ready to involve himself in anything,' Flora said a trifle bitterly.

'But you've told Miss Tessa?'

'She had to know. She will wear very dark clothes and slip away —'

'Seems like you're planning on a whole heap of slipping around the place,' Tina said. She laughed suddenly. 'You really think that Miss Tessa will be able to wander along the back roads without being spotted? Not everybody's coming tonight, you know. And when the two of you come walking up the drive — by then the men might be back already from Chicago if that meeting of theirs finishes early.'

'Then what can I do to help?' Flora

demanded. 'I can't sit here just doing nothing, just paying lip service to an injustice!'

'You stay right here,' Tina said. 'You stay
here and get yourself made elegant for this
night's festivities! I may be gone for a half-
hour before dusk but don't fret yourself.
You think that you're the only person that
can make plans? You stay here, Miss Flora,
and trust me to —'

'But Tessa expects —'

'No point in telling Miss Tessa what's
planned for her,' Tina said. 'Her face gives
every blessed thing away even if her mouth
doesn't. But hold on to those tickets for
Bloomington! That's something not thought
of!'

As she bent to pat the younger woman's
shoulder a thin chain slipped from beneath
the round neckline of her dress. There
dangling at its centre, was a small golden
star.

'But I have one . . .' Flora exclaimed. 'It
was in my purse . . .'

'Still be there,' Tina said, her face suddenly expressionless. 'This one I keep for
someone else. You rest easy now. I've matters to arrange!'

Sixteen

Perhaps it was customary here for lovers to exchange tokens, Flora thought. She was walking restlessly in the garden, having eaten a light lunch. She had looked in at the kitchen on her way out and seen the maidservants with extra help at hand hard at work on the final preparations for the evening's festivities. Platters of meat and bowls of fruit were being assembled on the long pine tables and the scent of baking bread wafted through the kitchen.

There was no sign of Tina. As she stood uncertainly in the doorway a couple of the maids looked up from their work and began whispering to each other in their own tongue.

Everybody in Pine Creek Ridge, she thought, must be aware that this evening was her uncle's way of bringing more men into his house to assess the charms of his niece. The mischievous thought that she could scandalize local society by turning up at the dance in her riding clothes brushed her mind but that would dishonour Uncle Frank who, whatever his failings, had genuinely made her welcome.

The weather was hurrying into winter. She could feel the bitter wind tear at the hood of her cloak and now and then came a faint dusting of snowflakes on the air. The maize fields were barren now and the occasional bird winging its way over them flew low in search of grain.

'Miss Flora, you'll be catching your death if you stand musing in this wind!' Mary Redfeather, for once without a troop of small children in tow, was coming along the road.

'I am killing time until the men return from the meeting,' Flora said.

'Me too!' Mary laughed. 'I'm hoping my John ain't shot himself in the foot like he did last winter. I tell you that man'll be the death of me one day. Not that he was hurt bad! A flesh wound the doctor said though it's a puzzle to me how he found any flesh. My John's one of the heartiest eaters I know and never puts on an ounce! Walk with me if you've a mind?'

'Where are the children?' Flora enquired as they set off along the track through the fields.

'Miss Minnie opened up the school and took the little ones in there out of the cold,' Mary told her. 'She has her good points does that one. Always kind to the little ones.'

Flora didn't particularly want to hear praise of Minnie Hargreaves but had in justice to admit privately that the overseer's daughter had her good points.

'You all ready for the party later on after the men get back?' Mary was continuing.

'The house is being turned upside down,' Flora said wryly. 'You know my uncle wishes me to find a husband and I have a feeling that I won't be able to oblige him!'

'I meant the party when our men get back from hunting,' Mary said. 'In a week or so they'll come riding home with what they've tracked and killed ready for the skinning and then burying in the snow holes.'

'Snow holes?'

'We divide up the meat and dig holes in the ground lined with tin and put the meat there,' the other told her. 'When the snows really come the holes get iced up and the flesh stays fresh. Then we dig it out when food gets scarce.'

'And there's a party? For Indians — ?'

'Anyone who wants to drop in,' Mary said cheerfully. 'We have a real good feast! Lots to eat and more to drink!'

'I like that idea,' Flora said warmly. 'Mary, I need to ask you something.'

'Ask,' Mary said simply.

'Each clan has a totem? I've read about that.'

'We do.'

'And individual people have small totems? Husbands and wives? Lovers?'

'Some do. Custom's not as common as it used to be,' Mary informed her. 'My John and I have a token each of us wears, has worn since he carved them — well, he says he carved them but since he's never carved anything else in his entire life it's my guess he bought them at the trading post! Not that I'd ever let on!'

She stopped to push back her sleeve and reveal a thin copper bangle from which dangled a little copper heart.

'Love tokens,' Flora said thoughtfully.

'Now don't fret because you ain't got any to wear or one to give,' Mary said in a consoling tone. A wink accompanied her words. 'When you find your mate he'll be putting a fine bright ring on your finger! And you will find him, Miss Flora! Oh, here comes Brent!'

Brent, wearing a heavy jacket with his hat pulled low, was driving the wagon towards them, its interior piled with heavy sacks.

'Good day, Flora! Mary!' He raised his voice against the wind as he drew up.

'You still working?' Mary said. 'Ain't you off to the dance later?'

'When I've got these potatoes sorted out. I'm putting the whole stack of them in my barn against the hunger later in the season.'

'And you are coming tonight?'

'All togged up in white shirt and string tie and my boots shining,' he said with a grin. 'See you later!'

His wave encompassed them both as he flicked his whip over the backs of the horses and went past the two women.

'Nice man!' Mary said.

'Yes,' Flora said soberly.

A nice man, friendly with everybody but not willing to engage closely in any disputes. An attractive man, she thought, and she felt a prickling of irritation because she had always regarded herself as a woman of good sense and women of good sense didn't allow their eyes to stray in the direction of men already engaged.

'We'd best be turning back,' Mary Redfeather said. 'Wind's blowing stronger. I hope my John had the sense to keep his buckskins on!'

They returned to the gates of Scott Place

where Mary left her to make her way back into the village and Flora went back indoors, grateful as she closed the front door behind her for the warmth that issued from every open door within where fires had been kindled in all the rooms.

'If this wind doesn't drop,' Tina said, coming down the stairs, 'they'll either end the meeting early and be here before we know it or get blown off course and end up in New York!'

'You were out before?' Flora questioned as they went up the stairs. Tina having turned in mid-flight, walking respectfully in the rear.

'Errands to run,' Tina said briefly. 'I've told the girls to boil up water. Your hair's going to take some drying.'

They entered Flora's bedroom and Tina shut the door firmly.

'Tessa . . .' Flora began.

'All in hand,' Tina said calmly. 'Miss Tessa won't be "slipping" over here when dusk falls so you can just settle to making yourself beautiful for the dance.'

'I won't have a husband pushed at me just because my uncle wishes it,' Flora warned.

'That's your business, Miss Flora,' Tina answered imperturbably, 'but you don't want to miss the chance of saying "No", now do you?'

Flora shook her head grudgingly, the thought crossing her mind that it might one day be rather wonderful to be able to say 'yes', and mean it!

The sounds of trotting hoofs and rumbling wheels sounded as the finishing touches were being put to her toilet. She went to the window, where she beheld a cavalcade of riders and ladies in pony traps and small wagons proceeding up the sloping drive past the flowerless terraces.

'You look real nice, Miss Flora!' Tina said in unflattering tones of surprise. 'I'll go down to get them all settled and in their right places and you make your entrance when you feel it's time. Reckon they started back real early!'

Flora turned from the window to survey herself in the long glass. She looked, she thought uncertainly, either completely unlike her usual self or like herself as she had never been.

The tall, slender creature in the mirror wore the ivory gown whose simplicity of cut drew attention to smooth arms and shoulders and narrow waist from which the silk flowed over its underskirts, catching the light that emphasized the subtle tints of palest beige and gold in the heavy silk. Her

344

thick, curly, brown hair had been drawn up into a coronet, each curl anchored with a tiny gold pin. Her cheeks were slightly flushed and her eyes sparkled as she gazed at her reflection.

She moved to the dressing-table and took out the garnet necklace and earbobs, fastening them carefully round her neck and in her ears, seeing the rich scarlet of them blaze against her skin.

There was a tap on the door.

'My dear, are you ready to join our guests?'

Her uncle stood on the threshold, his smile widening as he saw the jewels.

'Quite ready, Uncle. Please come in. You are early back from the meeting.'

'The weather's on the turn. Better to be safe than sorry,' he answered genially as he entered. 'My dear, I am delighted you chose to wear the garnets. They enhance your looks and your appearance, even without them, would at this moment be very far removed from plain. Indeed I would describe you as a handsome, even striking, young lady.'

'And you have invited several gentlemen to attend this evening?' Flora rejoined calmly.

'My dear Flora, for once there will be

more gentlemen than ladies at a social event in Pine Creek Ridge,' he told her. 'Hot toddies are being served in the dining room as soon as the guests have removed their travelling garments and been allotted their sleeping quarters. Your friends from the sewing circle are already divesting themselves of capes and shawls and will be happy for you to greet them.'

'Of course, Uncle.'

She went past him down the stairs and stood for a moment looking down at the throng below as the maids relieved them of their outer garments and ushered them past Tina who stood, smiling and respectful, outside the double doors of the long drawing room where the polished floor and the sight of three musicians tuning up on the dais in one corner made her realize with a little shock that this was going to be an elegant affair far removed from the barn dances she had read about in England.

'My niece will make you ladies comfortable while I check on my gentlemen guests,' her uncle was saying in a loud, slightly pompous voice. 'Mrs Eliot, what a pleasure it is to see you here.'

'Oh, Mr Eliot is never averse to a dance,' Mrs Eliot said, looking worried as if her husband had just been accused of something. 'He often tells me that exercise is food for the body and music food for the soul. Such a pleasant way for young people to mingle without any hint of impropriety.'

Brent hadn't yet arrived. No doubt he'd gone to fetch Minnie who had been looking after her young pupils for most of the day. Resolving to think well of Minnie Hargreaves, Flora moved among the ladies, finding the right things to say to them, signalling to the maids to serve the hot negus since many of the older guests looked chilled even though their drive here had been short.

At least they wouldn't be staying over, she reflected. Only the gentlemen her uncle had invited from Chicago would sleep over for a few hours before their return to town. So far only a few male guests had put in an appearance, among them, she noticed with a sinking of the heart, the egregious Harold Belmont.

'Flora, have you a moment?' Her uncle touched her lightly on the shoulder. His smile had fled.

'What is it?' she asked.

'Charles Fontaine has just ridden in to inform me that his sister is missing.'

'Missing? You mean Tessa — ?'

'There's no sign of her anywhere, but the

347

prints of an unshod horse are visible in that part of the ground where the frost has so far not hardened.'

'Are her belongings gone?' Flora asked.

'Everything seems to be there except her winter shawl.'

'She may have gone for a walk,' Flora suggested weakly.

'In this cold after dark? Even her outdoor shoes are still in their accustomed place. You went for a walk today?'

'Yes, this afternoon. I walked along with Mary Redfeather for a while.'

'You didn't visit the Fontaine house?'

'No,' Flora answered truthfully. 'I didn't go anywhere near it.'

'And you can promise me on your honour that you know nothing of her whereabouts?'

'Nothing,' she answered levelly.

'We shall have to mount a search party,' he began, but was interrupted by Charles Fontaine who had just entered, his fair hair blown back from his forehead, his face as white as the frost.

'No, there will be no search party,' Tessa's brother said, his voice clearly audible as small groups ceased their politely murmured conversations and looked in his direction. 'Tessa has never made any secret of the fact that she wishes to return to the

Peoria. She is a moral outcast, lost to any standards of decent behaviour, and having brought her back once and kept her close to home I'll not trouble myself a second time.'

'That hardly sounds like a concerned brother, Charles!' Brent's voice rang through the room.

'My brotherly concern has been flung back in my face too often,' Charles Fontaine said bitterly. 'Are you sure you didn't have some hand in this yourself, O'Brien? You always made it plain that I should've left her where she was!'

'I've always been her friend and I don't care who knows it!' Brent retorted. 'I've also never given anyone the slightest reason to think I'd help her in any damn fool escape!'

'Brent, language! Ladies present!' Harold Belmont had pushed his way forward. 'No sense in our losing all sense of decorum even in a crisis, as we doctors say.'

'If I were in Tessa Fontaine's place,' Mrs Eliot said, showing a sudden and most unwelcome intelligence, 'I would hide nearby and slip away later when the search had cooled down.'

'In that case a search of the village seems to me to be perfectly in order,' Brent said. 'My house keys are here. I've just locked my front door and nobody was in the house or my stables but you're welcome to go and look.'

'I didn't mean to imply . . .' Mrs Eliot flustered, reddening.

'Might the Indians be hiding her?' someone asked.

'They won't risk their jobs or their lands to help a runaway,' another confirmed.

'Forgive me.' Charles had flushed slightly. 'I had no wish to spoil the evening by blurting out my own troubles. I am sure that the savage whom Tessa insists on calling her husband rode up and simply took her with him. As far as I am concerned the matter is now closed. My sister has been a sore trial to me ever since she was returned and while I never will wish her ill I would never under any circumstances welcome her back.'

He bowed and walked stiffly out, a hubbub of shocked and excited chatter following him.

'This is a bad business!' Flora's uncle said. 'Unless we are careful it may cast a blight over the entire evening! Now you will appreciate, Flora, why I disapproved of your trying to strike up a friendship with her. She is quite lost, I fear. And I feel very much for poor Charles, who has always tried to do his duty by her. It sets a very bad example!'

He broke off, forcing a smile as a group of newcomers entered, evidently having been shown their night's quarters and tidied themselves for the evening's social event. Flora found herself in the midst of a circle of well-clad, for the most part tall, young men who bowed over her hand and were, most of them, erect in their bearing and attractive.

Uncle Frank, she decided cynically, had gone to some trouble to bring eligible suitors! Her mother would be absolutely delighted to witness her wallflower daughter becoming a social success! The musicians had begun to play a medley of tunes and since the space allowed for eight couples on the floor those who wished to dance had but a short time to wait before they too could join in, while others were already in the next room partaking of the various dishes laid out on the long tables, or admiring the elaborate arrangements of late flowers, berries and autumn leaves that graced the vases.

Her uncle's fear that Tessa's escape would cast a shadow over the gaieties seemed to have been unfounded, though to judge from the scraps of conversation she heard as she circled with first one partner and then another, everyone, almost without exception, was whispering about it.

Brent had left. Minnie hadn't yet arrived. Flora noticed their absence and mentally scolded herself for feeling a tiny empty space open up somewhere in the recesses of her heart.

'You will take a glass of negus, Miss Flora?' One of her uncle's Chicago guests was bowing before her as she sank on to one of the chairs placed at intervals around the walls.

'Thank you, yes.' Flora gave him a somewhat mechanical smile that faded as a figure just coming through the door approached her.

Minnie Hargreaves was handing her cloak to her father, on whose arm she had entered. She wore a low-cut dress of emerald green, its full skirt banded in black ribbon. Her hair was in its usual crown of plaits in which a pearl headband gleamed. She looked unusually pretty.

'My apologies for arriving so late!' she said in a hurried undertone. 'I had to see all my pupils safely off school premises and then hurry home to change. Brent was supposed to escort me but he sent word he was delayed and so my father has conveyed me here. Is it true that Tessa Fontaine has run away again?'

'Or ridden away,' Flora said. 'Her brother brought the news.'

'Poor Charles! She has been nothing but a disgrace to him since the soldiers restored her to civilization,' Minnie murmured.

'She must've gone of her own free will,' Flora said carefully.

'They are searching the village in case she is still hiding somewhere,' Minnie confided. 'For my own part I wish she had never come back at all! Ah here comes Brent now!'

Brent had shed his outer garments in the hall and looked elegant in evening dress, his thick russet hair curling slightly against his neck.

'Charles insists the search be abandoned,' he said, walking over to them. 'He declares that from now on his sister is dead for him. I suspect he may always have felt so. Minnie, my apologies for letting you down! I figured your father would get you here safely, but let me make amends by inviting you to dance. Flora, good evening!'

He and Minnie were dancing together. Like many tall men he was light on his feet but his height looked odd against Minnie's tiny, plump frame.

Which, Flora told herself firmly, meant nothing to her.

Another of the Chicago guests was edging

his way towards her. Flora rose and slipped out into the hall where the lamps were fewer and there were pools of shadow in between them. From the other rooms she could hear the music, the clinking of glasses and cutlery, the hum of voices. On the stairs where she seated herself there was a measure of tranquillity. She looked down through the balustrade into the hall, seeing the occasional figure cross from one room to the other.

'Ah, there you are! I've been wondering where you were hiding.' Brent had arrived at the foot of the staircase and was mounting to the step where she sat. 'Weary of so many suitors all at the same time?'

'I needed a few minutes' peace and quiet,' she confessed.

'Very sensible! May I join you?' Without waiting for an answer he seated himself beside her.

'Minnie . . . ?' she began awkwardly.

'Is dancing with Harold Belmont. She and I — our steps don't always match very well. She feels for Charles, who has however, gained his place in society again now that he has renounced his naughty sister.'

'Brent, where is . . . ?'

'The snow is starting to fall and will obliterate any tracks rapidly.'

'She isn't in your house?'

'She is not,' he said shortly. 'Flora, I want to talk about something else with you.' His voice was low and so grave that she felt a moment's unease.

'What is it?' she asked at last.

'The guests your uncle has brought with him from Chicago. He has introduced them to you?'

'Yes, but I'm afraid I didn't pay too much attention to their names,' Flora said apologetically. 'To be honest, they all look much of a muchness to me. Why?'

'I've recognized a couple of them and they're not from Chicago City,' Brent murmured. 'Unless my memory plays me false they're from Fort Dearborn.'

'Military men?' Flora stared at him, suddenly seeing the upright carriages and slightly formal manners in a new and unwelcome light.

'Hush, keep your voice down,' he warned softly, pressing her hand. 'They're state militia. Now why would your uncle suddenly fill his spare rooms with militia in civilian dress and not mention their profession?'

'He said he was going to introduce me to . . .' She felt herself reddening.

'Potential suitors? There doesn't seem to

be any need to send to Fort Dearborn for them.'

'Then why? Brent, perhaps an Indian attack is expected and they haven't informed the ladies.'

'They haven't informed me either,' he said. 'The last Indian attack at Pine Creek Ridge was more than twenty years back when I was a child and then it was a group of starving Kaskaskias. But an attack of some sort? That's possible.'

He spoke almost in a whisper and his face was grave in the shadowy gloom.

'Brent?' Gripped by a fear impossible to define she touched his hand briefly.

Her own hand was gripped tightly in return as, shaking himself out of what seemed like some private dream, he said, his voice low and tense, 'Something is wrong, very wrong. I'll start out first thing tomorrow and track down the Peoria hunting party. You must keep that to yourself.'

'How can you possibly . . . ? They're long gone by now!'

'With any luck they'll be on their way back. Anyway, I'm a good tracker.'

'But to ride alone? Brent, it's starting to snow quite hard. The tracks will be gone.'

'There will be a base camp at Spirit Wolf Place. Trust me to know what I'm doing.'

'Brent, at least take someone else with you,' Flora pleaded, filled suddenly with an apprehension greater than she could have described. 'Why, I could ride out with you —'

'On Bess who plods along or Moonlight, who'd take the greatest delight in tossing you into the nearest snowdrift?' He sounded amused. 'I appreciate the offer but I'll ride faster and get there sooner without having you to worry about! Flora, will you do something else for me?'

'You know I will.'

'As soon as it's light go over to Mary Redfeather's place and tell her to gather the children together and take them on to my land. Oh, and here's a key to my house. They will be warmer inside. Will you do that?'

'Yes,' she whispered, slipping the key down her bodice. 'But there's something I have to know.'

'Which is?'

'You said Tessa Fontaine wasn't in your house. Is that true?'

'Perfectly true.' He leaned closer, whispering in her ear. 'After the Indian attack my father dug a cellar under the barn, very well concealed and unknown to any neighbour. She's beneath the barn, well supplied with food and blankets.'

'And the tracks? The unshod prints?'

'I sometimes amuse myself by testing my skills at riding one or other of the Indian ponies bareback.'

'But Tessa couldn't just have walked over?'

'Certainly not before dusk.' His voice was still a whisper, his breath fanning her cheek. 'It's amazing what a wagonload of potatoes can also carry. You strolling along with Mary Redfeather this afternoon almost scared the wits out of me.'

'You said you would never risk —'

'Risk my good job? Risk my standing in the community? Flora, until you came along I held aloof from anything more than showing Tessa some friendship. You made it clear what you thought of that. So I flung my hat into the ring and decided to pay more than lip service to my beliefs.'

'Because of what I thought. But why?'

'Because,' he said very low, 'you're a lovely woman, Flora Scott. I almost forgot to tell you that.'

And kissed her cheek and the corner of her mouth just as Minnie swished into the hall and stopped at the foot of the staircase to stare up at them.

SEVENTEEN

There was no time to react, to move away before Minnie had turned and headed back into the midst of the gaiety.

'I'd best be off,' Brent had obviously not seen Minnie. He drew away and stood up.

'You said in the morning . . .' Flora began.

'It's already close on one o'clock and I've preparations to make.' He bent to touch her shoulder lightly with his fingertips and went on down the stairs.

'You are not dancing?'

Harold Belmont had planted his foot on the lowest step and was looking up at her.

'My feet ache,' Flora said.

'Dancing can overheat the blood as we doctors say.' He threw her a sickly smile which he probably intended to be arch. 'This is a splendid occasion, is it not? A pity that the news about Tessa Fontaine has rather overshadowed it. Her brother seems quite adamant that he will not seek her or try to bring her back. It's a great pity she was ever brought back at all, for it caused Minnie to break off her courting with Charles. Human nature is a fruitful field for study as we —'

'Would you be kind enough to get me a glass of wine,' Flora broke in. 'I feel quite thirsty.'

'Certainly, and then perhaps — ?'

'My uncle will expect me to mingle with his guests from Chicago,' Flora said.

'The snow seems to be settling,' her uncle informed her when she joined the others again. 'I fear some of our neighbours might be obliged to leave early or they may find themselves stranded. Those jewels become you. They are yours now, of course. No sense in my holding on to them until after I've gone. What do you say, Miss Minnie? Don't you agree my niece is in good looks tonight?'

Of all the people milling about in the downstairs rooms he'd chosen Minnie Hargreaves to ask!

'Flora looks charming,' Minnie said, smiling.

'But where's your partner, m'dear? Brent neglecting you?'

'He was called away,' Minnie said.

'But we cannot have our schoolteacher

360

hiding among the wallflowers!' Uncle Frank said heartily. 'Piers!' He nodded towards a tall gentlemen who had arrived from Chicago. 'Piers! If you lack a partner allow me to present Miss Minnie Hargreaves who acquits herself most gracefully on the dance floor.'

'Delighted, ma'am!' The tall gentlemen whisked Minnie away.

'Going to dance with your old uncle then, Flora?' Uncle Frank enquired.

He had regained his good humour completely, she noticed, aided by the sight of her obediently wearing the jewels and several hot toddies, but he held his liquor well and swept her into a waltz with perfect timing.

'It's a bad business about Tessa Fontaine,' he said as they circled the floor. 'In my view once a white woman has turned native there's little to be done. Charles arrived at the same conclusion and I cannot blame him. So how do you like my guests? A handsome bunch, don't you agree?'

'And most soldierly in bearing,' Flora said.

He shot her a glance and smiled.

'Indeed they are,' he said amiably. 'Indeed they are!'

He was holding a secret close to himself but not so closely that she couldn't discern that there was a secret to be discovered. Yet he hadn't drunk sufficient to loosen his tongue. Flora tried desperately to think of something to say that might persuade him to speak more openly but the dance was over before a single idea had occurred to her and then she was claimed by a Mr Allen who seemed unaware of the undercurrents in the room but held her gingerly and apologized when he took a wrong step. This limited conversation since he was obliged to apologize very frequently.

Brent hadn't reappeared and her thoughts flew to him, riding through the settling snow to bid the hunting party return quickly. And thinking about him brought the blood surging into her face.

'So sorry!' Mr Allen said again. 'Rather clumsy on my feet, ma'am.'

Some of the older guests were leaving. The Eliots were bundling themselves up in their outdoor clothes and shaking hands. Flora thanked Mr Allen for the dance with what she hoped sounded like sincerity and went to shake hands with them.

'A most successful evening,' Mrs Eliot said. 'Though it's unfortunate about poor Miss Fontaine. She is a lost soul I fear.'

'Come, my dear, we must be charitable,' her husband scolded. 'We must continue to pray for her. Miss Flora, our thanks again.'

The rooms were slowly emptying. Flora had been occupied with those who were returning to their homes and by the time she re-entered the long drawing room where the musicians, their instruments packed away, were bolting down a hasty supper several of the guests from Chicago had already sought their lodgings in the other wing. Flora looked around for Tina but couldn't see her anywhere.

'Flora, my dear. I've arranged for a stirrup cup to be served to the last of our guests,' her uncle said, joining her. 'If you wish to slip away to your room nobody will blame you. It's close on two.'

'If you don't mind, Uncle?' Flora said.

Her head had begun to ache a little and her troubled thoughts made it difficult for her to keep a polite smile on her face.

'You run along,' he said, patting her shoulders. 'Ah, here is Miss Minnie! My dear, your father just left. Is Brent to drive you back?'

He addressed the schoolteacher as she came down the staircase and across the hall, having evidently collected her outdoor garments from the little dressing room where some of the ladies had deposited cloaks and overshoes.

'Brent must've had business elsewhere, Mr Scott,' she replied, coming towards them. 'Mr Fontaine has offered to see me safely home.'

'Charles came back?'

Uncle Frank excused himself and hurried to the door.

'Goodnight, Flora.' Minnie shook hands. 'This has been a delightful evening.'

For a girl whose betrothed had departed so abruptly she looked uncommonly pleased with herself.

'Good morning rather!' Uncle Frank said jovially. 'I see that Charles has kindly come to escort you home. Your father —'

'Was hardly in a fit condition to get himself home,' Charles Fontaine said, 'and Brent is seeing to a mare that recently foaled. You don't disapprove of —'

'Now that poor Tessa has gone,' Minnie said, 'I believe you should involve yourself in society again. You ought not to suffer any longer for her errors. Goodnight again.'

She dropped a curtsy, laid her hand on Charles Fontaine's proffered arm and went out into the cold.

'She takes O'Brien's neglect very calmly,' Uncle Frank said, looking after them. 'He seems to have neglected to ask you to dance too. You should go to bed, my dear. You are beginning to look just a trifle jaded but you may congratulate yourself on quite a successful evening. Now I must see that my friends from Chicago are settled. I heard a few flattering compliments being passed about you. Sleep well, my dear.'

The last of the local visitors had gone. The maids were collecting plates and glasses. Flora turned towards the staircase and mounted slowly, tiredness seeping through her bones. In one part of herself she could still feel the touch of Brent's lips against her own skin, the firm clasp of her hand so tangibly that she almost expected, as she mounted the steps, to see herself and her companion still seated in shadowy outline on the step like living ghosts.

She reminded herself that she could afford to snatch only a few hours' sleep before she went over to see Mary Redfeather with Brent's message that the children were to be taken on to his land. And her own luck being what it was, she thought wearily, she would probably find that he had given the message personally by the time she arrived.

In her bedroom a lamp had been lit and the covers turned down. A plain, dark dress and her cloak were laid over a chair and would suffice for the morning, she decided. She removed her jewels and put them back into their case, then let her ivory silk dress slip down to the floor. Amid a froth of petticoats it billowed and then sank, as if it shared her exhaustion.

Then she pulled off her dancing slippers and lay down under the goose-feather eiderdown, too wearied to bother with a nightgown. She fell asleep almost immediately, without dreaming. There was nothing but blackness and herself floating in it.

She surfaced into wakefulness slowly to find the back of her throat was hurting. She became aware that the lamp on the bedside table was smoking and that her mouth felt parched. As she turned over her gaze fell on the little clock which showed six o'clock.

Six! She had planned to be on her way to Mary Redfeather's house by now. Flora hastily pushed back the bedcovers and reached for her dark dress and cloak. When she drew the curtains it was still dark beyond the window but there were streaks of grey in the sky and the snow had covered the ground with brilliant white marked by the hoofs and wheel-tracks made by the departing guests.

She sat down to pull on her riding boots, blinking as her eyes began to sting. For a moment the temptation to lie down again with the comfortable probability of Brent's having already instructed Mary Redfeather to take the children on to his spread proved almost overwhelming. The bedside lamp burnt out with a little splutter, leaving a delicate spiral of smoke to pierce the half-light.

But the room was filling with smoke! It crept inexorably from the minute cracks between the panels of the wardrobe, making her retch. Flora turned and saw the first tiny flames outline the wardrobe itself, breathed in, as she coughed into full wakefulness, the acrid smell of slow-burning fire.

There was a tall ewer of water in the adjoining room. She had the sense to fetch it and carry it into the bedroom. She wrenched open the wardrobe door with the tip of her boot as she flung the contents of the ewer into the space within where smouldering garments had twisted into grotesque and half-blackened shapes.

Had there been a draught the flames would have billowed out. As it was they sizzled horribly as they died, showers of sparks landing on the carpet where they pitted the wool with tiny black-rimmed holes.

There was water also in the basin. She lunged that in and drenched the remaining flames, which were sending wicked little tongues through every crack in the wood.

Flora bent and saw through the haze of diminishing smoke two candles, almost burnt out, which had been placed neatly at the back of the lowest section of the wardrobe. By some chance they had remained almost upright, their wicks blackened, their wax still fuelling the fire that ate through the wood and the long shreds of silk, wool and cotton which were almost all that remained of her new clothes.

The wood was still too hot to touch but she knew even before she seized the poker from the hearth and levered up what remained of the bottom of the wardrobe that the sheaf of papers she had secreted there would be nothing but blackened and fragile shards, the proof of Brent's land sales to some of his Peoria neighbours eaten away by white hot ash and burning pieces of wooden panel.

There was no point in raising the alarm. Flora emptied the last of the water into the wreckage of her clothes and stood numbly staring at the devastation.

The bedroom door opened and closed as a footstep sounded softly behind her.

'What happened here?' Tina asked.

'Someone set my garments on fire,' Flora

said, groping towards a chair and reaching for a handkerchief to wipe her streaming eyes. 'It burned very slowly but it did a great deal of damage. I slept heavily, because I was tired and maybe because of the smoke seeping into the room. Tina, I have something to do — a message to deliver.'

'I'll see to this.' Tina spoke calmly. 'I'll get it cleared before your uncle's about.'

'Who could have set a slow burning fire to damage my clothes?' Flora wailed in utter bewilderment. To her surprise the housekeeper nodded.

'Late last night when everybody was making tracks for home,' she said, 'I saw Minnie coming out of this room. I guessed she'd left a cloak here or something.'

'Minnie Hargreaves,' Flora said. 'Of course.'

She saw again in her mind's eye Minnie, coming down the stairs with a pleased smile on her face, shaking hands and thanking her for a pleasant evening. Minnie had come briefly into the hall and seen her intended husband kiss Flora as they sat together on the stairs. Minnie knew nothing of the copies of the land sale documents concealed in the wardrobe. She had merely acted out of spite and jealousy to deprive someone she viewed as a potential rival of her garments and had presumably never given a thought to what might have occurred had the fire spread beyond the wardrobe.

'I'd better go.' Flora said. She pulled on her cloak, tying the strings of the hood. Tina merely nodded, her expression unfathomable.

Flora left the room and walked quietly towards the back stairs that gave access to the stables by way of the side door.

A sound from below halted her. She drew back, flattening herself against the wall, hearing a male voice, quiet but filled with authority, from below.

'Detachment make ready to mount.'

Flora risked a swift glance through the banisters. In the side hall below half a dozen of the Chicago guests stood, evening dress and lacy cravats now exchanged for uniform tunics with insignia on the shoulders. They carried long rifles and pistols were strapped to their sides.

Flora edged back along the corridor, resisting the urge to reopen her bedroom door. Tina would find out what was happening soon enough if she hadn't already guessed it.

The main hall was deserted and dim. Flora went softly down the stairs and drew the bolts noiselessly on the front door, shutting it with equal caution behind her. It would be much too risky to go to the stables to saddle up Moonlight or Bess, since she had no desire to be seen by the militia — erstwhile guests at the dance who now, in the dark dawn of a winter morning, clearly had matters other than dancing on their minds.

At the main gates she turned towards the village, stumbling in the snow, her face already chilled by the bitter wind. Through the wind, like a melody sobbed in time with its wailing, came a low keening sound mingled with shouts and the occasional high-pitched cry of a woman.

Wagons were drawn up along the stream and elderly women, shawls over their heads and a few possessions spilling out of canvas bags, were being herded by a couple of soldiers. There were only four wagons, obviously for the very old, the very young and the sick.

Other Indians were being herded along the track, clutching what they had managed to salvage from their homes. Small children clung to their mothers' skirts, clearly wanting to know what they were doing out in the cold with men in uniforms to chivvy them along. A young woman with her baby in a birch-bark sling went past, an older child stumbling at her heels.

She guessed now what had been decided at the Chicago meeting. She knew now why her uncle's guests had ridden here, taking advantage of the fact that the able-bodied Indian men were away on their hunting trip. For a dreadful moment she felt her uncle's guilt reach out to stain her.

'Get a move on, do!' One of the militia spoke wearily as a woman lost her footing and fell to her knees, then scrabbled in the snow for the basket she'd dropped.

'Where are you taking these people?' Flora tugged at the soldier's arm.

He turned a face she recognized from the previous evening.

'Miss Scott, what gives you the right . . . ?' His bluster died as swiftly as it had risen and he said flatly, 'We're under orders, Miss Scott.'

'But the removal had been delayed until Spring!'

'The City Council decided differently, ma'am. Excuse me.' He turned away again.

Flora ploughed on towards Brent's spread. Surely he had managed to speak to Mary Redfeather before he'd ridden to Spirit Wolf Place!

'Mary Redfeather! Mary Redfeather!'

The wind blew the words back into her

face as she fought her way towards the house.

Mary Redfeather lay on the path, her cloak and skirt brilliantly red against the whiteness. Shaking her and crying over and over in his shrill little voice one of her smallest children crouched.

'Shot while resisting arrest, ma'am.' A soldier came up, pushing her aside with little ceremony and bending to lift the child. 'Can't help admiring some of 'em, can you? Kept on shouting that the O'Brien place was sanctuary. Well, there's no sanctuary now.'

'The child . . . ?' Flora found herself gasping.

'He'll go along with the others.' The soldier looked at her for the first time. 'This is no place for a lady. Miss Scott, isn't it? Very sad business but they'll be all right once they're out of the territory. Fine people some of them!'

'You've no right —' Flora said angrily.

'It'd be a good idea if you didn't go shouting about it,' the soldier said. He scooped up the crying toddler and strode towards the wagons.

Brent had obviously delivered his message before riding out to call back the hunting party but for Mary Redfeather the warning had been useless. There had been no sanctuary anywhere. Flora bent and tried to rouse her, knowing already it was useless. One of her arms was still curved as if it held a child.

There was no way of stopping this, no way of delaying it even.

She turned and walked back on to the track, resisting the temptation to go into the barn and find Tessa, who would still be concealed there in the cellar and must be terrified if any noises reached her from above ground.

The village proper was silent still, save for the glow of a lamp here and there. Flora saw that a few windows had been opened and she could discern faces watching in the strengthening daylight but word that the removals were to take place today must have already spread and most people preferred to remain prudently out of sight.

The Eliots, to do them justice, were not remaining aloof. Mr Eliot stood arguing fiercely with a soldier while his wife was busily handing up loaves of bread and bottles of what looked like hot coffee to those already packed into the wagons.

'This is against all justice, sir!' Mr Eliot was exclaiming. 'For years my dear wife and I have sought to care for the souls of these poor people, to lead them to the way of Christian compassion and goodwill to all races. We must not forget they are human beings, sir!'

'They'll be better off where they're going,' the militiaman said.

'My dear, we are doing no good here,' Mrs Eliot said. 'Flora! You have seen what is going on?'

Flora nodded curtly.

'To wait until the men were off hunting and then to bring in the militia!' Mrs Eliot shook her greying head in distress. 'Your uncle will be shocked to learn that some of his friends from Chicago are actually in the militia!'

'I don't think he will be,' Flora said. 'Excuse me.'

She went on past them, hearing the creaking of the wagons as they began to move, the cries of the women and children fading into a bewildered silence.

'Miss Flora!'

To her surprise she turned to see Charles Fontaine coming towards her.

'Mr Fontaine.'

'Minnie — that is, Miss Hargreaves,' he said, reddening slightly, 'is in the schoolhouse. Some of the children left drawings and suchlike there and she became rather upset when she realized that some of her pupils might not be returning. She is very fond of children you know.'

'Yes indeed.'

'She has asked me to convey an apology to you. Apparently she was a little out of temper last night, which is hardly surprising when O'Brien seemed preoccupied with other matters, but though she didn't specify I gained the impression she may have spoken harshly to you.'

'Please tell her the apology is accepted,' Flora said. 'Good day, Mr Fontaine.'

She walked on, finding a bleak humour in the situation. Minnie had set candles to destroy the fashionable dresses owned by the woman she regarded as a potential rival, a stupid action she must now be regretting and she would never know that she had destroyed something more valuable than garments — the copies of the land sales to those Peoria who had owned their little farms legally.

Tina was in the hall when she came up the steps, opening the front door and admitting her with a finger to her lips and a gesture indicating that she should go quietly upstairs.

In her bedroom the scorched, soaked wardrobe had gone and the open windows through which the wind now blew strongly had dispersed the smoke. What remained of her garments that might be wearable was laid out across the bed.

'The Peoria women, old people and children are being driven out,' Flora said tensely. 'Mary Redfeather is dead. Will the wagons meet the hunters returning, do you suppose?'

'No. Your uncle is at breakfast,' Tina informed her. 'He thinks you are sleeping late. He told me as we sat down to coffee that the Peoria are to be taken by a different route. The hunters are not due back yet — or did Brent ride out to warn them?'

'He rode out but there's no sign of them yet. How did — ?'

'He didn't confide in me,' Tina said, 'but since he left fairly early it didn't take much for me to guess. Brent always did do the right thing when it came to it. Miss Flora, there were a lot of burnt and sodden papers in the wardrobe. Were they important?'

'Not any more,' Flora said dully. 'Tina, you know where Tessa Fontaine is?'

Tina nodded. 'Brent showed me the hiding place under the barn on his spread a couple of years back,' she said. 'He's my stepson, remember, and he always was a friend to me.'

'And my uncle? Tina, do you mean to stay here now?' Flora pressed. 'You must be aware that my uncle knew what was planned — or did he tell you?'

'He told me nothing but I've eyes and ears and I know a military man when I see one,' the housekeeper said.

'And you didn't think to warn . . . ?'

'I learned a long time ago to look out for myself,' Tina said. 'I'm part Apache, Miss Flora. The Peoria mean nothing to me.'

'And you mean nothing to yourself either!' Flora said sharply. 'You have no respect for yourself if you continue to live here under my uncle's protection!'

'You're here,' Tina said.

'But not for very much longer! I shall inform my uncle that very soon I shall be going back to England since no suitors were found to offer for me.'

She stopped short, remembering the two tickets to Bloomington in her purse.

'What is it?' The other was looking at her enquiringly.

'Did Brent tell you that Tessa and I planned to catch the Bloomington stage at the second bend in the river?'

'He did and a damn fool idea he thought it. If the stage is ambushed then people will be killed, including yourself maybe. It's his wife Smiling Moon needs alive, not another white woman for the soldiers to bring back.'

'I cannot let her travel alone!'

'Her brother won't bestir himself to find her, you know,' Tina said. She spoke casually but her brow furrowed as if an idea wrestled for expression.

'Best go down and have your breakfast,' she said at last. 'I'll finish up here.'

Flora did as the housekeeper suggested. It was useless trying to argue with Tina, who cared more for her own comfort and security than for her self-respect or the plight of others.

Her uncle was just finishing his steak and eggs and looked up with a smile as she sat down.

'Did you sleep well after the excitement of last night?' he enquired genially.

'Well enough. Your Chicago guests left early, I understand?'

'Ah! You have already been listening to servants' gossip! It was decided at the meeting that the wisest course of action would be to start the removals —'

'I suspect,' Flora broke in irritably, 'that it was actually decided some time ago. Militia don't just turn up from Fort Dearborn equipped with evening suits as well as uniforms and weapons and their accommodation was made ready days ago.'

'And as an intelligent young woman you will understand the necessity to plan well ahead and to act once the final ratification was agreed. And the young men were indeed taken with you, my dear, though so far no offers have been received.'

'Too busy piling Indians into wagons,' Flora said. 'Uncle, I have decided that I will not be here for very much longer. Before next spring I hope to be bound for England again.'

'Naturally you will wish to visit your mother —'

'And I won't be returning,' she said stonily. 'I honestly don't want to inherit your grand house or your flourishing grain business or your horses or — or anything. And forgive me, but I've completely lost my appetite for any breakfast!'

She rose, dropped a curtsy and went out, leaving him to glower after her.

She would walk back into the village, she decided. The departing Indians had been given only a few minutes to collect their possessions. It might be possible to send some of their things after them.

The wheel-tracks were still deep ruts in the snow. A few Indians who had evidently avoided the exodus milled about aimlessly. They were elderly people who looked lost and bewildered.

'Flora, there you are!' Minnie Hargreaves was hurrying towards her. 'Mrs Eliot and I are going to check on the few who weren't taken west and try to set up some kind of relief centre for them and see if any possessions left behind can be salvaged from their houses and sent after them.'

'I had the same idea,' Flora admitted.

'Oh, Charles Fontaine is helping us organize everything in the schoolhouse,' Minnie said.

'Oh.'

'So there really is little you can do though your uncle might be willing to let us use a couple of wagons.'

'I'll ask him when I next see him.'

Feeling definitely surplus to requirements she walked on. Minnie Hargreaves was no female villain after all, she thought, but she was so pleased with her own desire to help that her very presence was an annoyance. As she moved off Minnie's voice echoed after her:

'Oh, and I'm sorry about — it was very stupid of me.'

Flora raised her hand in acknowledgement of the belated apology and went on towards

Brent's house.

There was a thin coating of ice on the stepping-stones of the stream. She crossed making her way as briskly as the slippery surface allowed to the dwelling where she saw that the motionless figure of Mary Redfeather still lay though someone had covered her with a blanket.

A solitary militiaman, rifle cocked, barred her path.

'Sorry, miss. I'm to wait here until the relief arrives. We aim to pick up a few strays that hid out in the woods and the grain barns and send them after the rest.'

'And Mary Redfeather?'

'The squaw? I covered her with a blanket,' he said. 'Seemed more respectful somehow. You know when I was a little lad we lived quite close to an Indian village and I used to play with the children there. Nice people they were too! Seems kind of sad that this should be going on. Still I reckon the bigwigs know what they're about.'

He broke off as a rider galloped past him and leapt from his horse followed by a slighter figure.

John Redfeather had knelt by his wife, tugging at the blanket while his son stood as if carved from stone at his side.

A long keening sound rent the air.

'Seems like they really do feel things badly,' the militiaman said.

'He was her husband and she was my friend,' Flora said.

'I reckon I'll take a short stroll, let him get his grieving over,' he returned.

Standing with his rifle he looked suddenly very young.

'John Redfeather!' Flora hurried to his side. 'There's nothing you can do for Mary. Your other children have been taken in the wagons. You will be taken too if you linger here. Go with your boy after the wagons. The children cannot survive out on the prairie without father or mother. At least they'll be adopted by others, perhaps from other tribes, but Mary would want her family to stay together.'

'I rode on ahead,' he said dully, rising but not looking at her. 'Brent and the others are not far behind.

'Will they fight?' she queried fearfully.

He shook his head.

'No, ma'am. The Peoria spent their shot in the hunt,' he said. 'They'll join up with their wives and young ones and share the meat.'

'I am so sorry,' she said helplessly.

'I brought down a fat buck,' John Redfeather said. 'First time I hit anything in my

life! I was all fired up to tell Mary about it.
Hell of a world, ain't it, Miss Flora?'

EIGHTEEN

It was too depressing to stay any longer in the village. People were venturing out of their houses now, many looking distressed as it sank in that their peaceable Peoria neighbours had gone, others with half-concealed smiles of satisfaction. Flora had reached the gates of Scott Place when she saw the hunting party riding across the snowy fields, the sudden glitter of the emerging sun flaming Brent's hair as he rode with them, his eyes fixed on the way ahead so that he would not have seen her, diminished in the distance, as she paused.

'There you are, my dear!' Uncle Frank was emerging from the study, cloaked and with his riding boots on.

'Nearly all the Peoria have been taken away!' Flora burst out. 'The men are just coming back from the hunt but there will be little they can do save catch up with their families.'

'Which is where they should be,' her uncle said comfortably. 'Believe me, but this will work out for the best. Have you spoken to Brent yet? I shall have a word to say to him myself when I see him. His conduct last night was far from gentlemanly. Minnie Hargreaves has just cause for complaint but on the other hand — Charles Fontaine having decided to disown his sister — ?'

He cast her a smiling glance.

'Minnie was sorry about the Indians too,' Flora said, not answering his question.

'We are all sorry,' he rejoined unctuously, 'but progress cannot be delayed for ever. Now I have an apology to make but necessity takes me back to Chicago. Some of those little farms abandoned by the Indians will be put up for auction very soon.'

'And you are going to bid for them? Uncle, haven't you enough land already?' she burst out.

'A man can never own too much land,' he replied. 'I shall be away for a couple of days. If you see O'Brien tell him that I expect to meet with him when I return. A manager ought to keep his employer informed of his whereabouts, don't you think?'

'Some of those farms were legally bought by the Peoria. Don't they at least deserve some compensation?'

'Bought by their parents,' he said. 'Very irregular transactions went on in the old days. Of course if any can prove legal ownership — but what use will they have for money, my dear? I must go. We shall have a chat when I return.'

Brent had sold small plots to the Indians and deposited copies of the deeds in Bloomington. The originals had been reduced to blackened, sodden shreds through an act of spite. Flora stood aside as her uncle went out, feeling numb and sick.

One of the maids came out of the dining room, her expression downcast.

'Will they be sending us away?' she asked in her strongly accented English.

'I'm sure your place here is safe,' Flora assured her.

'You didn't have no breakfast,' the girl said.

'Then I shall take a very early lunch,' Flora said.

Later, having forced down food she really didn't savour, she went upstairs and saw that the room now boasted a new wardrobe doubtless brought from another chamber. The spoilt clothes had gone and her remaining possessions looked somewhat meagre in the space.

'If Mr Scott asks any questions,' Tina said,

coming through from the bathroom, 'I shall say there was an accident with a candle, but I don't think he will. As long as the household runs smoothly he does not ask questions.'

'He's gone to Chicago,' Flora said. 'Mary Redfeather is dead.'

'Yes. I was told. The Indians must look out for themselves,' Tina said dispassionately.

'And Tessa Fontaine? She is still . . . ?'

'In Brent's cellar? No, during the upheaval when the soldiers came she was taken to a safer place,' Tina said, with a hint of satisfaction.

'Where?'

'One of the grain stores out on the edge of the village. Early tomorrow morning you can make your way to the stage.'

'For Bloomington,' Flora said blankly. Somehow or other the proposed trip to Bloomington had receded into the back of her mind.

'In dark cloaks and bonnets you will be safe enough. Mr Scott is away to Chicago and Charles Fontaine has made it known he has no further use for his sister.'

'Do you suppose the stage will be ambushed?'

'Who knows?' The housekeeper sounded

weary. 'I don't care.'

'You don't care about anything, do you?' Flora said. 'Not about the Peoria or Tessa or even yourself!'

'I've kept my place here for twelve years!' Tina flashed, with a sudden narrowing of her sloe black eyes.

'As a housekeeper companion to a man who would never dream of marrying you?'

'You think your uncle would marry a Mestiza?' Tina said angrily. 'Even Comanches would think hard before diluting their blood with Apache! As for half-breeds, why do you think I never told —'

She stopped abruptly, slim brown hand flying too late to her mouth.

'Never told whom what?' Flora demanded.

'The star the Kickapoo woman gave you . . .' She hesitated again.

'You wear an exactly similar star. Who gave it to you? Was it — was it Brent, Tina?'

She recalled in vivid and disturbing detail the picture of them dancing together in the dark.

Tina sat down abruptly on the edge of the bed and drew the chain with its glittering token from beneath the high neck of her day dress.

'Daniel O'Brien gave me this,' she said. 'On the day we were married, the day that he died.'

'And the one given to me?' Flora pressed.

'Mine was given to Daniel by his first wife,' Tina said. 'He gave it to me in memory of her though we never met. The one you have was given to his first wife by Daniel O'Brien. An exchange of love tokens.'

'But how did a Kickapoo woman get hold of it?' Flora asked, puzzled.

'That we shall never know for certain,' said Tina. 'But you will remember that I suggested to you that the Kickapoo woman was likely a shaman — a wise woman?'

'Yes,' said Flora, still puzzled.

'It is clear that the Peoria and perhaps some others have been aware of your arrival and your doings in this place — people you have met, perhaps become close to —'

'Tessa . . . ? You . . . ?' Flora was still trying to make sense of Tina's words.

'And the Indians have ways of communicating, even over great distances and tribe between tribe,' Tina went on as though Flora had not interrupted. 'They will have seen you with Brent —'

'With *Brent . . . !*'

'My stepson, Brent. I think I should tell you now that Daniel O'Brien's first wife was a Comanche. He bought her from a Comanche chief in New Mexico. Such deals were not — are not — uncommon between the Mexican and American traders and the tribal chiefs — it was a way not only of acquiring a wife but of buying favour with the local tribes. But Daniel loved her very much. Singing Star was her name though he gave her the name of Estella. He married her down in Santa Fe, Miss Flora, and they exchanged tokens as is the custom. She died within the year bearing her babe. Brent is half-Comanche, Miss Flora! He's a half-breed! That was why Daniel came to the United States, to Pine Creek Ridge, and left his wife buried in Santa Fe. He wanted his son to be regarded as white, as full Irish!'

'Does Brent know?'

Tina shook her head. 'No. He was reared as white, Miss Flora, and the red hair helped. Twelve years ago Daniel went back to Santa Fe to pay his respects to his wife's memory and he met me. He married me, Miss Flora, because he was lonely and craving female company. Brent knows nothing of his mother. She died thirty years ago and he has never seen her grave.'

'Hasn't he the right to know?'

'I think that Daniel might have told him one day,' she said slowly. 'I kept silent when I first came here and I went on keeping silent. I know how hard it is to make your way in the world when you're a half-breed or a Mestiza. Maybe I kept silent too long. Then he and Minnie Hargreaves started courting. Miss Minnie was very upset when Charles Fontaine stopped seeing her because of his sister — that was his idea of being noble, and Mr Hargeaves did not want his only daughter connected to a local scandal. So I kept quiet. I tried to be a good friend to Brent. He's educated, Miss Flora, and he's going to prosper.'

'And he dances with you in the garden.'

'I like to dance sometimes,' Tina said. 'I used to dance in the tavern sometimes. That was where Daniel O'Brien first saw me. It was a hard life but the dancing was special. When I'm feeling low Brent often turns up, sensing my mood, and we dance and for a while I'm a girl again. It's nothing more than that, Miss Flora.'

'Does anyone else here know that Brent's half-Comanche?' Flora asked.

'Nobody, I thought. But now we must suppose that the Peoria here have received word,' Tina said. 'They would keep silent, anyway. Anyway I've the one star and you have the other. Seems to me that you might as well have both. Then it's up to you whether you tell Brent or not.'

'Why up to me?' Flora demanded.

'He's going to wed Minnie Hargreaves,' Tina said, unclasping her chain and handing it to the younger woman. 'You think she'd marry a half-breed Comanche when she stopped going out with Charles Fontaine because his sister wed a Peoria? And you might ask yourself another thing! Why did that Kickapoo woman give you the other star?'

'She was a — shaman, d'ye call it?'

'Maybe yes and maybe no.' Tina shrugged. 'All I know is what Daniel O'Brien told me when we met. He said his first wife had a cousin, kind of a solitary creature who used to read signs in the stars and such like but that's not the point. Point is that she tended her when Brent was born and saw to her burial. I reckon she took the star her cousin wore. I reckon that Daniel was too upset to notice or maybe he told her he was going to bring up his child as white and she hung on to something that might lead him back to his mother's tribe.'

'But why give the token to me?' Flora began and hesitated, remembering the night she had huddled terrified on the sacking while the Indians had argued amongst themselves. That was when Brent had ridden up, demanding that she be freed. The Kickapoo woman could have seen Brent's resemblance to his dead father — the red hair, heard him make his demand and jumped to the conclusion that he'd arrived to save his love from an unpleasant fate. That would explain why she had slipped the token into her hand and told her to give it to her true love.

Now she asked abruptly: 'Is Brent like his father in appearance?'

'Taller and slimmer in the hips,' Tina answered, 'but the living likeness in every other way. Anyrate the cousin of Singing Star was there in Santa Fe when the baby was named. Daniel told me that he never gave his son any Indian name.'

'And never told him the truth about his mother,' Flora said slowly, 'and you think I would?'

'I think he's the one you'd give the token to if you could see your way,' Tina told her. 'I took a real close look at that painting you ripped up. Seems to me a woman don't paint a man from memory and then rip it up if she's no feeling for him and she don't sit quiet on the stairs when he kisses her without asking leave. Seems to me you have a whole heap of thinking to do, Miss Flora.'

She dropped a faintly mocking curtsy and went out, leaving Flora with the chain in her hand.

This was an intolerable decision to have to make! She had to admit to herself that despite their sparring she relished his company and conversation, had felt her heart leap more than once when she had seen him approaching even when they'd ended by arguing. He'd intruded into her dreams just as he'd intruded into the picture she had tried to paint. Perhaps her feeling of dislike when she saw Minnie Hargreaves was prompted by more than her irritation at the other's smug and overbearing manner.

And Brent? He had made it increasingly plain that he was in no hurry to lead Minnie to the altar. Now she had only to speak a few words and the engagement would be broken. Minnie's father had objected to her walking out with a man whose sister had married a Peoria. What would he say to his own daughter wedding a half-breed?

After a while she rose and donned a clean high-necked dress and slipped the twin token over her head, concealing both under the bodice; her mind was in a ferment as to how to act.

For the moment, it was plain, she was not in a position to do anything. What she ought to do, she decided reluctantly, was await events.

The snow had settled and the sky had lightened to a clear pale blue. Outside the air held tiny crystals of ice.

It was later in the afternoon when, gazing aimlessly through the sitting room window and half-wishing she was a servant who would at last have domestic tasks to occupy her she saw Brent clad in buckskins riding up the drive and round to the stables. She had only a few moments to compose herself before Tina was announcing him in her customary formal accent.

'This is a bad business,' he said without preamble. 'If I had started out after the hunting party sooner I might have persuaded them to return and mount some kind of resistance. As it is most of their shot is spent and it's two generations anyway since the Peoria went on the war path. Most of the men have collected what they could of what was left behind and ridden to catch up with their families. At least they have some fresh-killed meat to tide them over. You look tired.'

He broke off abruptly, staring at her.

'The dance,' she said, 'was somewhat fatiguing. My uncle is returned to Chicago.'

'To bid for the Indian farms. So I heard. Happily I registered half a dozen spreads in the council and you have the originals.'

'No,' Flora said in a small voice. 'I no longer have them.'

'What!' he took a step towards her, anger and astonishment mingling in his tanned face. 'What the hell happened? You weren't so foolish as to trust them to your uncle?'

She could tell him now that Minnie, spurred by jealousy and spite, had unwittingly destroyed them. But Minnie had apologized after a fashion and had no notion of the real damage she'd done.

'There was an accident with a candle,' she said at last. 'I'm terribly sorry.'

'An accident with a candle?' he echoed incredulously. 'You're a fool if you expect me to believe that! Did you hand them over to your uncle for safe keeping or decide not to risk hiding them yourself or what? What the devil possessed you — ?'

'Don't swear at me!' Flora said, breaking free of him as he seized her wrist. 'I did think I'd kept them safe but there was an accident with a candle and they — burned up. Brent, I am truly sorry but there are the documents in official hands still —'

'Which will count for nothing if the wrong people get hold of them! I should've given them to Tina to conceal but I was reluctant to subject her to the risk of having your uncle discover them, and Tina has little sympathy for the Peoria anyway.'

'And you have a great deal of sympathy with them,' Flora said.

'So did my father! He welcomed those who came to settle here, helped them with their sowing and reaping, lent them money when he had it to tide them over.'

'I said I was sorry!' Flora cried, suddenly terrified she was going to burst into humiliating tears. 'Meanwhile there's Tessa to be considered.'

'Where is Tessa?'

He seemed to be still holding a further explosion of rage within himself as he asked her.

'She has been taken —'

'By the militia? Surely not! You didn't take it into your head to send her off alone on a wild-goose chase to find Smiling Moon?'

'I take it you didn't find her in the hiding-space under the barn?' Flora said.

'I did not!'

'Tina has her safely hidden in one of the grain stores on the edge of the village. She could have told you herself if you hadn't rushed in here like a —'

She stopped abruptly, on the verge of saying 'like a wild Comanche'.

'Without being seen?'

'She says so.'

'Tina knew where she was since she helped smuggle her there,' Brent said. 'She would've been wiser to leave her where she was.'

'About that you'd best ask Tina!' Flora snapped, her courage returning. 'I think she was right. Brent, the militia were my uncle's Chicago guests, as you surmised. They weren't looking for Tessa but rounding up Peoria and the Peoria women were wailing and their children crying and there were shots fired. Even under the barn floor Tessa would've heard something of what was going on. And it's cold, Brent. She had food and blankets but no fire. How long could she have survived there?'

'Then Tina acted with good sense,' he said reluctantly.

'And you did not!' Flora said stormily. 'It was a crazy notion to go haring after the hunting party in the hope of reaching them in time to bring them back to resist the soldiers. How could they have stopped what happened? They are farmers, not warriors.'

Brent looked suddenly older and sadder, the faint lines about his dark eyes more clearly marked. He looked, she thought, in feature at least, more like an Indian. In years to come when the russet hair was grey and his skin more lined he would look less like an Irishman and more like the people of his mother. For the first time she felt fear for him. All his life he had lived with Indians around him, felt sympathy with them, worked with them. Had that been an instinctive emotion that had troubled him so that, without knowing quite why, he had held aloof from active defiance on their behalf?

'Brent . . .' Flora said tentatively.

'I must go and see Minnie,' he said. 'I neglected her last night. My mind and heart were . . . otherwise engaged. I wish you and Tessa a safe journey to Bloomington tomorrow. You will be gone before your uncle returns from Chicago, I suppose. You realize you risk losing the promise of his estate? Well, that's your choice. Good day, Flora.'

NINETEEN

The rest of the day and the night that followed dragged on. Flora suspected that Brent would have gone first to the grain store to find Tessa and ensure she was unharmed. The militia had gone and by now the hunting party would have caught up with their families. Had there been a skirmish between them and the armed guards? From everything she had heard there would not have been. The Peoria were peaceable.

The great house seemed silent as if it waited for something. Around it the deserted maize fields lay under their blanket of snow and when she opened one of the windows crisp cold air stung her face. She wondered what her uncle would say when he returned and found her gone.

He would surely guess that her journey to Bloomington held some secret purpose. About the journey itself she didn't want to speculate. At some point the stage might be ambushed and Tessa taken, but what they might do about the other passengers remained unclear.

She hesitated as to whether to leave a note for her uncle. What could she possibly say in it?

Dear Uncle Frank, I am taking a trip to Bloomington with Tessa Fontaine. She is hoping to rejoin her husband and I am going as her companion.

Better to slip away in silence and make what explanation she could if and when she returned.

Tina made no further appearance. It was as if, having told Flora the truth about Brent's mother, she had disposed of the star tokens and washed her hands of the whole matter.

When, weary with her own company, she went into the kitchen after a supper served by a downcast and obviously uneasy maid she found the housekeeper, the hem of her skirts damp with snow, warming herself before the fire.

'I took the liberty of sending the maids into the village to gather what news they could of the doings there,' she said. 'Some of them have families who've been forced out and they will have to choose whether to follow them or stay here and work for Mr Scott. I reckon that most will stay. Better a secure place than a cold prairie!'

'Have you seen Tessa?' Flora asked tensely.

'That's where I've just been. She's in the second grain store on the edge of the south field. I took her extra blankets since she's another night to spend there. She's all right, Miss Flora. She looks delicate but you don't live with the Peoria for ten years without toughening up. She was real upset about the soldiers coming and real relieved that her brother has finally washed his hands of her.'

'Brent?'

The housekeeper shot her a faintly mocking glance.

'Brent's been helping out all day, sorting stuff, getting Mary Redfeather buried. Not many of her people left to sing the death song for her soul but a few came and Mrs Eliot brought food and a shawl to be buried with Mary for her journey to the next world. I didn't reckon any of the ladies round here took any interest in Indian customs.'

'Was Minnie there?'

'Clearing the schoolhouse.' There was another mocking glance. 'Then she and Brent went off together; I didn't notice where. Maybe she's getting him to buy her a ring.'

'Thank you, Tina. I shall have an early night,' Flora said with some dignity. 'I shall rise before dawn and go over to the grain store —'

'I'll see nobody watches you leave,' Tina said.

Flora went soberly to her room. There was no point in thinking about Brent and Minnie. There was no point in wondering whether she was wise to accompany Tessa on the stage. There was some possibility that the Peoria would attack en route and not hang about in Bloomington to meet Tessa. Either choice held dangers for everybody. If they ambushed the stage they'd be unlikely to leave witnesses and in the town there would surely be a military presence who would keep a close eye on any gathering of warlike-seeming Indians.

The idea of tamely undressing and getting into bed to lie wakeful for half the night was not an appealing one. Instead when she eventually entered her room, where a fire burned brightly, she donned her warmest clothes — a thick riding skirt and long-sleeved jacket and a heavy shawl that would conceal her features should anybody be about.

She stretched out on the bed and closed her eyes. Clear images flashed before them. She saw herself arriving in Chicago and the young Indian lifting her cases aside; Brent offering her the whiskey-flavoured water as they drove to Pine Creek Ridge; herself and Brent frying supper in his house. She saw the glinting moon on the oak tree and Brent riding to find her when the Indians had abducted her. She heard Brent arguing with her, scolding her for giving Moonlight his head, felt him kissing her cheek as near to her mouth as made no difference. Brent, Brent. . . .

Someone was shaking her awake. She opened her eyes and sat up with a jerk as Tina, lamp in hand, stood back.

'It's gone six, Miss Flora,' she said. 'I reckoned the least I could do was walk with you to rouse Miss Tessa.'

'It's you who should be making the trip, not I!' Flora said.

'To travel to and then carry on further west to Santa Fe?' Something wistful lay beneath her quiet voice. 'Miss Flora, truth to tell I wish you'd never come here! First I reckoned you were all set to take over the house and then I found out you weren't about to push me from my place and that made me feel more friendly. But you have a managing way with you for all that! You say things that make other folk think, Miss Flora, make them discontented with their lot.'

'You were not contented with my uncle when I arrived!' Flora said, pulling on her boots.

'True, but I told myself I was,' Tina said. 'Now I'm not sure, not sure at all! But in New Mexico — what's there but the taverna. My family's long scattered. I've no money.'

'My uncle doesn't pay you?'

'He gave me a house to run and himself to pleasure. Maybe it's time to ask him for a regular wage when he gets back from Chicago. Then I can save a little until I can make a fresh start. Meanwhile, we'd best be getting over to Miss Tessa.'

'Wait a moment!' Impulsively Flora crossed to the dressing table and took up the flat case.

'We'd best hurry, Miss Flora. That stage won't wait for late —'

'My uncle gave me these,' Flora interrupted. 'Garnets set in gold. You could sell them in Bloomington maybe?'

'For a good sum,' Tina said, 'but they belong to you.'

'Now they belong to you,' Flora said,

pressing the case into the housekeeper's hands. 'They will buy you further passage down to Santa Fe, give you a fresh start there! Maybe you'll find some of your family or start your own with a man willing to offer you marriage.'

'Your uncle —'

'Isn't it time you fretted about yourself? Tina, you don't love —'

'I only stayed on because Daniel O'Brien asked me to be a friend to his son.'

'And Brent's a grown man, about to wed Minnie Hargreaves. Take them and the tickets and go with Tessa. If the Indians attack in order to get her they're less likely to attack a Mestiza surely?'

'I wouldn't go trusting one of these Indians as far as I could throw him,' Tina said.

'But you will go, take your future in your own hands?'

Tina stared at her for a moment, then suddenly laughed.

'Five minutes for me to pack a small bag,' she said. 'You ain't just managing, Miss Flora, you're downright bossy!'

Fifteen minutes later they were moving through the still-shadowed maize fields towards the grain stores. Tessa was waiting, pale as the snow with her blond hair smoothed under a dark bonnet and shawl.

'Is all well? My brother hasn't . . . ?' Her tone was anxious.

'Your brother won't seek you out a second time,' Flora said. 'You look cold!'

'I wish him well.'

Tessa's face was filled for a moment with sadness. Then her smile was like the sun breaking through the clouds as she said, 'But I want to return to Smiling Moon, to my own Peoria people.'

And so saying she hurried ahead of her companions over the freezing surface of the field, the ends of her shawl flying out behind her as if she were a bird winging her way to her mate.

The river lay quiet under the rising dawn. At its second bend the small hostelry, marking the spot where passengers might be picked up.

'If the stage is attacked,' Tina said in an undertone to Flora, 'you will surely hear about it. If not then you may hear nothing. I plan to go to Santa Fe if that's possible. Tessa must trust to luck. Goodbye, Miss Flora.'

They had barely arrived in time. The stage was making deep ruts in the snow as the horses strained towards them and the driver, greatcoat fastened and hat pulled low, drew them up.

'Two passengers for Bloomington,' Tina said, showing the tickets.

'Climb aboard, ladies.' He reached down for their small bags. 'I'm not hanging around this trip. I've a mind to get us down to Bloomington in one piece.'

Other travellers within the coach were sleepily making room for the newcomers as they got in, making it obvious from the window seat accorded to Tessa and the less comfortable centre place given up to Tina that they regarded them as mistress and maid.

Flora had time only to raise her hand as Tina, leaning from her seat, called through the half-open door:

'Miss Flora, we all have a right to know our beginnings!'

Then they were gone in a flurry of snow and the ruts made a track that was as quickly iced over again. Flora watched it out of sight and then turned back, bending into the icy wind that blew down from the ridges above the river where the trees lifted their snow-laden arms to the grey sky.

No doubt her uncle would be home either that evening or the next day. He would be annoyed to find that Tina had left — annoyed, Flora thought. Not sad, probably not even very angry. For twelve years she had been nothing more than a convenience after all.

The absence of the garnets might not even have to be explained. One did not, after all, wear such jewels to go and sit in the sewing circle or help out at a church fête. In time the restless energy within her would be tamed into the quiet resignation of settled spinsterhood.

That prospect cheered her so little that she broke into a run. Suddenly she felt the ground beneath her sliding away as her boot caught on the half-frozen stump of a felled tree and she slid inelegantly on to her back.

'Bed,' said Brent, riding to her side and dismounting, 'is the place for lying down. Not the frozen wastes of a ploughed maize field! What the devil are you doing out here anyway?'

'Admiring the scenery,' Flora said crossly, accepting his hand unwillingly.

'And seeing Tessa Fontaine off on the stage too, I daresay. At least you had the sense not to go with her!'

'Is that why you rode this way? To find out if I'd gone too?'

Flora scrambled to her feet and scowled at him. 'Tina went with her,' she said.

'Tina!' For an instant he looked startled. Then he nodded. 'Yes, Tina ought to have gone years ago but sometimes we make prisons for ourselves. I saw her briefly yesterday after I got Tessa Fontaine smuggled into the grain store. With all the commotion going on it was easier than I thought it would be. She didn't tell me she was leaving.'

'She only decided this morning. Did she say anything else?'

'She wished me well in my marriage,' Brent said. 'She also said you might have something to tell me.'

Under the high neck of her dress the tokens on their chain were cool against her skin. How easy it would be to tell him the truth, knowing that Minnie Hargreaves would never agree to marry a half-breed even in the unlikely event of her father approving.

'I wish you joy in your marriage,' she said.

'Tomorrow I shall set off for Bloomington,' he said, not responding to her good wishes. 'If the land rights are still properly filed there and haven't unaccountably disappeared then I shall press either for the right of my tenants to return or, if that's forbidden, for compensation. I doubt if I will get either but I must try.'

'And Minnie agrees?'

'I haven't discussed it with her. She's not

without heart, you know, even if she never went all the way in championing the Indians.'

'But you have. Will that trouble her after you are —'

'Minnie asked me to release her from our betrothal,' Brent said.

'Someone told her?'

'She was being courted by Charles Fontaine before his sister was found and brought back. It should've been an occasion for rejoicing but Tessa made it clear that she regarded her marriage as a binding one, thought of herself as a Peoria. Charles, who has an overdeveloped sense of what is proper, withdrew his suit and —'

'And now? She doesn't know that Tessa has left?'

'You forget,' he reminded her. 'Tessa's absence was discovered two nights ago. Charles declared publicly that he had disowned her and refused to organize a search party to find and bring her back. So, as Minnie reminded me last evening, that gives Charles the right to mingle freely in society again. In my view he might have mingled before with no more than a few raised eyebrows, but Fontaine was always very correct.'

'Minnie wants to marry Charles Fontaine?

Did you —'

'Gave them both my blessing with a feeling of relief,' he said cheerfully. 'I was so sorry for her when Charles withdrew his friendship — sorry for them both, actually. Their attitude is as out of date as anything I can imagine. Anyway I was fond of her, still am, but I was beginning to see that we wouldn't have suited. In due course Charles will propose and they will raise a brood of well-behaved children and lead happy lives. She was never really for me.'

'And now?'

They had reached the track that led past the gates of Scott Place to the village.

'When the spring comes,' he said, 'I've a mind to go down to Santa Fe.'

'To find Tina?'

'Tina is capable of looking after herself. Always was. No, I want to pay my respects at the graves of my parents. My mother died when I was born, you know, and my father came east again immediately, leaving her down there. It was eighteen years before he went back to Santa Fe to pay his respects to her remains and on that occasion he met Tina. Being lonely — but you know the rest. I would like to be reassured that the headstones are properly inscribed. My mother's name was Estella, you know.'

413

'Singing Star,' Flora said.

'Who?' Brent stopped and looked at her.

She had spoken without thinking and it was too late to retract. Planting her booted feet firmly on the icy ground she said steadily:

'Your mother was a Comanche woman, Brent. Her name was Singing Star but your father called her Estella. When I went to Chicago with you and Minnie and tried to find Smiling Moon —'

'And got captured and nearly married off for your pains,' he broke in.

'There was a Kickapoo woman there with the other Indians.'

'A wise woman — a kind of fortune teller. Saw her. What of it?'

'She slipped me a little gold star,' Flora said, drawing it from her neckline. 'Tina had been given its twin by your father. They were the tokens he had exchanged with your mother when he wed her. I don't know how the wise woman came to have the other star. Perhaps she tended Singing Star when you were born and took it then. Anyway she gave it to me.'

'Why?' he said blankly.

'I suppose she saw you ride up to demand my release and jumped to the —'

'Wrong conclusion,' he finished for her.

'Hardly likely she'd've recognize me unless her second sight is more powerful than I'm willing to believe. She meant you to give it to me, I daresay, as a token of —'

'She told me to give it to my true love.'

'Very charming custom. Well, when you find someone who's ready to make an offer for a self-willed young woman due to inherit a fortune, give it to him.'

'I'm giving them both to you. You may do with them what you will!' Anger had bubbled up in her, making her suddenly feel reckless. 'Both tokens were the marks of love between your parents and what use, if any, you make of them is your business.'

'Probably none at all,' he said.

'You're not ashamed surely of being part Comanche?' she challenged.

'I'm not exactly used to the idea yet,' he said. 'No, I think it probably explains a few things to me about myself. I've always had a sympathy for the Indians, for their way of life, but never felt I could give myself wholeheartedly to their cause. My father brought me up to be white, had me educated, civilized. I can't suddenly go on the warpath with feathers in my hair and a tomahawk stuck in my breeches. Happy Minnie! Think what her father might've said if she'd married me and he'd found out later that his daughter had married a half-breed! You didn't tell me about these before. Why not?'

'Because you were engaged to Minnie. It might have spoilt your plans.'

'My plans were so ill-defined that I never even got round to buying her a ring,' he said wryly. 'Well, I've no use for them. Exchanging tokens with young women isn't in my nature, any more than wedding prospective heiresses is!'

'Which makes you a coward,' Flora said coldly.

'Which makes me a sensible man who doesn't particularly care for the notion of being shot by Frank Scott!'

'That's ridiculous!' Flora snapped. 'Uncle Frank may have his faults — yes, very bad ones, but he doesn't go round shooting people! And as for my being an heiress! I've determined to return to England as soon as can be arranged. I can be a spinster just as comfortably there as here. So I won't be an heiress for very much longer once my uncle understands from me that I persuaded his Mestiza woman to leave and make a new start for herself.'

'And I won't be your uncle's manager for much longer once I've informed him that my mother was a Comanche woman. Here!

Take the tokens!'

He was thrusting them towards her again.

'I've given them both to you,' she said. 'Make of that what you please. I'm freezing to death just standing here.'

She broke off as he seized her, his mouth covering hers, his hands pulling her so close that had he loosed his grasp suddenly she would have fallen.

'You're stubborn and self-opinionated,' he said, flinging the words into her face. 'You came here full of romantic fancies about a new world where people behaved differently and women were free to please themselves and Indians and whites lived on equal terms! You're not a beauty, though a man could drown in the depths of your eyes, nor much of a lady for all your fine clothes, but you're truthful and foolhardy and a risk-taker. I daresay if I asked you to marry me you'd happily go ahead without even considering that you'd almost certainly be flung out of the sewing circle, not to mention being disinherited by your uncle.'

'I might if you asked me,' Flora said.

'I never will!' Brent said, the colour mounting in his face. 'No, it's not because the truth about my birth shames me. I've never felt fully at ease with myself and never understood why until now, and I don't intend to hide my beginnings! I won't ask you because we're too much alike you and I — stubborn and proud and not ready to give an inch.'

'If you took one step away from me,' Flora said breathlessly, 'you'd not be able to bear the space between us!'

'Go back to England, Flora!'

He sounded almost as if he hated her.

'Not until spring,' she said. 'The tokens I give to you. The wise woman told me to give the star she had to my true love. What you do with the other star is your choice. Give it to your true love when you find her.'

'You being — where?'

'Safely back in England!' Flora cried and started away from him through the gates.

From behind her he said loudly and angrily, 'You might as well know that you're right! I cannot endure a step away from you so you will have to give up your plans to return to England. The Atlantic would separate me from my heaven and my earth! So here's your token from me to my true love, though the Lord knows we may both live to regret it!'

TWENTY

August, 1848

Those who say that marriage is a happy ending have never been wed. Our union began in conflict and ten years later we still disagree passionately about many things. It makes for lively conversation, for the occasional slamming of a door and for a reconciliation in the sweetness of the dark. It makes for shared laughter and the meeting of minds.

My uncle returned from Bloomington with a look of satisfaction on his face. He had bought up many of the abandoned Indian homesteads and scarcely appeared to notice that Tina had left. To him she had been no more than a convenience after all.

What angered him more was the revelation that Brent's mother had been a Comanche. My uncle's sympathies for those with Indian blood didn't extend to employing them as managers and a niece who contemplated marriage with one was a disgrace to the family.

'A complete and absolute disgrace,' he told me coldly. 'If you persist in this course then I shall be forced to ask you to leave my house.'

'My things are already packed,' I said.

'And where will you go? There is no hotel here and even you might hesitate before moving into O'Brien's place,' my uncle said bitingly.

Happily my problem was solved in an unexpected manner. On the Sunday following Tessa's flight Brent appeared at church and, having evidently spoke to the Eliots, stood up to tell an avid congregation that he was part Comanche. He spoke clearly and briefly, telling the people whom he had known all his life what he himself had recently learned and giving them the choice to accept or reject him.

'I was reared as a white man, educated as a white man, believed myself to be of Irish blood entirely. What I recently learned was that the mother who died in the bearing of me was a Comanche. If that makes any difference to any of you then I am sorry but there is nothing I can do to alter the facts.'

He sat down amid excited whispering.

Uncle Frank, his face like thunder, rose in

his seat and snapped out:

'I have already accepted O'Brien's resignation as my manager!' Then he walked out, not even glancing at me.

Mr Eliot, fumbling with his spectacles, rose to announce the next hymn. Never had I heard anything sung so out of tune!

'Flora, may I have a word?' Minnie Hargreaves, Charles Fontaine hovering in the background, touched my arm as we left the church and went out into the icy whiteness.

'Yes?' Try as I might I couldn't put much friendliness into my voice.

'Charles Fontaine has asked me to marry him,' she said in a rush. 'We shall have a quiet ceremony in a week or two. The school will be closed now until spring and . . .'

'And what?' I asked as she hesitated.

'There is a rumour that you and your uncle are at odds . . .'

'On practically every subject,' I told her.

'If you are not yet ready to return to England,' she said, 'the school building will be empty over the next two or three months. There are two rooms and one could serve as a bedchamber. I would like to do something to —'

Make up for her spiteful act that had destroyed more than she intended or would ever know?

'Thank you,' I said. 'I shall be glad to accept the offer.'

So for a few weeks I dwelt in the schoolhouse, ignoring Brent's jibes that I might be happier as a spinster after all. We both needed a little time, he to accustom himself to the knowledge of his roots, me to refrain from rushing into anything at all.

We married shortly after Christmas, myself in the ivory silk dress that had escaped the wardrobe fire and Brent in his smart suit with boots polished to sparkling brilliance.

Word about the Bloomington stage had been gleaned by him. The coach had stopped for a long halt during a fresh snowstorm some miles north of its final destination and during that time the two women who had joined the passengers outside Pine Creek Ridge had informed the driver of their intention not to proceed further. As the blizzard faltered and ceased they had walked away together, but where to remained unclear.

In the years since no word has come from either Tessa or Tina. Sometimes I wish I knew where they were. Did Tina find a new life for herself in Santa Fe? Did Tessa find Smiling Moon and does she live now with her fierce husband, happy in a life already familiar?

Pine Creek Ridge is flourishing as more people settle here. Minnie, after her marriage, reopened and extended the school. Brent tried in vain to get compensation for those who had been evicted from their farms but at least he has paid off his mortgage and made a success of his own spread.

In May and June of 1838 most of the Cherokees who had not already left were forcibly removed from their sacred lands in Georgia, many at gunpoint and all with great brutality. They, together with many of their slaves, were forced upon a journey of over 1200 miles to the Indian Territory, far to the west of the Mississippi. They were miserably provisioned, taking no more than the clothes on their backs and what they could carry on horses or small wagons. Some travelled partly by boat, but the land route came north for some distance, and actually crossed the southern part of our state of Illinois. We had word of their plight from some who had witnessed it. They were stricken with disease, and many were dying from exhaustion. They called it *Nunna daul Isunyi* — the Trail Where We Cried — we heard this from some of our own Peoria who had been able to stay on their farms, but white Americans call it the Trail of

Tears, which is more impersonal, perhaps because they do not like to think too much about the suffering. They say 4,000 of them perished — about a quarter of those who trekked.

'There's talk of the gold being exhausted in Georgia', Brent tells me, unfurling his newspaper and scowling at it, 'though no doubt the Cherokees would have been forcibly removed whether or not the speculators had come so greedily for their gold.'

He sounds bitter and my heart falters because in recent years I have sometimes heard that bitterness in his voice mingled with a touch of yearning. We are happy together and our two children, Daniel and Estella, are healthy and bright so I wonder for what he yearns. The remembered laughter of the other children bundled into wagons so long ago grows ever fainter in the mind and new immigrants tend the farms and harvest the maize.

Three years ago they gave a name to the doctrine that drove that policy — that Divine Providence which Brent once explained to me. Now they call it Manifest Destiny. Where will it lead, I wonder?

I see my uncle rarely, as he rides over his estate. He never turns his head or acknowledges my existence in any way. When he dies his great house, won in a game of poker from a man who had drunk too deeply on his wedding day, will stand empty and forlorn.

Once a year a letter, cool but friendly, arrives from England with a banker's draft for the allowance willed to me by my father. The family is well and enquires kindly after my own husband and children but no suggestion of any visit in either direction is ever made.

Our neighbours here, perhaps mindful of Mary Redfeather's solitary grave, have not turned their backs on us. I am still welcomed in the sewing circle and our children are never short of young companions to play with. I suspect a shared sense of guilt has something to do with that but I accept it. Life is good and my marriage strong.

'Going to be a good crop provided the weather stays mild,' Brent said, coming into the house and dropping a kiss on the back of Flora's neck as she closed her journal.

'Any news from anywhere?' she enquired.

'One bit of information that might interest you.' He gave her a teasing glance. 'I just spoke to Mrs Eliot who just had it directly from Mrs Belmont that Harold —'

'Passed his final medical examinations?'

Flora guessed.

'He has signed on as a ship's surgeon on a clipper bound for San Francisco. He had apparently heard vague rumours that there might be gold in California. He had not done very well in his final examinations, it seems, and this looked to him like a favourable opportunity for getting himself employed as a doctor with the prospect of making a fortune at the end of the voyage. A likely prospect indeed!'

'While there's life there's hope, as we doctors say.' Flora grinned.

'Don't you wish you'd encouraged his suit now?'

'About as much as I wish I was still living in my uncle's house!' she returned.

'We are happy, aren't we?' He spoke suddenly quietly with a serious note.

'Don't you think we are?'

'Most of the time but then something tugs at me. When I was a boy I used to ride out with the Peoria on their hunting trip in spring. I never felt different from them, never felt myself to be an outsider.'

'That was because you had more in common with them than you knew,' Flora said.

Inside her a little flutter of apprehension was growing.

'You know, I would like to get to Santa Fe

to honour my parents' last resting places,' he said.

'Perhaps one day soon you will be able to take the stage to Santa Fe. New lines are opening up now.'

'I want to find my mother's people,' he said. 'Possibly I have relatives still living.'

'But the Comanches are split up into small roaming bands. How could you hope — ?'

'The wise woman found you, didn't she?'

'You want to leave Pine Creek Ridge?'

'I've been offered a good price for the farm.'

'And the house?'

Her heart was thumping.

'For that too,' he said.

'You want to leave us?'

'No, of course I don't want to leave you or the children!' he said roughly. 'Do you really believe that after ten years I was preparing to ride off into the sunset and abandon my family?'

'Then what do you want?' Flora demanded. 'I can understand you want to find your mother's people, visit her grave and your father's grave, maybe discover what happened to Tina and to Tessa and Smiling Moon. But this is your land and you've worked hard to prosper, and the children are doing well in school. Everywhere Indians are being pushed off their lands by miners and gold prospectors and immigrant farmers and every couple of years a new fort springs up along the ancient trails. The Comanches aren't even united. One of their chiefs —'

'Ten Bears?'

'Is already in his fifties and more of a poet than a warrior.'

'And we have security here,' Brent said. 'I'm forty years old and accepted by nearly everybody in the community and you're due to be elected President of the Ladies' Committee. You are quite right, sweetheart.'

He nodded, patted her shoulder and went out. It seemed to her that his tread was heavier than usual and there were flecks of grey in the russet hair.

She rose to her feet, went over to the door and stood there, watching him leaning on the picket fence. The restlessness within him he would fight and suppress for her sake.

When she had first arrived here, she thought suddenly, she had hoped to escape the conventions of London life, had been disappointed to find the people still hidebound by outdated notions of propriety. She had flouted those conventions, helped Tessa and Tina, defied her uncle and practically badgered Brent into admitting his feelings for her.

Now she was settled and happy and could remain so, for Brent, having spoken his piece, wasn't one to nag or reproach.

She pulled the door wider and went across the garden to stand by him, pulling her lace cap from her head and letting the wind tangle her hair.

'The schoolbooks I could take along with us,' she said. 'I'd not want the children to fall behind too far and you'd best brush up your camping skills. I shall expect a snug lodge in the winter and a good horse to ride in summer.'

Brent caught her to him, kissing her passionately.

'Are you sure?' he said at last.

'Sure?' Flora echoed. 'Brent, I am sure of only one thing. You will never be content until you have tested the other side of your nature and I will never be content until you are completely happy.'

'You've been settled here for ten years,' Brent said.

'And you for much longer!' she retorted, wrapping her arms about him. 'Time we were moving on together, my Comanche love.'

It seemed to her at that moment as a long

arrow of late afternoon sunshine struck them that someone somewhere approved their decision.

ABOUT THE AUTHOR

Maureen Peters was born in Caernarfon, North Wales. She is a prolific author who has had many books published.

We hope you have enjoyed this Large Print book. Other Thorndike, Wheeler, and Chivers Press Large Print books are available at your library or directly from the publishers.

For information about current and upcoming titles, please call or write, without obligation, to:

Publisher
Thorndike Press
295 Kennedy Memorial Drive
Waterville, ME 04901
Tel. (800) 223-1244

or visit our Web site at:

http://gale.cengage.com/thorndike

OR

Chivers Large Print
published by BBC Audiobooks Ltd
St James House, The Square
Lower Bristol Road
Bath BA2 3SB
England
Tel. +44(0) 800 136919
email: bbcaudiobooks@bbc.co.uk
www.bbcaudiobooks.co.uk

All our Large Print titles are designed for easy reading, and all our books are made to last.